W9-AAU-206

HER
DAUGHTER'S
CRY

BOOKS BY M.M. CHOUINARD

HER DAUGHTER'S CRY

M. M. CHOUINARD

bookouture

Published by Bookouture in 2020

An imprint of Storyfire Ltd.
Carmelite House
50 Victoria Embankment
London EC4Y 0DZ

www.bookouture.com

Copyright © M.M. Chouinard, 2020

M.M. Chouinard has asserted her right to be identified
as the author of this work.

All rights reserved. No part of this publication may be reproduced,
stored in any retrieval system, or transmitted, in any form or by
any means, electronic, mechanical, photocopying, recording or
otherwise, without the prior written permission of the publishers.

ISBN: 978-1-78681-828-7
eBook ISBN: 978-1-78681-827-0

This book is a work of fiction. Names, characters, businesses,
organizations, places and events other than those clearly in the
public domain, are either the product of the author's imagination
or are used fictitiously. Any resemblance to actual persons, living or
dead, events or locales is entirely coincidental.

For Bobby

PART ONE

Saturday, April 6th – Tuesday, April 16th

CHAPTER ONE

The woman stumbled through the woods, face burned from the sun, feet aching with fatigue. She forced herself to keep moving forward as she fought to keep sight of the paved road, but after hours with no sunglasses, she could barely manage hurried glimpses through narrowed eyes. The trees in front of her blended into a wavering green-brown image. She coughed, and her throat seized. How long had it been since she'd veered from the river to follow the road? Two hours? Three? If she didn't get water again soon, she'd pass out.

Something brown and white danced back and forth in front of her.

She shielded her eyes and forced them open against the pain. The lines took form—some sort of building? Adrenaline coursed through her and sped her steps. She rubbed her eyes and peered out again. Two buildings on either side of the road. Maybe more. Maybe a town?

She hobbled as quickly as she could. When she couldn't avoid it any longer, she stepped out onto the road. A red-lettered sign topped a quaint country storefront—Treasures From My Attic.

She pushed through the door, the cheerful tinkling of the bell at instant odds with the darkness that engulfed her. Her panic spiked as she froze, struggling to see. But within seconds, the black turned to dark gray, then lighter gray. After hours in sunlight, her eyes just needed to adjust.

Movement pulled her attention. The outline of a man rushed toward her, knocking over his chair in his hurry. She turned, ready to run.

"Oh my God!" he cried. "What happened to you? Are you okay?"

She could make out his face now, and his shocked expression. He was staring at her torso.

Because her blue-and-white-checked shirt and jeans were caked with dirt and blood.

"What happened?" he asked again.

Her eyes raked his face. "I don't know."

CHAPTER TWO

An hour and a half later, Detectives Josette Fournier and Bob Arnett pulled into the lot of Sacred Heart Hospital's emergency room in Larkville. The cool air had a biting breeze that, despite a spate of mild weather and daffodils peeping up in front of the red-brick-and-glass hospital, reminded Jo spring hadn't fully sprung. Even though she'd moved from New Orleans to Massachusetts when she was a young teen, she still fell prey to the first deceptive signs of warmth in a way no truly native New Englander ever would.

As they crossed the tarmac toward the sliding doors, Jo's gait stiffened.

Arnett shook his head. "You and hospitals."

"What? I'm not bad."

"Like hell. You hide it well, but you go two shades paler and walk like you're made out of sticks and rubber bands."

She scrunched up her face and pulled her head back. "What does that even mean?"

He laughed and gestured up and down her frame. "You know you do. Look at yourself."

He was right. Ever since she'd had to accompany her father through his second bout of chemotherapy, hospitals had become synonymous with fear and desperation for her. She took a deep breath and tried to shake off the memories.

But he'd glimpsed her face. "How's your father doing?"

"Better. They think they've eradicated it, so he's in remission."

"You don't sound happy about it."

"Of course I'm happy about it. I just wish he'd let them remove his prostate."

"Ah, well. Anytime you're talking about surgery in that particular location, the subject gets a little sensitive."

She shook her head, and strode past the rows of yellow plastic chairs to the annoyed blonde triage nurse behind the counter. "I'm Detective Josette Fournier from Oakhurst County SPDU, and this is Detective Bob Arnett. You have a Jane Doe we need to see?"

The nurse's annoyance deepened. "One minute."

She slid the frosted glass window back into place, and disappeared for several minutes. Without warning, the door next to the window buzzed like a giant angry mecha-wasp. Arnett pulled the handle and they stepped through.

The nurse pointed back and to the right. "Room three. The officers said you'd need to talk to her privately. Lucky for you we're slow today so we had a room to spare."

Jo nodded her thanks. "We appreciate it. We'll be as fast as possible."

The nurse gave one short nod, expression slightly mollified.

Jo tried to ignore the antiseptic smell as they followed the beige-and-white hall to the target room. They opened the door and waved out the two uniformed officers, a medium-height brunette in her early thirties, and a tall man with a spray of salt at his temples and just the hint of a starter paunch. Jo glanced at Arnett and hid her smile—in ten years the pair would be Fournier-and-Arnett body doubles. Over the twenty-odd years of their partnership, Arnett's hair had flipped to more gray than black, and he'd put on about thirty pounds when he quit smoking, although he'd lost ten of that when his marriage nearly ended. While Jo's stylist kept her own gray permanently covered, she surely had other signs of her own transformation—a reality she quickly blocked herself from dwelling on by leading the introductions.

"So what exactly happened?" she asked when she finished.

The brunette officer, whose badge read Gonsalves, answered. "Woman walked into an antique store over in Taltingham, clothes covered in blood, with leaves and sticks in her hair, scrapes and bruises and sunburn, with no idea who she is. She nearly gave the guy who owns the shop a heart attack. He called the paramedics and they examined her and brought her here."

"No ID on her?" Arnett asked.

"Nope. No wallet, no phone, nothing. Just the clothes on her back, and barely the shoes on her feet. They're some sort of slippers, not real shoes, and they're so shredded they're nearly falling off. Looks like she walked a fair distance before stumbling into that shop."

"You said they found her in Taltingham?" Jo asked. "Why didn't they take her to Suffolk General?"

"There was a five-car pile-up right before the call, so they had their hands full. Since her life wasn't in immediate danger, they brought her to the next closest hospital. Since nobody in Taltingham knew who she was anyway, now she's our problem."

A doctor appeared around the corner and hurried over to them, several strands of auburn hair trailing her severe bun. She addressed Arnett. "I'm Doctor Brodie. The nurse told me you'd arrived."

Jo answered her, and introduced them. "Can you update us on our Jane Doe?"

Doctor Brodie glanced at her, then physically turned toward Arnett. "She has a concussion, but no laceration, so it can't be responsible for all the blood on her. No other significant injuries."

Jo sighed internally. She'd met far too many women like this before. Successful, professional women, who, whether consciously or not, assumed Arnett was the one in charge. It was bad enough when men treated her that way, but when women did it, especially women who'd certainly battled far too much of their own gender discrimination, it just plain pissed her off. "Did you do a rape kit?"

"There was no reason to." The doctor turned a withering glare on her.

Jo kept her face neutral. "Of course there's reason to. She wasn't able to tell you what happened, which means she doesn't know, and you don't know. We need to recover any potential evidence as soon as possible."

The doctor's cheeks tinged slightly red. "We'll do it now."

"Swab inside and out, trim the fingernails, all of it," Jo said.

The glare turned to daggers. "I know how to collect a rape kit."

"That'll help. Blood samples?" Jo said.

The doctor's sharp intake of breath was satisfying, as was Gonsalves' muffled laugh. Arnett shot her a questioning glance, which she ignored. Yes, she was being bitchy, and no, it wasn't like her. Especially on the job.

"Already sent off for bloodwork," Doctor Brodie said.

"And the extras? For our lab?"

The doctor's tinge turned to a full flush—she'd been caught in a second mistake. Would she own up to it, or try to BS her way through?

"No need. We're doing a full screen on her," she said.

Jo held her eyes. "Right. Except the woman is covered in blood that Officer Gonsalves assures me *you* said couldn't have come from her wounds. So my lab will need to compare the blood on her clothes against the blood in her veins."

"I can do a typing right here."

Jo had reached her limit—the doctor's ego was so big she was doubling down on her bullshit, even if it meant playing intentionally ignorant. "We both know that tells us next to nothing. Even if the blood types match up, we won't be able to say for certain the blood is hers. And since we have no way of identifying her, we'll need to submit her DNA into the system to see if she matches any missing cases."

"I'm not a mind reader, Detective. I'll have the nurse take another sample as soon as possible."

Arnett shifted, eyebrows up. Jo stopped herself from asking the doctor if this was her first day in the ER, and chastised herself for even having the thought. What on God's green earth was wrong with her today?

She took a breath and forced herself to smile. She'd made her point, over-made it in fact, and she needed as much information as she could get. "Thank you. Can you tell what caused the injury?"

Relieved to be on solid ground again, the doctor's flush abated. "My guess is she was in a car accident while not wearing a seat belt, and was thrown from the vehicle. Which is why a rape kit really is a waste of time and money."

Jo fought to stay civil. "We'll search for any crashes that match up. This type of memory loss, is that common with her type of head injury?"

"It happens. I've called in a neurology consult, he should be here shortly. He'll be able to tell you more once he examines her."

"Great, thank you." Jo pointedly turned her side to Brodie, and spoke to Gonsalves. "Can you make sure all the evidence makes it back to Marzillo at SPDU headquarters?"

Gonsalves smiled. "Sure thing."

Arnett grabbed the doorknob. "Ready to go talk to her?"

Jo nodded and he opened the door, then waved her through.

CHAPTER THREE

The woman's head shot up as they stepped through the door. She was small, probably no more than five foot five, and the hospital gown made her look smaller. She wore no jewelry other than two rings, a simple gold wedding band, and a faceted figure-eight turquoise ring on her right hand. The pale, sunburned skin dramatized her dark brown hair and highlighted the beginning web of middle-aged crow's feet around her eyes. Confusion and fear filled her wide brown eyes, reminding Jo of a trapped fox.

Jo pulled a plastic chair next to the bed. By unspoken agreement, Arnett followed suit, but stayed a foot farther back. "You've had quite a day," Jo said.

"I'm sorry if we know each other, I'm having problems remembering." Her eyes flicked between them, and to the door behind them.

"No, don't worry." Jo introduced herself and Arnett. "We're here to help figure out what happened to you. The doctor says you don't even remember who you are?"

Tears filled the woman's eyes. "No."

Jo leaned in and slowed the pace of her voice. "Don't worry, we're going to get this all figured out as soon as possible. In the meantime, what would you like us to call you?"

A cloud passed over her face, deepening the anxiety there. "They've been calling me Jane Doe. They use that for dead bodies, don't they?"

"Yes, exactly. It's a horrible name for someone who's alive and going to be well soon. So what would you like to be called until you remember your real name?"

"One of the nurses' names is Zoë, that's really pretty. Can we use that?" She searched Jo's face.

"Zoë it is," Jo said. "Now I'd like you to think back as best you can. What's the first thing you remember?"

The door to the room swung open, and a tall, black-haired, brown-eyed doctor strode in. His eyes swung to each of them, then settled on Zoë with an accompanying thousand-watt smile. "You must be my new patient. I'm Doctor Soltero, and I'm a neurologist. I hear tell you have a big lump on your head and you're not remembering much?"

Zoë sat up, cheeks flushed slightly, and absentmindedly ran her fingers over her hair. Jo hid a smile. She couldn't blame the woman. Dr. Soltero's square-jawed good looks must have charmed more than a few patients in their time, even those in far worse shape.

"Yes, that's right." Zoë wrung the hands clasped in her lap.

Dr. Soltero nodded. "And you are Detectives Fournier and Arnett?"

"Our reputations precede us," Jo said.

"Yours does, anyway. Quite a bulldog, I hear." He raised one eyebrow at Jo, a smile playing at his lips.

She refused to be embarrassed. "We just decided Zoë would be an excellent temporary name, and were asking Zoë if she can remember anything about how she got here."

"In that case, hello, Zoë." He stepped around the bed and examined her as he asked questions about how she felt, and checked the extent of her memory loss. "We find ourselves back at the detectives' question. What's the first thing you do remember?"

Her eyes darted back and forth over the ceiling. "Waking up in the woods. I was lying under some rocks, like a little lean-to made out of the space between them. I was horribly cold and my head was throbbing, and the bright light made it worse. I had no idea how I got there or what to do, so I got up and started walking. I found a river, which was good because I was really thirsty. I drank some water, which probably means I have some sort of parasite now, but I didn't have anything to boil it with…" She looked up at the doctor.

He smiled, and patted her hand. "I'm sure you're fine, but we'll monitor you. You did the right thing. Dehydration was a much bigger problem just then. Go on."

She smiled wanly. "Then I followed the river downhill, the direction it was running. I figured, people live near water, right?"

Jo shot Arnett a look. Not just anybody would have put that together.

Dr. Soltero nodded. "Very smart."

"By that time, though, I was struggling to keep going. I was thirsty and hot and tired, and felt like I was going to pass out. But I didn't have any other choice, so I just kept walking until I came to a dirt road, and then I followed that until I hit a paved road. Then I followed that until I got to a town, just trying to put one foot in front of the other."

"Didn't any cars stop to offer you help?" Dr. Soltero asked.

Zoë quickly looked down before answering. "I, uh, didn't walk out on the actual road."

"Trying to stay in the shade? Also very smart. But you should have come out when you heard the cars." He laughed.

Jo glanced at Arnett again, and registered the change in his expression. He'd also seen Zoë's flicker of hesitation. She looked back at her. "Is that why? Or were you scared?"

Zoë's eyes darted over to Jo's face, and then down again. "Yes."

"Afraid of the person who did this to you?" Jo asked.

"I—I know it sounds crazy, but I don't know what I was scared of. I just know I was scared. I mean, I didn't know what happened, or where I was, or anything, and I was just trying not to let myself get hysterical because I knew that wouldn't help anything. Because you don't just find yourself out in the woods covered in blood, there has to be something that—" Her throat seized, and she struggled for words through panicked tears.

Jo squeezed her hand. "That must have been terrifying. But you did the right thing, and you're safe now. Take a deep breath for me."

Zoë nodded, and took several breaths.

Dr. Soltero continued when she'd calmed. "Then what happened?"

"That's it. I just kept going. By the time I found the town, my vision was blurry and I could barely walk anymore. I managed to reach the first building, and the guy called an ambulance for me. They brought me here."

"Got it." Dr. Soltero circled around the bed and patted her arm. "I'm going to order a few more tests for you, including a CT scan. Then we'll chat again once I've had a chance to look at the results, okay? In the meantime they'll put you in one of our deluxe suites upstairs. We'll get everything figured out, and before you know it, you'll be angry at me because you remember all your childhood traumas."

Zoë smiled at his joke, and flushed slightly again.

Jo put on what she hoped was a reassuring smile. "With any luck, we'll have you identified even before that. Someone must have noticed you missing by now, and must have filed a report. We'll be back to tell you your real name in no time." She turned. "Doctor Soltero, may we speak to you?"

"Of course. I'll see you again soon, Zoë."

*

Jo and Arnett followed Dr. Soltero into the hall. "We'll keep it quick, Doctor Soltero, we know how busy you are," Jo said.

Dr. Soltero turned on the thousand-watt smile. "Matt, please."

"Matt. I know head trauma can be deceptive, but is it possible for someone to lose all their memory from an injury that small?" Jo asked.

He wagged his head back and forth. "Memory is complicated, especially cases of pure retrograde amnesia like this. A small injury can trigger a minor stroke or epileptic episode we need test results to detect. And, yes, it's common with even minor insult to have some memory loss. But generally speaking, in a case like this with relatively moderate injury but dramatic memory loss, I'd expect an accompanying psychological component."

"Like when someone blocks out something traumatic that happened to them during childhood, but then recovers the memory later?" Jo asked.

The doctor raised his eyebrows. "The whole issue of adults recovering memories of childhood trauma is very controversial. But your gist is right. You're asking about dissociative amnesia— people who experience something traumatic, even without an accompanying injury, and have extensive memory loss."

"So this probably wouldn't just happen as the result of a random car accident?" Arnett asked.

Dr. Soltero grimaced. "I don't want to say it couldn't happen, because it *could*. But I'd say in that case it's more likely the memory loss would be limited to a few hours, maybe days, surrounding the crash."

"What if the patient had been attacked and crashed their car in the process of getting away from something traumatic?"

"Definitely closer, yes. Probably the best way to put it succinctly is, you can get this type of memory loss from a traumatic brain injury, or for psychological reasons without any injury at all. So the less severe the injury is, the more likely I'd hypothesize something traumatic accompanied the event."

Jo nodded. "Got it. And I'm guessing there's no way of knowing when or if she'll get her memory back?"

He shook his head. "Excellent guess, that's also complicated. Most likely it *will* come back, but there's no telling when. Sometimes within hours, sometimes not for years, and sometimes only partially. Older memories are more likely to be recovered than newer ones, and more likely to be recovered sooner."

Jo and Arnett both nodded.

The doctor reached into his lab coat pocket and pulled out a card. "I'd like to keep her overnight for observation, but if her memory doesn't come back by tomorrow, we'll need to place her in some sort of care."

Jo traded him a card of her own. "Right. So you'll keep us updated?"

"I'll contact you as soon as I get a look at her test results." He smiled, and held her eye a moment longer than necessary.

CHAPTER FOUR

"So, who pissed in *your* Wheaties today?" Arnett asked as they walked back to the car.

Jo stared at him blankly for a moment before connecting the dots to her conversation with the ER doctor. "Oh, that. I'll admit, I came down on her a little hard. But she had it coming."

"Of course she had it coming. But normally the bigger assholes people are, the less butter melts in your mouth."

Jo laughed. "Look at you, stealing my favorite sayings. But you're right. I'm not sure why it got under my skin that way. Maybe Hill of Beans gave me decaf by mistake."

"Lucky for you, I know the perfect remedy." He reached for the driver's side door of the undercover Chevy Cruze. "Double meatball sub from Sal's makes everything right with the world."

She slipped into the passenger seat. "What about your dinner?"

"Laura's got her book club tonight, so I'm fending for myself," he answered. "And besides, that blood on Zoë's clothes isn't sitting right with me, I'm worried about who it belongs to. I'd like to find out who Zoë is tonight, if we can."

"You don't have to ask me twice. Make it so." She pointed in the direction of Sal's. "And I agree. That much blood means someone somewhere may need help, but the question is where? She could have come from any direction out in the woods before she hit that stream she followed, and who knows how long she ran before she passed out last night. This could have happened anywhere in the county, behind God only knows what tree or in what house. We're looking for a needle in a forest full of haystacks unless Zoë remembers who she is. But I'm not going to be able to sleep tonight until we check for a missing persons report on her, or any accidents that might be related."

They took their food to go, and jumped into the search. Half an hour later, Jo wiped a glop of marinara off her desk as she broke focus with the database in front of her. "From what I can see, there aren't any crashes with abandoned vehicles, or that would otherwise fit Zoë's situation, anywhere near the Taltingham area in the last two days. Pretty much all of the roads in the area would have been traversed by now, so anything like that should have been reported. I don't think she could have been out in the woods longer than that?"

"Seems unlikely, but we can check with Marzillo to see if she can zero in on the timing any better," Arnett said, referring to one of the senior medicolegal investigators in their lab.

"Maybe she drove off the road where nobody can see the vehicle? If so, who knows how long before it'll be reported." Jo shook her head, frustrated.

"True. On to missing persons." Arnett wiped his hands and pulled his keyboard closer.

"What do you think, radiate out by county?" Jo asked.

"Probably best, she could be from anywhere. Lots of camping up there even this time of year among the hard-core set. Time frame?"

"I say start with cases reported yesterday or today, but we may have to go back farther. She may even have been abducted and held, for God knows how long."

Arnett shook his head, expression grim. "You take Oakhurst, I'll take Hampden."

The work was arduous, and disheartening. Although Zoë looked to be in her forties, they had to keep their age range wide. Visual estimates of age could be wrong, especially after the ordeal she'd been through. Even with the tragic reality that most missing women were under the age of eighteen, a considerable number of cases remained to slog through.

When Marzillo called them two hours later, they'd only found two possibilities, who, when viewed through squinting eyes, might have been Zoë. But phone calls to the families in question had quickly ruled them out.

"I hate those calls," Arnett said as they strode down the corridor to the lab. "You raise the family's hopes, even if it's only for a second, then the pain's back in their voice, fresh like the day it happened."

Jo nodded, and pulled open the door.

"Guys, how's it going?" Christine Lopez whipped around toward them from her now-permanent set-up on the right side of the room, sending her long black ponytail swinging. During a brief period when Jo had been lieutenant of the department, Lopez had partnered with Arnett. When Jo asked to be made detective again, Lopez, still new to the force, had been assigned to another partner. When he'd been hospitalized the previous fall, Assistant District Attorney Rockney asked Lopez to use her considerable computer and internet savvy to help out in the understaffed lab, working with whichever squads needed her. After a few months on that detail, she'd asked interim lieutenant Martinez if she could make the switch permanent.

"Frustrating. Still enjoying lab life?" Jo asked.

"Happier than a dog in a vat of peanut butter."

"I always did think you missed your calling. Whenever I picture you, I see you in a room surrounded by five monitors and stacks of illegal high-tech gadgets." Jo dropped into the desk next to hers.

Marzillo emerged from the back of the room perched on her usual cork platforms, several pencils spearing her dark curls into a tight bun. "Only problem is, now I gotta listen to her music all day. And I use the word music very, very loosely."

"Still hate headphones, huh?" Arnett asked, grabbing another chair.

Lopez grimaced. "You can't hear anything around you. Anybody can sneak up on you, zombies could overrun the room, you name it, and you'd never know it."

Marzillo stared at her. "Seriously. Stop it with the *Resident Evil*, I'm begging you. It's warping your mind."

Lopez pointed at her with a zombie troll doll. "Classic directional causality error. I play *Resident Evil* because my mind is warped, not the other way around. And, bee-tee-dub, if you think *Resident Evil* is the only shooter with zombies in it, you've got another think coming."

Marzillo stepped closer for a better look at the doll. "Oh my *God*, that's horrifying. Please tell me where you found it so I can never, ever shop there."

"Psh. I didn't find it, I made it. I am a woman of many talents." Lopez grinned.

Marzillo held up a hand and turned away. "Yep, done with you. Fournier. Arnett. Let's get down to it, since time may be of the essence."

"Even grumpier than usual." Arnett glanced at Jo. "What, there some sort of epidemic going around?"

Jo shot him a laser glare.

"Nope, I'm not even gonna ask," Marzillo said. "So, you got the same rundown of Zoë's injuries I did. Contusion on the back of the head, several scrapes and bruises, sunburn. You mentioned the doctor thought this was caused by a car accident?"

Jo nodded. "She said most likely Zoë wasn't wearing a seat belt, and was ejected from a car during a crash. But I wouldn't trust her to diagnose a wart on a witch's nose."

"Excellent call, because it's total bullshit. The only way she could sustain these injuries from a car accident is if she'd been driving, or riding, while sitting backwards. And in the very unlikely event that happened, she'd have serious soft tissue injury, neck or spine issues, and nothing here mentions that."

Arnett shook his head. "The doctor didn't mention anything like that, and Zoë said only her head hurt. She was moving around just fine, and they hadn't medicated her because of the concussion."

Marzillo pulled up a folder on her main computer and opened a file. A picture of Zoë's left shoulder appeared. "Also, these bruises. This I don't blame the doctor for, because the shapes might have still been developing when she first examined Zoë. You can only see the shape faintly."

Jo's brows popped up. "Fingers."

"Maybe someone pulled Zoë from the car?" Lopez had come over to look at the pictures.

"You can't have it both ways. Either she was ejected from the car and that's how she got the injury to the back of her head and the cuts and scrapes, or she was pulled from the car, and couldn't have sustained that head injury. And how do you pull someone out in a way that leaves that mark?"

They all thought for a moment, miming reaches and holds, but came up empty. "Maybe whoever left the mark did it first, and then she crashed her car getting away from him—but no, that can't be, or those bruises would have been just as developed as the others."

"Nicely caught." Marzillo smiled at her.

"So you're thinking some sort of attack?" Jo asked.

She nodded. "I can't say for sure, but that's what seems to fit best. Look at the location of the contusion, *above* this curve on the back of her head. It's hard to fall in a natural way and hit your head like that, you'd have to slide into something. Not impossible, but unlikely. My guess is there was some sort of altercation, maybe an attempted rape. My guess is the attacker, who I'd bet was taller than her, hit her on the head at some point, and they struggled, but she ultimately got away."

"*Attempted* rape. So there's no evidence of rape in the kit?"

"No evidence of any recent sexual activity at all, forced or otherwise."

"What about the blood she was covered in? We're worried about the source."

"The blood isn't hers, which we knew before I tested it, since there's no way that much blood came from a contusion with no laceration."

"So maybe she hurt her attacker?" Arnett asked.

"Could be. But whoever it was, it's very possible they're dead or dying somewhere. You don't lose that much blood without needing medical help. Especially considering the patterns." She clicked on another picture, of a checked button-down shirt and jeans. "Look here, and here." The bloodstain ran from the top of the collar to the hem of the shirt, and down the length of the jeans. Marzillo pointed with a pen to an area near the shoulder.

"Blood spatter?" Arnett asked.

"You win the zombie Kewpie doll. This top part is spatter. The kind you get when someone's being bludgeoned, or hacked at."

"Any chance someone was only bleeding from an arm, say, and flung that arm during a fight or some such, causing the spatter?"

Marzillo's eyebrows popped up. "Interesting. It's possible. I can't rule that out."

Jo nodded. "Either way, this happened right in front of her."

"You sure she was the victim?" Lopez asked.

"No. But since she ended up on the run with a head injury that took out her memory, I'd say it's more likely she was fighting back than attacking," Jo said.

"Do you stick around long enough to do that much damage if you're just trying to get away?" Arnett asked.

"Sure. I'm a big fan of the principle of double tap, myself." Lopez pointed two fingers in a gun shape. "And her wounds, especially the bruises, suggest someone was pulling at her rather than pushing her away. That's defensive." Lopez tapped the Kewpie doll's foot on her desk.

Jo nodded. "Let's pull it apart. Scenario one, someone is attacked in front of her. Maybe she and someone else were tied up together by their attacker, who killed the other party, but she managed to get away before it was her turn. Scenario two, someone came up behind her and bashed her on the head but didn't knock her out, or some such. She fights back, somehow gets the upper hand, and does considerable damage to her attacker. And scenario three, she's the attacker." Jo paused, and pointed at the picture. "There was enough blood to soak through her shirt onto the jeans?"

"The rest didn't come from spatter, but yes. Through to her panties, as well. So you see what I'm saying—this wasn't some little cut."

"Right. Which means whoever belongs to that blood is seriously injured or, more likely, dead," Jo said.

Marzillo took a deep breath. "Some injuries, including head injuries, bleed profusely but can close up just fine with a couple of amateur stitches. So there's hope."

"In which case, that other victim could still be alive and in serious danger," Jo said.

Arnett nodded. "So we have ourselves a crime scene, and time may still be of the essence."

"No doubt about that. I'll put a rush on the analysis of both Zoë's blood, and the blood on her clothes. Even so, I can't see us getting it back in less than a week." Marzillo clicked open two more photos. "And just to be thorough, here's the full shot of her shoulders, neck and back. You see what I mean about the bruises—"

Jo interrupted her. "What the hell. She has a tattoo?"

Marzillo gawked. "Doctor Clueless didn't mention that?"

Arnett leaned forward. "No, in fact, we had to remind her to take pictures at all."

Marzillo zoomed in on the tattoo below the left shoulder blade—a baby's footprint with script just inside the heel.

Jo stepped up to peer at the picture. "Can you make out what it says?"

Marzillo zoomed in on the photo, then shook her head. "Too much ink bleed. This part is most likely a name, because this part is formatted like a date. I think that first letter is an S."

"Or possibly a fancy P," Lopez said.

"And there's nowhere near enough detail to identify the print?"

Marzillo shook her head. "Nope. Even if the artist had been fully accurate when they put it on, which I doubt, it's too blurred out and faded now. We'd never be able to run it through a database of baby feet, even if such an animal existed."

"But that's a good point—any chance you can tell how old the tattoo is? That might give a clue to their ages."

Marzillo tilted her head. "Hard to say for sure, but with that degree of ink migration, I'd guess no less than, what, ten years, Chris?"

Lopez nodded. "At least that. Unless the artist was really incompetent, I'd say most likely longer."

Jo stood up. "Well, at least the tattoo should help us confirm when we've found the right missing person. I don't suppose Doctor Brodie also forgot to mention a convenient label sewn inside her jeans, complete with her name and address?" Jo asked.

Marzillo shook her head. "Sadly, no. And all of this makes me think I should have my tattoo guy put my actual name somewhere on me this weekend."

Lopez pointed her can of Rockstar at Marzillo. "I'll pay for it if you make it a tramp stamp."

Marzillo closed her eyes and shook her head. "What makes you think I don't already have one?"

"Aaand, that's my cue to go." Arnett stood up and left.

"You're too easy to mess with," Lopez called after them as Jo followed.

CHAPTER FIVE

They started early on Sunday searching hospitals in western Mass for someone whose injuries might match up with the amount of blood found on Zoë's clothes. When they found nothing, they searched all reported deaths in the county for the same, then checked to see if any new missing persons cases matching Zoë had been opened.

Jo pushed her keyboard away in frustration. "How is this possible? She was wearing a wedding ring *and* she has a baby's footprint tattooed on her back. How can *nobody* be looking for her?"

"I get that most people believe the BS that you have to wait at least twenty-four hours before you file a report, but someone should have reported *something* by now." Arnett bounced his palm on his desk. "There has to be something we're not thinking of here—"

Jo's phone rang, and Dr. Soltero's name flashed on the screen. She answered and identified herself.

His voice was as warm as she remembered. "Hello, Detective. I hope you're well. It's good to talk to you again."

"I am well, thank you. How can I help you?"

"You asked me to call and update you on Zoë. Do you want the good news first, or the bad news?"

"I'm the let's-get-on-with-it type."

"The bad news is, Zoë still doesn't remember anything. The good news is, I've had a look at all her tests. Everything looks excellent—no evidence of a stroke or any other insult other than the contusion to the back of her head. No swelling, nothing. So, no additional physical reason we can find for her memory loss."

"Dammit. So we're back to some psychological trauma. Here's our problem, Doctor Soltero—"

"Matt, please."

"Matt. Our problem is, not only do we need to find out who Zoë is for her own sake, we need to figure out what happened to the person who bled all over her. Someone somewhere may be in danger, but we have no idea where to start a search. Is there any way we can help her get her memory back?"

"The best way is to find the right trigger. And the more, the better, so getting an amnesiac back to a familiar environment, surrounding them with people they know, that sort of thing, is best. But, of course, since we don't know where she's from or who she is…"

"We find ourselves in a catch-22."

"Exactly. Which brings me to my second reason for calling. We obviously can't release her when she doesn't know who she is. In cases like this, we discharge the patient to a government-funded care facility. However, the closest one with an opening is in Springfield. That's a bit difficult for me to get to with my other responsibilities, and I'd like to keep Zoë under my observation. So I've pulled some strings to get her into one in Northampton I've worked with before, Sunset Gardens. We'll be transferring her over there in about an hour. If you want to talk to her, it's late enough that it's probably best to let her settle in tonight and visit tomorrow."

"Got it." Jo jotted down the address he gave. "Will you keep us updated about any changes?"

"Will do. In fact," he cleared his throat, "I'd love an excuse to talk to you again."

Without a doubt, she was tempted. He was good-looking, he was charming, and he seemed compassionate and kind. And, she could stand to blow off a little pent-up sexual energy. She hadn't had a date since Eric, the last man she'd casually dated, had broken things off with her.

"Murdered anyone lately?" she asked.

His laugh was deep, throaty, and sexy. "If that's what it takes. Or, maybe we could save a life and just have dinner Saturday night?"

"I'll let you know." She hung up, a smile tugging the corners of her mouth.

Arnett stared at her with an amused expression. "I'm not even going to ask," he said.

"Smart choice." She summarized the rest of the conversation for him. "Normally I'd say the next step is to plaster her picture all over the news and wait for someone to show up looking for her, but…"

"But the someone who showed up might be the person who did this to her, looking to finish the job," Arnett said.

She tapped her pen on the desk. "Maybe that's exactly what we need to flush them out. But my worry is, if they're a husband or a relative, I don't think we'd have any legal way of preventing them from walking off with her before we figure out if she's safe or not, and before we've found out who lost all that blood. Can we legally prevent her from leaving the care facility if she wants to?"

"I doubt it, but I've never seen anything like this. Maybe you should call back Doctor Loverboy and ask him if this falls under anything like a mandatory psych hold. No way we'll get away with putting her in gen pop when she can't even remember who she is."

"Doctor Loverboy. Very cute. But make no mistake, keep it up and I *will* cut you." She tapped the pen on her leg. "I'm thinking we have to find a way to trigger her. Maybe while we're there we can check with the administrators at Sunset Gardens about what they can legally do and what they can't."

"Great. But how the hell do we trigger her?"

"I have an idea we can try out tomorrow."

CHAPTER SIX

Jo woke so exhausted the next morning she fought to get out of bed. She showered in water as cold as she could bear, but still struggled to get through her morning routine. Which was odd—she was generally a morning person unless work disrupted her normal pattern, and her caseload was relatively quiet at the moment. Was she getting the flu? She'd had her shot, but these days they never could guarantee how effective the inoculations would be. She sighed. Probably the best thing would be a stop off at Jamba Juice for some type of immunity-boosting smoothie. She eyed her espresso machine and made herself a double-shot quickly before she could talk herself out of it, then jumped in the car and drove to HQ, stopping off for the drinks.

She laughed at the grimace on Arnett's face when she handed him his matching smoothie. "I know, I know. But I think I'm getting the flu, and if I do, you know you're gonna. Drink up, and we'll stop through the Dunkin' drive-thru on the way."

"You're driving, then," he grumbled.

Sunset Gardens was surrounded by a ten-foot gray wall with intermittently dangling fronds of ivy. They pulled up to the gate and identified themselves through the speaker, and an anonymous man buzzed them in.

Jo surveyed the property. An expansive lawn ringed the main building, lined with a walking path and burgeoning flower beds. "Very pleasant," she said. "Except for the huge looming wall trapping you in."

"Promise me that if I ever end up in a place like this, you'll shoot me," Arnett said.

"I call *not it*. But I'm sure Lopez will be more than happy to accommodate."

The building opened into a small foyer with a check-in counter. A blonde woman in her mid- to late-twenties wearing a name tag labeled 'Julie' looked up as they entered. "Hello. How can I help you?"

Jo introduced them, and explained the purpose of their visit.

"Oh, right, the director said to expect you. Follow me." Julie came out from the back of her counter, and led them down one white-painted, white-linoleumed hall and around to another. "She's in B wing, our lily wing. So far, she hasn't left her room. Normally we try to get everyone out for a walk in the morning if the weather's cooperating, but they told me to leave her alone for now."

"I can't imagine any transition is easy when you can't remember who you are," Jo said.

Julie's brown eyes widened. "No-oo." She paused in front of a white-paneled door marked 6B. "Here we go." She rapped on the door and chirped, "Zoë? You have visitors! Isn't that nice?"

There was a pause before Zoë answered, "Come in."

Jo opened the door. The room, wallpapered with pink-and-white lilies, was larger than she expected. In addition to a bed draped in a pink-and-white coverlet, it featured a large bureau, a television bolted to the wall, a writing desk with chair, and a cushy armchair in the corner. On the wall opposite the door, a large double-paned window overlooked a garden courtyard with paths meandering through manicured lawn and shrubs. Off to the right, an open door revealed a private bathroom.

Jo stepped in toward Zoë, who sat in the comfy chair, staring out the window. "Zoë, do you remember us?"

She turned, and smiled. "I do, thank goodness. I remember everything that happened since I woke up in the woods. At least so far."

"How are you settling in?" Arnett asked. "Have you remembered anything?"

"Nothing." As Zoë looked around the room, her eyes filled with tears and the traces of confusion and fear in her expression intensified. "And I'm not really settling in. The room is fine, but it makes me feel like I'm twelve and like I'm in prison all at the same time. And everyone has been nice to me, but the way they talk to me, like I'm some sort of mental patient, scares me even more." She met Arnett's eyes, then Jo's, with a pleading expression. "Have you figured out who I am?"

Jo pulled over the chair from the writing desk. "Not yet. Nobody has reported you missing."

Zoë held up her wedding ring. "But how can that be? I'm married, shouldn't someone be looking for me?"

Jo nodded again. "That's hard to say. It's only been a few days since you made it to the hospital. Especially because you were up in the woods, maybe you were on some sort of vacation or getaway and aren't expected back yet. Hopefully someone will realize soon that you haven't come home, so we'll keep checking."

Zoë's face contracted. "Or maybe my husband was with me, and he wasn't lucky enough to get away. Maybe that's whose blood is on my shirt—maybe he's lying out there, dead or dying, while I'm sitting here, helpless."

Jo took a deep breath, and made a quick choice. "You're right, that's a possibility. Which means the sooner you get your memory back, the better. So we'd like to try something out, if that's okay."

Her eyes widened further. "What?"

"The doctor mentioned the best way to help someone with amnesia is to bring them to familiar surroundings, to trigger their memories. But we can't do that, since we don't know where to bring you. So we thought we'd try taking some guesses."

Zoë looked between the two of them. "I'll try anything you think will help."

"Great. Then the first thing I want to ask you about is your tattoo."

Zoë eyes widened. "What tattoo?"

Jo did a mental double take. "The tattoo on your back. Of the baby's footprint?"

Zoë bolted up and dashed into the bathroom. Once in front of the mirror she pulled up her green T-shirt and twisted around. "A baby's footprint." She whipped back around to Jo, a cascade of emotions flooding her face. "I have a baby? What does it say at the bottom? I need to find him—or her? They must need me—"

Jo led her back to the chair. "Please, sit back down. We don't know anything for sure, that's why we wanted to ask you about it. We think that's a name and a date at the bottom, but it's no longer legible. And it doesn't mean you have a child for sure—sometimes people get a tattoo like that for a niece or nephew, or a godchild. But no matter what, our techs assured us the tattoo is at least ten years old, probably older, so they're not a baby anymore." She paused while Zoë perched on the edge of her chair. "Take a deep breath for me. If you're upset, it'll be harder for the memories to flow. Then think about the possibilities, one at a time, and see if they bring anything up for you. We think the first letter of the name may be an S or a P."

Zoë rubbed her hands together in her lap. "A baby. Or a niece or a nephew, which means I'd have a sister or a brother. Or a godchild? S… or P?" She shook her head, and tears flowed down her cheeks. "None of it means anything to me. How is that possible? They meant enough to me that I tattooed the name on my body, how can I not remember them?"

Jo grasped one of Zoë's hands with both of hers. At the touch, Zoë doubled over, forehead on Jo's hand, and sobbed.

"It's okay, let it out," Jo whispered as Zoë clung to her hands. "I know you're scared, I know. But we're going to fix this. We're going to find out who you are, and we're going to find out why you have that tattoo, okay? We just need your help to do that. When you're ready. Can you help us?"

Zoë's sobs crested and slowed. She sat back up, took the tissues Arnett had pulled over from the side of the bed, and sniffled. "Please. Whatever I can do to help, I need to do that."

Jo squeezed her hand. "Okay, let's try. Tell us if it gets to be too much and we'll stop."

Zoë nodded.

"We think it's possible you were on some sort of camping trip in the woods, since that's the main reason people go to the area around Taltingham. Does anything like that ring a bell? Driving up to the woods in an RV, or maybe putting up a tent? Building a campfire?"

She pulled her arms around herself. "No, not camping, not a tent, nothing."

"Maybe if you try to visualize it? Call up a campsite in your mind?"

Zoë squeezed her eyes closed for a long moment, then reopened them. "Nothing."

"How about a cabin out in the woods? Maybe driving out in the country? Maybe carrying bags into a house?"

She closed her eyes again, then shook her head.

Jo continued with several related scenarios, all with the same results, then sent a glance at Arnett. He nodded his agreement.

"Okay, let's shift gears a little," Jo said. "This may be a little harder, but I think we need to try it."

Fear flashed across Zoë's face. "What do you mean?"

"We think someone may have hit you on the head. Can you try to picture that, someone hitting you on the back of the head?"

"Nothing's coming to me."

"Okay. We think you may have run away from someone. Does that bring anything up?"

Zoë's eyes danced under her eyelids, and her face tightened. Jo jumped on the change. "What do you see?"

Zoë's face scrunched as she concentrated. "I'm not sure. I mean, I'm not sure when it's from, exactly. I just got a picture of running through the woods, trying not to crash into the trees, but I couldn't stop because I was terrified, like something was chasing me. And I had to fight not to slip because I didn't have real shoes on, my toes were cramping because I had to curl them to keep my slippers on, and I was so scared—" Her eyes flew open. "But it's gone again."

"Keep your eyes closed, see if it comes back. Was it light out or dark?"

"Dark. It must have been nighttime."

"Maybe the night before you found your way to Taltingham? Do you recognize anything?"

"No, it was all just blurry trees flashing around me— Oh—"

"What?" Jo asked.

"I just had another, like, flash? Of slipping and falling, then tumbling down a slope out of control. But now it's gone again." She opened her eyes and stared at Jo with fear and suspicion. "None of that makes any sense. The doctor says I was thrown from a car."

Jo shook her head. "We aren't sure that's what happened. In fact, your injuries don't really match up with that possibility. What you just described fits them much better. Can you see anything else? What was the terrain like?"

Zoë pressed her palm into her eyes. "I can't, I'm sorry. It was so dark, I couldn't see more than a few feet in front of me."

"Do you have any sense of why you were running? Who was chasing you?"

"I don't know, I just know I was afraid, and for some reason I felt like they could catch up with me at any second. I'm really sorry, that's all."

"Please don't be sorry. That tells us quite a lot." Jo smiled a reassuring smile. "One more question. We think you may have had to hit someone to get away from them, and that's what caused the blood on your clothes. Can you picture that, hitting someone?"

Zoë tried again, but shook her head.

Arnett asked, "Maybe slashing at someone with a knife?"

She shook her head again, and her eyes flew open. "I'm sorry, I need to stop, it's just making me scared all over again, and my head is throbbing. Can we stop? Maybe try again later? Maybe if you leave me a list of things that you think might have happened?"

"Of course we can try later. We're so sorry to have to put you through this." Jo crossed into the bathroom and poured a glass of water, then set it in front of her.

Zoë sipped the water. "No, it's okay, I understand. We have to do it if I'm going to remember. I think I just need to rest, then I can try again."

"Please, don't worry. It will all come back, and we'll have you home before you know it. But please call us if you think of anything, no matter how small, okay?" Jo stood up, and crossed to the door.

Zoë followed behind, arms wrapped around her midsection. "I will."

Once they were safely in the car and out of earshot, Arnett turned to Jo. "It was worth a shot. Too bad it didn't work. Back to square one."

Jo fingered the necklace at her throat.

CHAPTER SEVEN

As soon as the detectives left, Zoë ran back into the bathroom. For the umpteenth time, she stared into the mirror, this time turning to look at the tattoo. But otherwise, nothing was different—the frightened-mouse brunette dressed in oversized clothes could have been any stranger off the street.

She returned to the bedroom and snatched up the notepad she'd been filling up with details, trying to paint a picture of herself. She crossed off an item near the top, *Thrown from car in accident,* then jotted several new items at the bottom of the list.

A child—my own? A niece or nephew or godchild?
Ran from someone through the woods. Who? Why?

She considered each item on the list in turn, hoping the sum of the parts would yield some new insight.

She wore a wedding ring, so she was married. When the nurses brought her a stack of donated clothes to wear, she'd realized she didn't like pastel colors, or, ironically given the room's decorating scheme, any shade of pink. The jewel tones called to her, especially the forest green shirt and the deep purple cardigan. She'd instantly reached for the pants over the skirts or dresses. When walking around the grounds the day before, she noticed a gardener trimming roses, and without even thinking had blurted out that it was the wrong time of year for that—and when she reached one that was in early bloom, she knew its name, Kardinal, and that it was a hybrid tea rose.

When she found the library in the common area, it'd been like finding a chest full of gold. She'd snatched up all the mysteries and thrillers she could find; the orderly had laughed and said she must like to solve puzzles. Television had been helping, too: she loved the reality TV shows, especially documentaries and informational shows, but hated sports, anything animated, and war dramas. And as she watched some crazy guy who stranded himself repeatedly out in the wilderness, she realized she knew the basics of camping, along with how to fish and trap small game.

What sort of woman did all that suggest? Not a girly-girl, closer to a tomboy. Intelligent and eager to learn. Outdoorsy. Someone who knew about keeping a home, if gardening counted. A woman who was loved by someone, and loved someone. A husband and at least one child, whether the child was hers or not.

A sum total that added up to barely more than you'd know about someone after a five-minute chat at a cocktail party.

She threw the pad back down and crawled onto the bed, curling up around one of the pillows as she fought back the flood of tears. How was she here alone, frightened to death, when she had a husband and at least some sort of family?

The brief flashes of memory didn't add much to the picture, other than more to fear—and not just fear of the emptiness that filled her when she tried to remember who she was, but fear of *something*. Of *someone*. That morning in the woods, she'd woken terrified, and had stayed terrified until she was safely inside the ambulance. Which made zero sense if she'd been thrown from her car in some accident—so she wasn't surprised to discover that wasn't true. She'd already known it was wrong on some level anyway, because every time she'd tried to analyze her fear and considered a car wreck, she had a vague sense of not-quite-right. Like when you have a word on the tip of your tongue and someone offers you the wrong word—even though you don't know what the *right* word is, you somehow know the one they gave is *wrong*.

Which really sucked, because if she'd been thrown from a car, that would have been the beginning and end of her troubles. She'd have nothing to worry about, other than the bump on her head.

But running through the woods? That felt ominously correct, and brought her terror right back. Because you didn't run through the woods unless someone was chasing you. And if someone had been trying to find her *then*, they could be trying to find her *now*. Sure, it was possible the attack had been random, and the attacker had decided it was too risky to keep after her once she'd disappeared. Maybe he'd gone on looking for greener pastures, for some other woman who wouldn't escape from him. Or maybe whoever the bastard was, she'd killed him.

But maybe not. And maybe he didn't like the idea of her running around, able to identify him.

She sat up and glanced around the room. Was she safe here? This was the sort of place meant to keep the patients from getting *out*, not to keep anyone from getting *in*. But there was no way her attacker would think to look for her in a place like this, right? More than likely, if he was trying to find her, he'd just wait for her to return to her normal life. She wouldn't do that until she remembered who she was, and once she remembered who she was, she'd also remember what happened and could protect herself.

She lay back down. Problem solved. She'd stay here until she remembered, and when her memory returned, she'd know what to do from there.

But no, it wasn't that simple. She jumped up and paced the room. She arrived in Taltingham without a wallet or a phone— which meant whoever did this to her had them. Which meant they knew where she lived. If she didn't show back up in her normal life, they'd realize something was wrong. Then what would they do? Check with the police? Check with hospitals? Describe her, and be told about a woman fitting her description who'd lost her memory? And all she could do was sit here, completely vulnerable with no memory and no ability to help herself.

She stared out the window at two elderly women wending their way along the garden paths. But the little flashes of memory were a good sign, they had to be, and the rest might come back any minute. Yes, that was good. But who knew how long she could afford to wait passively? If the doctor and the detectives believed triggering her memory was the best way, she'd do everything in her power to trigger it herself.

She snatched up the remote control from her nightstand. The only real options she had while sitting in this room were books and television, and books took too long. So she'd try as many different channels and shows as it took until she managed to trigger *something*.

CHAPTER EIGHT

Back at HQ, Jo's phone buzzed as she walked to her car. She checked it, and found a text from Eric, the last man she'd dated. Nausea roiled through her.

I don't like how we ended things. We need to talk.

Really? Suddenly out of nowhere, after six weeks?

The last time she'd seen him was on Valentine's Day. They'd had an amazing dinner at an upscale-Italian restaurant, then gone back to his place. They'd raced each other to the bed with a playful, burning passion that stayed lit well into the night.

After the second round, he'd rolled over and pulled open his nightstand.

"You can't be ready *again*." She'd laughed, hoping he was.

But instead of a condom, he pulled out a box wrapped in red paper and tied with a white ribbon.

Something told her she didn't want to open it. But he hadn't gone down on one knee, so she figured she was safe. She kissed him, then started to pull apart the ribbon.

His hand shot out to stop her. "No, you have to untie it or slip it off. If you break the ribbon, it's bad luck."

She'd rolled her eyes and ripped the ribbon right out of the knot, ignoring the flash of *something* on his face. "You can't possibly believe that."

She lifted the lid from the small box. On the inside, sitting on a small square of batting, was a key.

"To the house," he explained when she didn't speak.

"Right." She cleared her throat. "Eric, I appreciate the sentiment, but I don't think I'm ready for this."

His face went blank. "We've been together for six months, Jo."

The conversation had spiraled downward predictably from there. She said she'd always been clear that she wasn't looking for anything long-term. He said he had a right to expect more by now, and he wanted a commitment, or they were over. She said she was happy the way things were. He told her the relationship was over, and asked her to leave.

That, followed by six weeks of silence, said all that needed to be said. What had he thought was happening all this time? Had he been bluffing, thinking she'd run to him and say she'd changed her mind? That she wanted to get married and have his kids? Wasn't that just the teensiest bit completely passive-aggressive?

Jo closed her eyes and took a deep breath. Why was her reaction to this so dramatic? Yes, the timing was odd. But her therapist had taught her that when surface emotions seemed stronger than they should be, something else was at the root of the issue. So what was she really upset about?

Not the timing. The implication that she somehow owed him a conversation.

Her hand flew to the diamond at her neck, originally the central stone in the engagement ring her murdered fiancé had given her, and her eyes squeezed shut. She'd fallen in love with two men in her life, and both had been violently murdered—after going through all of that, she just couldn't invest in everything a serious relationship entailed. So she'd been extremely careful to be clear with Eric, and not send the wrong signal. She never saw him more than once a week. She rarely stayed over his house, or allowed him to stay over hers. To be fair, during the holidays and after, his hints had become more brazen, and she'd compromised several times to keep the peace. But still not enough to imply a long-term commitment. And although she'd been sorry when he'd broken things off, if he wanted more than she could give, he'd been right to walk away. And she had respected that choice, not insisted on something he couldn't give.

"It's bullshit," she said aloud, and grabbed the phone. She placed a call, then tapped her finger against her leg while she waited for the line to pick up.

"Hello?"

"Matt. I've decided to take you up on that dinner Saturday."

*

Twenty minutes after confirming the time and location of her dinner with Matt, Jo pushed through the door of Fernando's Bar & Grill. She spotted Lopez and Marzillo at a wooden table in the far corner, huge margaritas and chips already in front of them. She pointed to let the hostess know she'd found her party, and grabbed one of the two remaining chairs.

"You already started without me?" She feigned indignation.

Marzillo pushed a third margarita toward her. "You're half an hour late! And, we got your kick-start right here. Appetizers on the way."

"Sorry about that. I got a text from Eric as I was leaving the station. And I think I'm going to pass on the margarita, I've been feeling a little off today."

"Well if you hadn't been feeling like shit before, I'm sure the text would have taken care of that." Lopez tossed back a huge gulp of her margarita.

"You're not wrong. I got nauseous the moment I saw it." Jo signaled to a waitress, who held up a single finger to say *one minute*.

"This is the whole reason I avoid relationships in the first place, so I don't have to deal with emotional fallout."

"What'd he say?" Marzillo asked.

"That we *need to talk*."

"What'd you say back?" Lopez asked.

Jo dipped a tortilla chip into the salsa. "Nothing."

"So what, you're gonna ghost him?" Marzillo said.

"Psh, men invented ghosting," Lopez said.

"That doesn't mean they like it when it comes back at them." Marzillo laughed. "But come on, Jo. You're better than that."

Jo fought the temptation to drown her frustration in the margarita. "I'm really not."

Lopez and Marzillo laughed. "Seriously, though," Marzillo said. "Golden rule? Karma?"

Jo rolled her eyes. "Hey, he broke things off with me. Not that there was really much to break off—we were basically fuck buddies. That doesn't buy you anything, golden or other."

Lopez jabbed the air with a chip to hold the floor while she swallowed. "I don't know about that. My feeling is, if you get it on more than three times, you at least need a conversation to end things."

Marzillo lifted her margarita. "Cheers to that."

"Hold on, ladies. We *had* a conversation. The one where he told me he couldn't see me anymore, and kicked me out of his house."

Lopez shook her head vigorously. "Nope. That was the fight itself. I'm talking after."

"If he wanted to talk, he knew my number. Now all of a sudden, after six weeks, I'm supposed to jump when he snaps his fingers? And I'm sorry, but I cannot stress this enough: there was never any exclusivity. There was never even a *discussion* of exclusivity. I never met any of his friends. He never met any of mine. And I think the whole time we were seeing each other, we went out in public together twice, once on the ill-fated Valentine's date."

Marzillo's eyebrows shot up. "And I quote—'we were seeing each other.' Plus, I know there were at least two weekends where you holed up together. Whether you like it or not, that's a little more intimate than casual sex."

Jo grumbled under her breath and looked around for the waitress. "Yeah, fine, I see your point. I still don't think I owe him anything, but I'll consider it. Subject change—how's everything going with Zelda?"

"I think she's cheating on me," Marzillo said.

"What the hell?" Lopez's head whipped around.

"Why do you say that?" Jo asked.

Marzillo counted off on her fingers. "One, her sex drive has disappeared. Two, she's been taking her phone into the bathroom for the last couple of weeks. And three, I followed her and saw her kissing some guy."

Jo choked on the chip she'd just put into her mouth. "You could have just skipped to three."

"No, because then you'd have judged me for following her, and I would've had to explain it, anyway."

Lopez laughed. "True. But can we back up to the part about how you caught your lesbian wife with a man? And don't give me the lecture about sexuality being fluid. I understand fluid."

Marzillo swiped at the salt lining her glass. "Not gonna lie, it hurts more than if it had been another woman. And I don't even understand why."

"Did you confront her?"

"Yeah. I thought she'd deny it and I'd have to pull out the pictures—"

"You took pictures?" Jo asked.

Marzillo blinked at her. "Of course I took pictures. What do I do all day? I process *evidence*. You think I'm gonna go into something like that without cold, hard facts? Anyway, she didn't deny it. So I told her to get the hell out."

"Are you okay?" Jo asked.

Marzillo tossed back the rest of her margarita. "I will be. We'll both take some time to think, and then we'll talk. If there's a problem we can fix, we'll fix it. If not, better I find out now when I'm thirty-seven than in fifteen years when my vagina's shrinking and I'm having hot flashes every five minutes. Not cute."

Jo and Lopez stared for a moment, at a loss for words, before a wide-eyed Lopez broke the silence. "Please tell me that vagina thing isn't real."

CHAPTER NINE

The next morning, Jo pushed Eric as far to the back of her mind as she could while she and Arnett scoured the new missing persons cases for anyone that matched Zoë's description.

Arnett stared at his monitor. "Absolute bupkis, still? I get why her job isn't looking for her if she took a vacation week or some such. But how can a husband be okay with not hearing from his wife for days in this age of cell phones?"

"Maybe he thinks she's not getting any signal? Or maybe he went off on a boys' trip while she was on a girls' trip? Or maybe she's recently divorced? An ex wouldn't be looking for her."

"Or maybe she killed her husband," Arnett said.

"Maybe *he* tried to kill *her*." Jo leaned forward and smacked her desk. "No. Either way, we can't just sit here waiting for someone to report her. I say we start canvassing as best we can. She was running through the woods in her slippers, which means she wasn't out hiking for the day. She was either living up there or camping up there. I say we assume camping, because we can start with the area campsites. Luckily, most of them haven't opened yet for the season, so that'll cut down on the work."

"Let's do it." He stood and grabbed his coat.

After asking the Berkshire County SPDU to keep an eye out for any empty houses or campsites that should have residents, they spent the rest of the day and the following morning checking the sites closest to Taltingham. Nobody recognized Zoë's picture, or reported an abandoned campsite of any sort.

They'd just begun to widen their circle when Jo's phone rang. "Marzillo. I have you on speaker. What's up?"

"You remember I put a rush on Zoë Doe's DNA results? I didn't want to get your hopes up, so I didn't tell you I called in a favor to get the results back fast. They just came in."

"Remind me to send them a few dozen doughnuts," Arnett said.

Marzillo continued, "First, and not surprising, they confirmed that the blood on Zoë's shirt was not her own."

"As you say, not surprising."

"Second, we can't find a match for either sample in CODIS."

Frustration pricked at Jo. "Damn. It's good she doesn't have any priors, but I was hoping the blood would pull up a known rapist or murderer."

"Nope, neither she nor the blood donor is known to us. However, don't despair just yet." Marzillo paused.

"You're enjoying this a little too much." Jo's eyes narrowed.

"It's not often I get a twist like this. Zoë's related to the bleeder." Jo sat up in her seat. "Related? How?"

She could hear the smile in Marzillo's voice. "She's Zoë's daughter."

"You're sure?" Arnett asked.

"Positive."

A slew of thoughts flooded Jo's mind. "Here's a question for you. I've heard about some cases where analysts were able to identify the race of an offender from a DNA sample, even eye and hair color. Any chance we can do something like that?"

"Not cheaply, and not quickly, and I have to warn you, the technology isn't quite as advanced as you might think. The lab we use doesn't do that sort of analysis, so you'd have to get an approval from Lieutenant Martinez to justify the expense. And since we're not even sure a crime was committed…"

"It's not likely he'll go for it. Got it. I don't suppose you have another bomb you're waiting to drop on us?" Jo asked.

"Nope, that's it."

Jo thanked her and hung up, then turned to Arnett. "At least that has to narrow down the problem space to some degree, if we're looking for a mother-daughter pair, or two women likely from the same area rather than just one?"

Arnett tilted his head skeptically. "Maybe, if everything is aboveboard. But if it isn't, I'm not so sure. Because we haven't seen anything that looks even close to that in all the missing persons files we've gone through."

"Not aboveboard. You mean like, if she gave the daughter up for adoption and their reunion went terribly wrong, something like that?"

"Roughly. And normally I'd question how likely that was, but given these circumstances…"

"Your normal preference for simplicity and rejection of coincidence is turned on its head. In an odd way, Occam's razor is still preserved, if you believe that the best way to explain bizarre circumstances is bizarre coincidence."

Arnett glared at her. "Keep going like that and you're gonna give me a migraine."

She laughed. "I'm already giving myself one. So our question is, how do we use this to our advantage? And I think the first thing we need to do is have another chat with Zoë."

CHAPTER TEN

They found Zoë watching TV in her room, slouched in the cushy chair with a throw blanket pulled up over her shoulders.

"Hello again," Jo said from the doorway.

Zoë sat up. "Please, come in. Have you found anything out?"

"Yes and no." Jo stepped inside the room.

A worried expression flashed across Zoë's face, and she started to stand. "Please take my chair."

"No, please, I can sit here." Jo perched on the edge of the bed while Arnett took the smaller chair. "How are you? Are they treating you well?"

"They try to give me whatever I need. But…" She turned to stare out the window. "It's hard to explain." She turned back and met Jo's eyes. "I can't get my feet under me. Like I'm floating in the ocean with no land in sight. Bobbing, hoping desperately that something appears. With no idea how I ended up in the middle of the ocean, or how I'll ever get out."

Jo nodded. "My grandmother had Alzheimer's disease. Pretty different, I know, but there were times when I could see on her face that she didn't know where she was or who she was, or even who I was, and she was terrified." She fought back the tears that came into her eyes, surprised at her reaction—her grandmother had been gone nearly fifteen years, but in this context, the memory of her grandmother's fear and helplessness were as clear as if they'd happened yesterday.

Zoë nodded, and spoke quietly. "But it's even weirder than that. See this scar right here?" She pulled the jeans up off her ankle, revealing a white slash. "I can't tell you how I got that. But this morning? They gave us pancakes that were raw on the inside, and I mentioned to the young intern who made them that she has to wait until the bubbles pop on the first side before flipping them, and make sure her pan isn't too hot. How did I know that?" She gestured toward a deck of cards on the table. "I know how to play solitaire. I know how to use a curling iron to style my hair. How is that possible?"

Arnett chimed in. "We did some googling. Turns out there are different memory systems in the brain. You've lost your autobiographical memory, but your semantic and procedural memory are intact. Facts, and how to do things."

Zoë shook her head. "Whatever it is, it's really weird, and scary. Like a stranger's living inside my head."

Jo nodded. "Well, we have some news for you. We can confirm you're a mother." Jo braced for her reaction.

A combination of fear and pride played on Zoë's face. "So that footprint is my child's?"

"That seems most likely. Does it call up anything for you? Any memories of a baby, or a little girl, or…"

Zoë stared out the window, eyes flicking left to right, then filling up with tears again. "Still nothing. How is that possible? What kind of a mother can't remember her own daughter?"

Jo hurried to reassure her. "During our research, I read about a woman who didn't recognize her husband. She refused to go home with him because she didn't believe they were married, and kept screaming that she felt nothing for him. But when she did finally remember, she was just as much in love with him as before. So don't worry if you aren't feeling anything right now, it's normal."

Zoë jumped up, shaking her head. "Oh, I'm feeling plenty. I'm angry because I can't remember my own flesh and blood, and I'm terrified that I never *will* remember her. She needs her mother, and I'm stuck in here, useless!" She whirled around to face them. "How old is she? Do you have a picture?"

Jo shook her head. "We don't know any of that."

Zoë stuck her hands on her hips, head jutted forward, and her tone took on an accusatory edge. "Then how do you know I have a daughter?"

Jo took a deep breath. "There's no easy way to tell you this. You remember how the clothes we found you in were covered in too much blood to be your own? We analyzed it, and compared it to a sample of your blood. The DNA results indicate the blood belongs to your biological daughter."

Zoë's hands flew to her face as the implication hit. "If all that blood was hers—oh, God—is she dead?"

Jo winced at the pain and fear in Zoë's voice, but she had to plow forward. "It's very possible she's perfectly fine. Plenty of non-fatal injuries bleed profusely. But it won't help for me to sugar-coat this—no matter what, she was hurt badly. And I know all of this is a shock, but, this also means you were with her when she was bleeding, so we need you to think. Do you have any memory of that at all?"

Zoë's head dropped back into her hands, and shook back and forth. "No, I— Oh God. No— No."

Jo sensed a shift, and stepped forward. "Did you see something?"

"No, nothing," she said, her voice muffled through her fingers. "It's just—oh God, what could have possibly happened? What would cause her to bleed like that?"

Jo laid her hand on Zoë's back, and realized the woman was trembling. "It's okay, don't push yourself. We'll figure out what happened."

Zoë's head shot up, her expression angry. "How? When you don't even know how old she is? When you can't even figure out who *I* am?"

Jo reached out for Zoë's hand, but she snatched it away. Jo gave a quick rundown of the steps they'd already taken, trying to calm her. "We can expand our search now that we know you have a daughter. She may have been reported missing, which gives us another avenue to investigate, and—"

Zoë cut her off. "You just said nobody with matching injuries turned up at any area hospitals. But she'd need help if she were still alive, right? Which means she's in danger." Tears filled her eyes. "What if she's dead? What if she's dying? We need to find her, I need to help her—"

Jo's heart sank—she'd been hoping Zoë wouldn't go down that path. "The only way you can help her is by staying calm and not jumping to any conclusions. It's very possible that she's just fine. But you're right, she may need help. Which is why our next step is to release a picture of you to the media, see if anyone recognizes—"

"No!" The word ripped from Zoë's mouth like buckshot.

Jo froze, and watched Zoë's mouth open and close, searching for words that wouldn't come, until they all came out in a sputtering rush.

"You can't. I mean—" Her glance darted between Jo's and Arnett's. "Don't you see? Someone tried to hurt us. They might still be looking for us, especially if they think I can identify them. If you go to the media, that will lead them right to me!" The final words burst out in a sob.

Jo put an arm around her and led her back to the chair, shooting Arnett a questioning look over her shoulder. "I know this is scary for you, but I need you to stay calm."

Arnett brought a glass of water from the bathroom, and held it out to Zoë. "Please, drink."

Jo waited while Zoë sipped, then sipped again.

"I'm sorry, I didn't mean to yell at you. I know you're trying your best," Zoë said. "But please, you just can't. It's not safe."

"I understand you're afraid. We threw a lot at you just now, and you need some time to process it all," Jo said. "We want to make sure you feel safe, okay? So let's talk it through."

Zoë nodded, and took another sip of water.

"First of all, the media report won't mention where you're located. Second, this is a secured facility." Jo pointed to the visitor badge hanging around her neck. "Not even police can get in here without permission. Nobody's going to reach you."

Zoë's eyes flashed to the window. "You think that, but look. There are no bars on the windows, and someone could push right through those hedges. They could climb right over that wall with a ladder."

Jo peered out at the fifteen-foot hedge and the wall. Crossing it would be nearly impossible, but Zoë's reaction wasn't fueled by logic. Jo needed to switch tactics.

"I promise you, it's designed to look pleasant from in here, but it's very secure. And we have a bigger problem—if your daughter's in trouble, we need to find her as quickly as possible. To do that we need to figure out who you are as quickly as possible. We need to get you to people and places that will trigger your memory, so you can tell us what happened."

Zoë reached out to set the glass on the table, her hand shaking so hard that water spilled from the glass. She took another deep breath, and looked up at Jo, her face rigid. "You're right, it doesn't matter what happens to me. Finding her is the most important thing, and that's the fastest way. I'm just going to have to push down the fear and trust you. But can I at least get a guard or something like that? Or maybe I can talk to another doctor besides Doctor Soltero? Maybe someone that can hypnotize me or something?"

Arnett took the glass from Zoë and set it down for her. "Tell you what. We'll talk to our lieutenant about a guard for you, okay? And we'll have Doctor Soltero call you as soon as he can to talk through your options. And we'll talk to the director here to make sure the staff is alerted that the information about you is going out to the public tonight on the news."

Zoë wrapped her arms around her abdomen, and nodded. "Yes, okay, thank you so much. Just do whatever you need to do to find my daughter."

"Don't worry, we'll find her *and* keep you safe," Jo said. "And please, if you remember anything at all, let us know as soon as possible, no matter what time it is. Even a small thing that seems meaningless to you might help, okay?"

Zoë nodded, and took another sip of water. "Okay, I will. Thank you so much."

Jo and Arnett left the room, and asked the nurse at the security desk to check on Zoë once they'd gone.

Then, as soon as they exited the building, Jo turned to Arnett. "She remembered something."

CHAPTER ELEVEN

Arnett pulled open the passenger's side door of their vehicle. "Are you sure? She seemed pretty upset. Maybe the patented Fournier instinct doesn't work on people who have no idea who they are."

Jo slid into the driver's seat. "Maybe. But she balked for the tiniest moment, then suddenly panicked at the idea of us going to the media. I think she remembered part of the attack—not her attacker's face, because she would have jumped to identify whoever did this. But maybe a glimpse of him from behind hurting someone else, something like that. Whatever it was, she's terrified he'll come after her again."

"Or maybe she saw herself murdering her own daughter," Arnett said.

Jo shot him a sharp glance and tapped her nail on the steering wheel. "Maybe, but what would that scenario look like? She kills her daughter, then runs off into the woods for some reason, hits her head, and can't remember who she is? Except why would she run off into the woods in the first place?"

"Maybe she's faking this whole thing. Maybe she killed her daughter and realized she'd never be able to make it look like self-defense, so she figured she'd pretend it was a random attacker."

"And you're saying she's been faking the amnesia the whole time?"

"I'm not saying it's likely, I'm just saying it's possible."

"But why? Wouldn't it be easier to just say from the start that someone attacked your daughter, and you got away? Why add the additional complication of the amnesia? And if that's so, why is she so terrified of us going to the media?"

Arnett wagged his head. "You're right, it's a stretch. And it doesn't really matter in terms of our next step anyway. She gave permission to go to the media, but we don't need it. This isn't just about her."

Jo switched on the ignition. "I agree. Whatever else happened here, her daughter's the main victim."

Arnett nodded. "If we hurry, we can get her picture up on the local news affiliates tonight."

As they hurried to put together the information for the public appeal, Arnett's theory nagged at Jo. When she was able to break away, she stepped into an empty conference room, and put through a call to Matt Soltero.

"Jo. What a nice surprise."

"I'm sorry to disappoint, but I'm calling about work."

"Ah, well. But I'm still happy to help."

"We talked before about the psychological reasons for amnesia, particularly someone wanting to forget something traumatic that happened to them. But what if rather than the victim, the amnesiac were the perpetrator, say if they killed someone? Could that lead to amnesia?"

He paused. "It would definitely count as something to be upset over. Do you think Zoë was the attacker here?"

Jo tugged at her necklace as she considered her answer. "Bob suggested it. But it doesn't seem plausible when I follow it through and I don't get a sense of anything like that from her. So I thought I'd see if I could rule it out from a psychological perspective. Would the memory loss be more consistent with something traumatic happening *to* her than with something she did?"

"I've seen both types of cases. One in particular involved a Vietnam vet who lost his memory shortly after setting fire to a village full of women and children."

"So guilt can trigger the amnesia."

"I'd be careful about making judgment calls on the underlying emotional attribution, but in essence, yes."

"Damn. Well, that's good to know, even if it doesn't help limit the possibilities."

"Anything else I can help with?"

"That's it for now."

"Then I'll look forward to Saturday."

She said her goodbye and hung up. Jo hurried back inside to watch the news segment, praying someone would come forward in time to help Zoë's daughter—if it wasn't already too late.

CHAPTER TWELVE

The man turned up the volume on the hotel TV.

He'd been watching every local news broadcast for days, googling every search term he could come up with, and scouring the local newspaper for any mention of her. Just as he was beginning to believe she'd died somewhere in the woods, there she was, large as life, filling up his screen.

The police had found her, and she was alive.

"Not much is known about the woman, who police are referring to as Zoë. She's five-five, one hundred twenty pounds, and somewhere between thirty-five and forty-five years old. Police believe she has a daughter, name also unknown, who may also be missing. If you recognize this woman, Oakhurst County State Police Detective Unit ask that you call the hotline shown below with any information you have."

As the news anchor segued to a story about a string of gas-station robberies throughout western Mass, he lowered the volume, but kept an eye on the screen in case they came back with more information.

She couldn't remember anything? That was an unexpected stroke of luck. In that case he just had to get to her and kill her, then everything would be okay.

The report hadn't given him much to go on, but he could work with what it had. Oakhurst County detectives were asking for information, which gave him a general sense of where she was. He'd find some untraceable way to call them—not hard to get a burner phone. They'd get a deluge of calls from cranks, and his call would meld in with the masses. He'd find out who was on the case and follow them until they led him to her.

But he had to move quickly, before she remembered.

CHAPTER THIRTEEN

For the next three days, Jo and Arnett became a task force of two, fielding a barrage of calls claiming to have information about Zoë, and checking on her when they were able. Most of the calls were easily eliminated as irrelevant or cranks, and by Saturday they'd narrowed it all down to several dozen they needed to follow up. Several of those turned out to be deeply disturbing, like the twenty-five-year-old man who showed up at the station claiming Zoë was his wife, with no pictures or other proof. After a very short investigation, they'd discovered he was married—to another woman who was at home cooking his dinner.

Arnett slid back into his desk chair when they returned, shaking his head. "What the hell did he think was going to happen? That we'd trot her right on out and hand her to him, no questions asked?"

"Preferably in handcuffs, so he'd be able to quickly tie her up in his basement," Jo added.

Arnett ran his hand up and down his face. "Nearly thirty years on the force, and people still manage to surprise me."

Jo waved her hand in a circle toward him. "That's because no matter how much you try to disguise it, you, my friend, are an eternal optimist. You believe in the fundamental goodness of people."

"Lies and slander." A grin tugged at his lips. "Anyway, back to it. I have to leave in about an hour, I promised Laura I'd be home in time for us to eat dinner together."

Jo glanced at the time on her computer. "I've got to head out, too, so that works out well. I can manage by myself tomorrow if you'd like—" Jo's phone rang, and her brow creased. "It's Sunset Gardens."

Arnett looked up from a stack of messages as Jo connected the call and put it on speakerphone. "Fournier."

"Hello. This is Dolores Chambray, I'm a nurse at Sunset Gardens care facility. I'm sorry to disturb you, but a man just showed up claiming to be Zoë's husband, and she's extremely upset. She asked me to call you."

Jo came up out of her chair, and grabbed her blazer. "Is he still there?"

"No, he disappeared when I went to get Zoë."

Jo shot an annoyed look at Arnett, who was shrugging into his coat. "We'll be there as soon as we can."

Fifteen minutes later, Jo pushed through the front doors of Sunset Gardens. A guilty- looking woman rose from behind the counter. "Dolores Chambray?"

"Yes. Thanks for getting here so quickly, I wasn't sure what to do."

Jo crossed quickly to the counter. "Where's Zoë now?"

"She's in her room. Julie's calming her down."

"Walk us through what happened."

Dolores' worried expression intensified, and she threw a nervous look at the security guard sitting next to her. "Okay, well, I was catching up on paperwork while Jerry was on his break, and a man came in. He said he thought his wife was here, the woman who'd lost her memory, and asked to see her."

"Then what?" Arnett asked.

"I went to get her, and when I got back, he was gone."

"Just like that you went to get her, because he said she was his wife?"

Dolores flushed. "He was convincing. He said he saw her picture on the news, and that it was his wife. I know you've been trying to get her to remember, and I figured her memory would come back if she saw him. If not, no harm done."

"No harm done unless he pulls out a gun. We had a long discussion with Director Rosen about safety protocols. Did she not pass that down to you?"

Dolores' color deepened still further. "I'm sorry, I wasn't thinking."

Jo took over. "What did this man look like?"

Dolores looked relieved to be on firmer ground. "Tall, about six feet I'd guess. Dark hair. I couldn't see his eyes, he had sunglasses on."

"Did he give his name?" Arnett asked.

"He said it was Oscar Snow."

"But you didn't check ID?" he asked.

"No." She looked like she was about to cry. "And when I told Zoë, she refused to come out, and asked me to call you, and to get his address and telephone number."

At least someone had common sense. "And when you got back, he was gone?"

"Yes. I ran to the door, to see if he was just outside for some reason, but he wasn't. So then I came back in and alerted Jerry"— she motioned to the guard—"then checked the other wing. I'd have noticed him in the hall if he'd come down Zoë's wing."

"Unless he hid in one of the rooms when he heard you coming back out," Arnett said.

Dolores' face turned sickly white. "Jerry checked every room after that."

"I did. Everything was clear." Jerry nodded.

"You have a security camera on the gate. We'll need to see the footage," Jo said.

Jerry stood up. "I'll pull it for you."

"Thanks. In the meantime, we need to talk to Zoë." Jo rounded the corner before Dolores could respond, and strode down to Zoë's room, Arnett at her side. When they reached the door, they knocked gently, then opened it.

Zoë sat in the oversized chair, wrapped in her throw blanket, with Julie encouraging her to drink what appeared to be herbal tea. As soon as she saw them, she set the cup down, and started to rise.

"No, please stay where you are." As Jo crossed the room, Julie stood up and offered her chair. "Thank you. Dolores told us what happened. Are you okay?"

Zoë nodded her head and looked down into her mug. "I'm fine, just shaken up. They want me to take a sedative, but I don't like how they make me feel. Have they searched the building?"

"They have, every room. Whoever the guy was, he's gone. We're pulling up the security footage, and we'll find him. But we need to ask you. The man said his name was Oscar Snow. Does that sound familiar at all to you?"

Zoë met Jo's eyes. "No. But that doesn't really mean much."

"No, right. We'll check into it, but it's almost certainly a fake name. And I'm sure the man was just some random person. We always get a few of those when we have a situation like this."

Zoë nodded, and looked back into the mug.

Jo threw a look back at Arnett, who looked just as confused as she felt. "I know you're shaken up, and I would be, too. But the good news is, the security worked. He didn't get into the building, and he didn't get anywhere near you. And, now we'll be able to convince our lieutenant to get that guard for you. We'll talk to him about it first thing in the morning, okay?"

Zoë's eyes shot up to Jo. She started to say something, but stopped. "Okay," she finally said.

Jo searched her face. "Or, I can talk to Doctor Soltero about moving you to another facility if that would make you feel safer?"

Zoë turned to stare out her window, and shook her head. "No. You're right. Everything worked the way it was supposed to. Dolores stopped him at the counter, and he's gone now."

Jo reached out to squeeze her hand. "You're going to be fine. And don't take that sedative if you don't feel like it—but it might help you sleep."

Zoë looked back at her, and smiled. "Thank you, Detective. I appreciate all your help."

Jo smiled back. "That's what we're here for. If you have any concerns, or anything else happens, call us right away. That card I gave you the first time we met has my direct cell number written on the back."

Jo watched Zoë over her shoulder as she and Arnett left.

CHAPTER FOURTEEN

Back at the front counter, Jerry had a memory card waiting with the relevant security footage. Jo stuck it into the front desk computer terminal, started the file playing, and realized almost immediately the footage was useless. Shot from an almost ninety-degree angle, there was no chance of seeing the car's driver, or the license plate number. And, it was in black and white—all they could tell was the car was a dark Toyota, most likely a Corolla. When they'd expressed their frustration, Jerry sheepishly replied that they'd never had to worry about people getting in who shouldn't be there—they'd only ever used the footage to alert them when a resident with dementia was wandering where they shouldn't.

By the time they left, Jo had to hurry to make her date with Matt. The process of getting ready brought to mind Eric's text—she still hadn't responded to it. She promised herself she'd do it the following day, and that she'd make it an actual phone call.

More excited about seeing Matt than she'd expected to be, she slipped on a red sheath dress that never failed to get a reaction from men—only to discover it fit just a titch more snugly across her middle than was flattering. She berated herself for one too many meatball subs as she changed into a more forgiving black-jersey A-line dress. She took her time applying a dark red lip to set off her green eyes and dark brows, and then, satisfied with the result, headed out.

She found Matt waiting for her in the bar of Chez Lumiere. He rose at the sight of her, as handsome as she remembered. His black suit was well made but didn't scream designer, and the cream shirt underneath warmed the olive undertones in his skin. He broke into a smile and held her gaze as he kissed her hand, then turned to tell the hostess they were ready to be seated. As they walked through the champagne-rose tables and armchairs, his fingertips rested ever-so-slightly at the small of her back, and he pulled out her chair before she sat.

"Quite a gentleman. You don't see that very much anymore."

"My mother taught me the secret to winning a woman's heart is to treat her like the treasure she is." He sat, and picked up his menu. "I think I'm in the mood for a steak tonight. They have magnificent filet mignon here. What looks good to you?"

The waiter appeared, and they gave him their orders. Once he filled their water glasses and left, Matt turned to her again. "Have you found out anything else about Zoë?"

"Yes and no," she said, and filled him in on the blood results, and their attempts to trigger her memory. "So far, no luck."

He nodded. "Clever approach."

"And, we had some drama tonight." She told him about the intruder. "Normally I'd say he's just a weirdo, but what's really bothering me is how he knew where to find her. There's no public record you have to keep of where you placed her, is there?"

His brow creased. "No, all information like that is kept strictly confidential. And I trust my staff implicitly."

Jo nodded. "That's what we assumed, but I told Bob I'd check. So that means someone went to some extreme length to figure out her location, which suggests something more nefarious."

"As in, the person who attacked her and her daughter is coming after her again?"

"That's my worry. But Sunset Gardens is on high alert now. Nobody's going to get through that gate, let alone past the front counter. Still, I wonder if it would be worth moving her to a different facility?"

"I can check into it. If it's safer for her, I'll find a way to work it out."

Jo reached over and put her hand on his. "Thank you. I realize that makes things harder for your schedule."

He waved her off. "Completely irrelevant."

She knew that wasn't true, and found him all the more appealing for claiming it was.

The waiter appeared and set their food in front of them, then asked if they needed anything more. They said they didn't.

"That's taken care of, then. So, tell me more about yourself," Jo said.

For the rest of the meal, they chatted easily about their careers, their childhoods, and their families. He was the oldest of four, with two sisters and a brother. He was one of the very few doctors on the planet with parents who disapproved of his career choice, because his father owned a chain of furniture stores he'd hoped Matt would take over. Luckily, his younger brother Raul had been happy to step up to the plate. But while his siblings had several children between them, his mother was still devastated he hadn't married and produced offspring of his own.

Jo laughed. "Never met the right girl?"

"Something like that." He glanced away across the room, then met her eyes again. "Same for you?"

"Something like that." She raised her glass. "Here's to having families that care about our happiness, even if they vocalize it a little too much."

He laughed, touched his glass to hers, then changed the subject.

Throughout the evening, Jo sipped her wine and watched him. The way he spoke, the expressions on his face, even his movements were infused with a natural assurance that drew her. She could easily lose herself in those arms, let his body carry her mind far away, leaving work and family behind. And the way everything seemed to take so much out of her lately, that would be a very welcome getaway.

As they left the restaurant, meal finished, Matt again guided her with a hand gently rested on the small of her back. The gesture, combined with the wine, sent a rush of warmth through her. They handed their stubs to the valet, and he turned to her.

"Coffee at my place?" The tilt of his brow and the corner of his mouth were a gentle tease.

"That sounds perfect. I'll follow you."

The instant his front door closed behind her, he gathered her in his arms and kissed her. Soft and lingering at first, but when she buried her hands in his hair and tugged, the kiss became hungry, and passionate. She savored the taste and feel of him for a long moment, then, heart racing and heat flashing through her, she gently bit his lower lip. He answered by pulling his hips into hers, and when she moaned, he pulled away to lead her to his bedroom.

For once, Jo completely forgot about the coffee.

CHAPTER FIFTEEN

When Jo woke Sunday morning in Matt's bed, the familiar rush of disoriented dread hit her. Waking in someone else's bed, especially the first time, was always a shock to her system. And, despite the cozy eiderdown blanket and the soothing blue of the walls, the emotion was oddly magnified this time, hitting with a side of nausea.

She grabbed her phone from the purse she'd cast aside the night before, and checked the time. Seven-thirty a.m. She'd never be able to sneak out this late without waking him.

She sat up slowly and when he didn't stir, slipped out of bed. She gathered her clothes and tiptoed into the bathroom, her bladder far too full to wait until she got home. When she emerged, fully dressed, he was awake.

"Going somewhere?"

"Work." She slid back over to him and covered her lie with a kiss. "I promised my partner I'd be there at six."

He narrowed his eyes at her, but his half-smile remained. "Far be it from me to interfere with the safety of Oakhurst County. But while I normally love being used for my body, I have to admit I'd like to see you again."

Jo ran her hand down his chest, and kissed him again. "I'd like that, too. I'll call you."

She slipped out the door and into her car, confused when the disorientation didn't dissipate as his house disappeared in the rearview mirror. In fact, it magnified, and—

She yanked the wheel as she rounded the corner, threw open her door, and vomited into the gutter.

She pulled several napkins from her center console and cleaned her face, then poured the half cup of leftover coffee waiting in her cup holder over the vomit, washing away as much as possible.

Something wasn't right. What sort of stomach flu came and went like this? She had sushi the week before, had she picked up some sort of parasite? Or—her father flashed through her mind—could it be some sort of cancer?

She fought down the irrational panic that gripped her chest and redirected to the nearest CVS. Nothing here would solve the underlying problem, but it would get her through the weekend until she could see a doctor. She located the anti-nausea medication, and, dazed by the selection of options, picked one at random and read the back.

A line from the warnings jumped out at her: *Do not use while pregnant.*

Pregnant.

The world retreated into a tunnel around her as she stared at the word. That explained everything: the moodiness, the fatigue, the tight clothes, the nausea. But it couldn't be. She used birth control religiously. And she hadn't had sex since Valentine's Day.

Oh, shit. She hadn't had her period since two weeks before Valentine's Day, either.

She set the anti-nausea medication back on the shelf, hand shaking so hard she nearly knocked it over. She scoured the signs hanging over the aisles and located the one she needed.

An hour later she sat on her bathroom floor, gaping at the second stick to show the same results.

She was pregnant.

When her phone rang, she barely registered the number from Sunset Gardens. She answered, eyes still on the pregnancy test, as Director Rosen's frantic voice broke over the line.

Zoë was gone.

CHAPTER SIXTEEN

The security gate buzzed Jo and Arnett through before they could push the button, and Director Susan Rosen waited for them outside the front entrance of the main building. Dressed in athletic shoes and a navy pencil-skirt suit, she flung back the doors with a strength and purpose that belied her five-foot-three stature and her late-sixty-something age. Once inside, she turned to Arnett, hand extended.

"I spoke to Detective Fournier on the phone. I assume you're Detective Arnett?"

"Correct." He shook her hand. "When did your staff notice Zoë was missing?"

Susan turned to direct her comments to them both. "When she didn't come out to breakfast this morning, one of our orderlies went to check on her, around eight-thirty, and found her room empty. But, to be blunt, the situation is far more complicated than just that. Normally we have breakfast at eight, not eight-thirty. It was delayed because two of our night-shift staff found their purses stolen when they went off shift this morning, and that threw everything into a tizzy. Dolores Chambray then realized her car had been stolen. They called the Northampton PD and had finished the process of giving a statement before anyone realized Zoë was missing."

Jo nodded, and strode over to the women. "When was the last time anyone saw Zoë?"

Dolores looked at Julie, who answered. "About half an hour after you left yesterday. She refused to take a sedative, and said she just wanted to sleep. So I made her a cup of chamomile tea and left her in peace. Since dinner was already over, there was no reason for anyone to bother her again."

Jo calculated. Zoë had been gone for as long as twelve hours.

"And when was the last time you saw your purses?" Jo asked.

Dolores answered this time. "When we clocked in last night at six, just before I called you. We're required to keep personal items locked up." She gestured to a cabinet under the counter.

Jo and Arnett walked around for a better view. "Including your phones?" Jo asked.

"Cell phones aren't allowed out in the building for patient privacy reasons," Susan said.

Arnett pulled on a surgical glove and carefully opened the cabinet to peer at the lock, which was intact. "So how did she get your purses without breaking the lock?"

Dolores looked at Julie, who shrank farther into her seat. "I, um. Sometimes I forget to lock it."

Arnett's head snapped around. "I need the full truth here. Did you really have your purses put away?"

Dolores tensed. "Yes, sir. We'd never break the rules like that. There was nothing disobedient here, it's just that Julie—well, she has a lot on her mind, and she's forgetful on a *good* day."

Julie's neck turned beet red, and Jo pushed down her annoyance. "What happened once you realized they were gone?"

"We did a quick search of the common areas, and the patients who were awake. We figured one of them may have stumbled on the purses when we were on break, without meaning any harm. When we couldn't find them, Susan told us to call the police. Then I called my husband and asked him to bring his car keys, because mine had been in my purse. When he got here, we realized my Suburban wasn't in the parking lot, and we found Julie's keys dropped on the ground next to her Civic. We called the police back, and that's when Todd came running out asking if anyone knew where Zoë was."

The entry door opened, and Marzillo entered.

Jo raised a hand to greet her, then turned back to Dolores. "Did you search her room when you realized she was gone?"

"We didn't. Todd and I checked her bedroom and came right back out. I told him we shouldn't touch anything. But I did notice the window was open, and her lamp and some other stuff was knocked over." She searched Jo's face as she spoke.

"That's good to know, thank you." She introduced Marzillo. "She and her techs will need to analyze the room, this cabinet and counter, and Julie's car keys and car. Can you start her off in Zoë's room?"

Dolores nodded, and led Marzillo down the hall.

Jo turned to Susan. "We're looking at two possibilities here. The most likely is that our friend from yesterday learned enough during his visit to figure out how to come back and kidnap her. The other is that Zoë fled. We'll need to see the gate's security footage, to see if she left alone, or with someone."

Susan produced a memory card. "I've already checked it. Nobody came in, the only car that left was the Suburban." She slipped the card into a computer and pulled up the clip.

Jo and Arnett leaned in as she played and rewound several times. A light-colored Chevy Suburban drove out of the gate and turned right. A portion of the driver's torso was visible, showing a large dark shirt, and the passenger seat appeared to be empty.

"Doesn't mean anything. That could be a man or a woman driving, and Zoë could be tied up in the back of the car. And Oscar could have slipped onto the grounds somehow, then needed a vehicle to get away quickly," Arnett said.

Zoë'd been wrapped up in a blanket when they'd seen her the night before. "Do you have any idea what she was wearing last night?" Jo asked.

Dolores, who'd returned while they searched the footage, looked at Julie, who shook her head. "I *think* she was wearing a dark green sweatshirt, but I'm not sure," Dolores answered.

Jo instructed Dolores and Julie to write down what information they could about their phones, credit cards, and other identifying items in their purses, then stepped out of the building with Arnett to call Lopez. Jo caught her up over speakerphone. "I'm sorry to have to call you on a Sunday, especially Palm Sunday, but I figured you might want to be involved. I can call someone else in if you prefer." For the past few years, Lopez had lived with her mother, who struggled with alcohol-dependency-related health issues, and was also a devout Catholic.

Lopez's voice was bright. "Don't worry, I took my mom to mass last night before I came in to check out Zoë's visitor. I'm free as a bird, and hell no I don't want someone else taking over on this."

Jo smiled. "Excellent. First of all, did you find anything yesterday on Oscar Snow?"

"Nope. I found five currently alive Oscar Snows in Massachusetts. One's a child, one's a teenager, and one's in his eighties. The other two have blond hair and alibis for yesterday afternoon and evening."

"Pretty much what I figured. Marzillo's already here working the scene, so hopefully she'll get some evidence that'll let us know what exactly happened here. Arnett and I will get out an APB for Zoë, our mystery man, and the stolen Suburban. Can you track the phones and such? We should also flag the driver's licenses and the Suburban's plates." She dictated the relevant information.

"Not a problem. Hopefully I'll have something for you shortly."

Jo hung up, then sent out the relevant APBs. When she finished, she turned to Arnett. "Okay, so, what are our next steps? One scenario is Oscar never really thought he'd get close to Zoë, and took advantage of Dolores' absence to do a quick search. He knew security was going to be on the lookout for him and his car, so he climbed the fence, got in through Zoë's window, snatched the purses for the keys, and drove off in the Suburban? Left behind the Civic because it's hard to hide someone tied up in the backseat?"

"I find it hard to believe Zoë'd have her window open after how freaked she was," Arnett said.

Jo's brows shot up. "You're right, that is strange. Maybe he forced it, but that would be hard to do without breaking the window, and they'd have noticed that. You think she bolted?"

He rubbed his forehead. "Not really, because where is she gonna go when she doesn't know who she is? If she wanted to leave, why turn down your offer to relocate her to another facility?"

"I don't know, but I do know she was acting strangely yesterday. Like she'd given up or something. Dammit, I shouldn't have left her alone."

"What were we going to do, sleep at the foot of her bed? And the more I think about it, Oscar probably snuck in some other way and left the window open to confuse us."

"Well, regardless, she may be in danger and we can't afford to wait until Marzillo and Lopez find something. What do we know that we can act on?"

"We've got nothing on Oscar, so that's a dead end. All we have is what we had before, following clues and canvassing the camping spots out in that area of the Berkshires."

Jo's spine straightened. "Wait—you're right. All we can do is go back to where this started. If Oscar kidnapped her to kill her and dispose of her, he's most likely headed back to the Taltingham area. And if she bolted but can't remember anything, the only place she'd know to go is back to Taltingham."

Arnett nodded. "So either way, we need to alert the locals up there asap, and head over ourselves."

They hurried back into the building to let Marzillo know where they were going, then headed back to the car.

"I'll call the local police on the way," Jo said, but as she dropped into the passenger side of the Cruze, her phone rang. "Lopez. Tell me you have something for us."

"Just GPS locations for both cell phones," Lopez answered. "They're showing up just off the Pike, heading east out of town."

CHAPTER SEVENTEEN

Five minutes later, Jo turned off the portable siren as the Cruze closed in on the exit flashing across their GPS screen. Jo recognized the location—it was a service plaza, not an actual exit. Arnett screeched into the parking lot.

"That way." She pointed right, to the far corner of the parking lot, near the restrooms. "And they're not moving."

Arnett slowed. "No way they can get past us now, anyway—this is the only way out."

They both scanned the area for movement as they approached. Arnett parked, and they stepped out of the car. Jo referenced the GPS screen on her phone. "There."

They crossed the pavement, each ready to draw their weapon.

"Shit." Jo's heart sank. "The two dots are on top of one another, right there." She pointed to a trash can.

"Motherfuck. He dumped them." They continued their cautious approach, then gazed down at the red-topped brown can. "Yup. We're standing right on top of them now. Of course."

"I'll call for a tech. He probably realized we could track them and dumped them as soon as possible. But maybe we'll get lucky with some prints or DNA."

Arnett stood, hands on hips, his expression dark. "Maybe Christmas'll come early and he'll have been stupid enough to use them."

"So, he was traveling eastbound, away from Taltingham. Or is that just what he wants us to think?"

"Doesn't really matter. We're back where we started."

Jo pulled out her phone. "I'll alert the locals up there. Can you set up a perimeter around the can?"

He barked a dry laugh. "On it."

Half an hour later, as another of Oakhurst County SPDU's techs, Vince Pepper, arrived to recover the bag of garbage from inside the can, Jo's phone rang. "Lopez. Please tell me you have news for me."

"Some very intriguing tidbits, yes. First up, Dolores Chambray's credit card was used at Walmart just before midnight last night. The charge includes toiletries, food, a thermal sleeping bag, a Swiss army knife, a backpack, mace bear spray, a hunting knife—chime in here when you guess the theme—"

"Survival gear."

"Ding. I'll e-mail you the complete list, but I also want to specifically mention the six five-gallon gas cans. Someone's on a road trip and doesn't want to have to stop off at gas stations. And, by the way, there's another charge, a considerable one, at a gas station out by you guys about an hour after that. My next step is to check their security cam footage."

"So he's heading out to the woods after all, and *is* trying to misdirect us," Arnett said.

Jo tapped the hood of the car with her fist. "Something's not right. If he was on the Pike for any period of time, the cameras would have picked up the plates," she said.

"Maybe he ditched the vehicle, and stole a different one?"

Jo nodded, and paced in front of the car. "Or maybe he realized back streets were a safer bet."

"Doesn't matter. We're back to square one, again." Arnett peered out over the highway. "Taltingham's our only lead."

"Agreed. If he did head in that direction and we move fast enough, we may be able to catch up with them. We need to move, now." She pulled open the car door and jumped inside. "But I have another idea, too." She tapped her phone to call Lopez. "Hey, can you set up a three-way call with Marzillo?"

"I can try, but she might not pick up while she's processing a scene. Hold, please."

Jo listened to the silence until something clicked back over, and Marzillo's voice came on the line. "Jo, Bob. What's going on?"

"Sorry to interrupt you."

"Not a problem, I just finished the main work, because there isn't much to process. No forced entry, nothing like that, which made things easy. Mehil can take care of the rest. What's up?"

"Have either of you heard of GEDmatch?" Jo asked.

"Sounds familiar—" Lopez started.

Marzillo spoke simultaneously. "Brilliant. How did I not think of that?"

Jo laughed. "Probably because CODIS is all you ever need. And we didn't realize Zoë would go missing." Jo turned and acknowledged the confusion on Arnett's face. "GEDmatch is an open-source database of DNA profiles, used mostly by people who are doing family tree research. I've been considering submitting to it to help trace my mother's family. You can upload a DNA profile and find people related to you. I'm hoping we can upload Zoë's profile, and find someone who can tell us more about her."

Lopez drew in a loud breath. "Oh, right, I remember now. That solved some high-profile case in California, right, by triangulating back to shared ancestors?"

Marzillo jumped in. "Yep. Well, two cases that I know of, and both took many months to triangulate to shared ancestors, then build a tree forward from those ancestors to identify potential suspects. Which resulted in lots of suspects because each subsequent generation has more people, who then all had to be located and vetted. But what we're doing should be far easier because we have pictures of the right person, we just need to find someone who can identify her."

Jo nodded with excitement. "That's what I'm hoping."

"But there's bad news, too. You need a different type of DNA profile than we use for CODIS. I'll have to get the lab to work one up for me, and I'm not sure if I can call in another favor this fast. It may take time."

"Wheedle, beg, borrow, steal, whatever you have to do, because we don't know how much time we have here. I don't suppose we can play on your contact's heartstrings by mentioning there's potentially a young girl hurt somewhere that we're trying to find?"

Lopez balked. "We don't know how old the daugh— Oh, I get it. Heartstrings."

"I can try," Marzillo said. "I'll go now."

*

As Arnett sped to Taltingham, Jo contacted the Berkshire County State Police Detective Unit for assistance. She e-mailed pictures of Zoë for dissemination along with information about the stolen vehicle, and the Berkshire detectives assured them they'd get the local police departments on it.

Then, when she couldn't put it off any longer, she called Matt Soltero.

"Well, hello. I'm pleasantly surprised to hear from you so soon," he said.

Her body responded instantly to the sexy purr of his voice— until a vision of the pink line on her pregnancy test slammed the reaction down. She squeezed her eyes shut and kept her voice professional. "I'm sorry it has to be about work yet again, and bad news this time." She caught him up on the situation. "If you hear from her, can you let us know immediately? Of course I'll do the same."

His voice switched from sexy to concerned. "I will, and I'll put my staff on alert."

"Thanks. I'll call you either way later this week." Jo hung up, still trying to push the conflicting emotions from her mind as they pulled up to the tiny 'downtown' area of Taltingham.

They talked to each of the shopkeepers, but no one had seen or heard from Zoë since the ambulance sped her away. They asked Evander Gibson, the owner of the antique store Zoë had stumbled into, to recount again what he'd seen the day she showed up, but learned nothing new. He hadn't laid eyes on her before she entered his store, and couldn't even say which direction she'd come from.

"Looks like we're on our own. Where do we start?" Jo said.

Arnett scanned the short street, and pointed out toward the forest. "Gibson's shop is the first you'd hit if you came from that direction. She said she followed the creek to a dirt road, and then to this paved road. So, let's go find ourselves the first road that intersects in that direction, and hopefully it'll lead to a creek."

"That's the best guess we've got. And if we can be reasonably certain we have the right creek, we can estimate the point where she picked up the creek based on the amount of time she claims to have been walking, and canvas from there."

Back in the car, they turned uphill at the first dirt road, then came almost immediately to a creek. "This can't be it—she mentioned walking for quite a while parallel to the dirt road. This wouldn't have taken her more than fifteen minutes to get to town," Jo said.

"Agreed." Arnett drove on.

With his eyes largely on the road, Arnett missed the second stream, but Jo caught sight of the water, half-hidden from the road by a high bank on the nearest side. "Here's one," she pointed, and Arnett pulled off the road. They scanned the area, and followed the creek uphill. "Looks large enough to follow for a fair distance," Arnett said.

Jo stepped carefully toward the lower bank, then pointed to it. "Hold on, check this out. The vegetation's crushed down. I'm no tracker, but that has to be recent, or it would have sprung back up by now."

Arnett followed, careful to step where she stepped. "Over there, in the mud—a partial footprint."

Jo pulled out her phone, zoomed her camera in, and shot pictures from several angles.

Arnett pulled up a map on his phone. "I'm not seeing anything nearby, no houses, nothing. No reason someone would just happen to be out here tramping around."

Jo twisted to examine the surrounding area. "I agree. And there are several other spots of crushed vegetation leading upstream. But why would Oscar come here? He has to know where the crime scene is. So maybe it *is* Zoë out retracing her steps?"

Arnett grimaced. "That still doesn't make sense to me. Maybe she had something Oscar wanted, and dropped it when she slid down the slope, and he's trying to find it again? Maybe that's why he attacked her and her daughter in the first place?" Arnett said.

"Interesting possibility. Either way, if we track them, we may be able to catch them."

Arnett scanned the area, hands on hips. "What do you think, follow the trail ourselves, or get a tracking dog up here?"

"There's too much underbrush and detritus. Unless they stuck right by the side of the creek, I'm not sure how far we'll be able to track them, and we'll just waste time."

"And contaminate the trail."

Jo pulled out her phone and made two calls. An hour later, an officer from Northampton PD dropped off the nightgown Zoë had been wearing at Sunset Gardens; a tracking dog arrived shortly after. Jo introduced herself and Arnett to Ivan Geary, the handler.

Ivan introduced the white-and-tan pit bull, then exposed him to the nightgown. "Rocket, find it!"

The dog picked up the trail immediately and took off up the creek a few hundred feet—but then made a right turn back in the direction of Taltingham, parallel to the dirt road. Confused, Jo followed Ivan until, half an hour later, Rocket stopped and sat in place.

"This is the end of the trail," Ivan told her.

"The creek runs up the hill, this goes back to town. This should be the starting point, not the ending point. Is it possible we followed the trail in the wrong direction?"

Ivan shook his head. "No way. She follows the intensity of the smell, the direction the scent was laid down, unless I tell her otherwise. Your target walked in this direction."

Was this a residual trail from when Zoë had originally walked into Taltingham? "Is it possible she continued on, but the trail just stopped here for some reason? Could something be interfering with it?"

"No, ma'am. She stopped walking here."

Jo turned in place, surveying the area. "There—tire marks. Someone did a three-point turn here."

Ivan bent to inspect them. "That'd be why. Once the target gets in a car, Rocket can't follow the scent anymore."

Jo crunched a few hundred yards back down to the parallel road and called Arnett. A few minutes later he pulled up, parked, and tramped back with her through the forest to where Ivan waited.

"So we have confirmation she was here, at least," Arnett said.

"But she, or they, didn't retrace her steps, they just found the creek and then drove off," Jo said, brow creased.

Arnett shrugged. "We weren't planning on hiking up it, either, just following it back on a topographical map. No reason Oscar wouldn't do the same, then drive close to where she woke up and hike from there. If they were searching for something, she'd already lost it before she woke up that next morning."

"Good point." Jo stared back toward the creek. "So now that we know they're out here, we approximate the starting point, head there, and hope we can run them down." She grabbed her phone, and pulled up the app they'd consulted earlier. "Okay, if you look here, this is the road from Taltingham, and right here's the creek. How long was she following it?"

"We guessed about six to eight hours from her description, although we don't know how long she walked before she found the creek. But, we'll just have to radiate out from our best guess."

Jo checked the scale of the map, then measured. "That best guess would be somewhere right about here." She touched the screen and a red teardrop appeared. "Two closest towns are Pelhaven and Redville."

CHAPTER EIGHTEEN

After updating Berkshire County SPDU with the new information and redirecting the search to radiate out from the target area, Jo and Arnett had spent the rest of the day canvassing campgrounds, beginning in the Redville area. By evening, they'd managed to talk to the employees and campers at the three southern-most sites, but nobody recognized Zoë's picture, or reported any accidents or other unusual circumstances of any kind.

As Jo climbed back into her car at HQ, frustrated and worried time was slipping away from them, a text from Matt appeared on her phone.

Any news?

She sent him an update, then backed out to her messaging page, where her eyes landed on Eric's last text. She groaned. She'd promised herself she was going to call him tonight.

But that was before the pregnancy test.

She leaned back against the headrest and closed her eyes. She'd managed to shove the test results aside all day by directing her attention to searching for Zoë, but now, alone in her car, she had nothing to hide behind, and it all came crashing down on her.

How had she let this happen? She was on the pill, and she used condoms. But condoms broke, and she'd been known to forget a pill or two when work kept her out until all hours. And what did it matter how it happened, anyway? It *had* happened, and that was that. What was she going to do about it?

She opened her eyes and scanned the lot to be sure nobody was watching—HQ wasn't a smart place to have a nervous breakdown. She flipped on the radio and found a talk show to distract herself, backed out, and headed for home. Ten minutes later she shut her front door behind her, shrugged off her blazer and kicked off her shoes, then plodded into the kitchen. She pulled down the calvados and poured her usual two fingers into a snifter.

Halfway to her mouth, her hand froze.

"What the hell?" She set the snifter back on the counter and stared at it like it was a rattlesnake.

Why did it matter if she drank the brandy? There was no way she was keeping the baby. But something had stopped her, and was stopping her still.

Just drink it, she told herself. But she couldn't bring herself to do it.

She slid down the cabinet and sat on the floor, head in her hands. Surely she wasn't considering keeping the baby? She'd never wanted a child, and she didn't want one now. When she thought about holding a sleeping baby in her arms, it sent waves of panic through her. How the hell was she supposed to take care of a child with the hours that she worked? She'd have to put it in day care all day and half the night, and what kind of life was that for a baby, never getting to be with its mother?

But no way was she going to have the baby and give it up for adoption, either. No way would she abandon a child she brought into the world. If she gave birth to it, it was her responsibility. And that wouldn't solve the interference of the pregnancy, anyway—as soon as the Assistant District Attorney found out she was pregnant, they'd pull her off of any hazardous duty, for liability reasons. She'd spend the next seven and a half months behind a desk.

So if she wasn't going to keep it, she wasn't going to give it up for adoption, and she wasn't going to abort it, then what the hell was she going to do?

She considered calling Eva. Her best friend had been there for her through all of the major traumas in her life—especially the death of her fiancé, Jack. Despite their shared high-school proclamations that they'd never have children, she was the mother of two, so she'd surely have some relevant advice.

But Jo rejected the possibility. She was so tired, she told herself, and it would be so difficult to explain it all. She just didn't have the energy right now.

She caught a glimpse of herself in the reflection of the glass oven door, huddled on the floor, face petulant and afraid. She barked a sarcastic laugh—who was she kidding? The real reason she didn't want to make that call was because as soon as she told someone about the baby, it would be *real*. Right now it was just a theoretical baby, an intellectual puzzle to be solved, and she could still convince herself she'd wake up tomorrow and this all would turn out to be a bad dream. And if she did decide to abort the baby, she didn't want to have to explain that choice to anybody, didn't want to deal with the judgmental looks she'd know mirrored her own soul—she'd rather just do it and pretend it never happened.

And, if she was going to get put on desk duty, she sure as hell wasn't going to allow that to happen until they'd found Zoë and her daughter.

Her phone chimed the arrival of a text, and she reached up to the counter to retrieve it.

Eric. *Damn, damn, damn!*

She'd resigned herself to the inevitable *we-broke-up-and-I'm-good-with-that* conversation, but what would that conversation look like now? If she kept the baby, didn't he have the right to know he was the father? And if she needed to tell him that, it would be a hell of a lot easier if they hadn't had a nasty conversation the last time they'd talked.

She dropped her head into her hands. She knew Eric well enough to know he'd propose to her if he knew she was pregnant. And he'd be pissed when she said no, and would insist on being in the child's life. He loved children, had mentioned several times how he wanted them someday. That was one of the reasons she'd always known they had an expiration date, even if she changed her mind about having another long-term relationship at some point.

She pushed herself up and trudged into the bathroom. She gave the shower knob a vicious twist and waited for the stream to warm up. She'd had a long, taxing day, and she wasn't in a fit state to make decisions about anything at the moment, let alone something this important. She'd take a shower, go to sleep, and think about it later.

But as the hot water rushed through her hair, an inconvenient truth pulled at her. She couldn't afford to postpone her decision for long.

CHAPTER NINETEEN

Jo woke Monday morning nearly as exhausted as she'd been the night before, and as awareness of the pregnancy came flooding back, an oppressive weight sank onto her chest. She dragged herself out of bed, glad she'd showered the night before, and brewed two shots of espresso. She couldn't bear the thought of food, so at least the coffee would hit her system quickly.

Arnett met her at HQ with a large mocha from Hill of Beans. "I stopped for the best, since today's most likely gonna be a long one."

She rubbed her eyes and sipped the coffee, grateful that chocolate and coffee soothed her stomach rather than aggravated her nausea. She pulled out the paper map they'd marked up the day before, and pointed to one of the red Xs. "Start here today?"

"Sounds good."

They spent all morning and half the afternoon canvassing, with no results. As they finished up their third campground of the day, Aspen Ranch, the sense of dread Jo had woken with combined with a building frustration. This was futile, they were looking for a needle in a haystack, and she had to force herself not to picture Zoë lying dead by the side of a Berkshires road.

"We saw her yesterday, right down the path over there."

Sure she must have heard wrong, she pushed the picture farther toward the pretty blonde woman who'd introduced herself as Kathy Miller. "Are you sure? You saw this woman?"

"Absolutely. We ran into her yesterday when we first got here, when we were bringing everything in from the car. See, I told you something was weird about her, honey." She threw an annoyed look at her husband Todd, then glanced out the filmy plastic window to where her children were playing in front of the cabin. "What has she done?"

Jo followed her glance, adrenaline erasing her dark mood, and automatically pulled up a reliable half-truth. "Don't worry, there's no reason to be concerned. She was in an accident and she lost her memory. She wandered away from her care facility and we're trying to find her."

She looked relieved. "Oh, thank goodness, I was about to pack up and leave."

"Was she with a man?" Jo asked.

"No, she was walking alone."

Jo exchanged a glance with Arnett, then asked, "Did she say anything to you?"

Todd Miller cleared his throat. "She said she was lost, and that she was looking for a different cabin and got confused. Then she went down the path toward cabin four. But when we got back to the car to get the rest of our stuff, we noticed the car closest to ours was gone."

Jo's head turned from the playing children. "What sort of car?"

"It was an SUV, I remember that for sure." Todd's brow furrowed. "Light color."

"A Suburban. I noticed because I've been wanting to get one for us," Kathy said.

"Did you notice if anyone else was in the car?"

Kathy and Todd looked at each other, both shaking their heads. "But I wasn't really paying attention to that," Kathy said.

"Do you remember what she was wearing?" Arnett asked.

Kathy's head bobbed. "Jeans and a dark jacket. Athletic shoes."

Jo and Arnett thanked the couple, and jogged back down the trail to their car. As they drove back to the registration building,

Jo spoke. "Okay, so maybe you were right. Looks like she was here alone."

"Unless she was being coerced somehow."

They climbed out, and pushed through the Dutch door into the building. James Roy, the barely-out-of-high-school assistant manager they'd spoken to when they first arrived, looked up as they entered.

"Mr. Roy? Sorry to disturb you again, but we think we may have a lead on our missing woman. Can you tell us who was registered in cabin six before the current occupants?"

"I should be able to." He ambled over to the computer on the counter, wafting a subtle draft of cannabis through the room. He typed a few commands into the computer, then pulled over a pad and pen. He jotted down the contact information, ripped off the sheet, and slid it across to them.

"Pat Morita, 1345 Macchio Lane, Boston," Jo read out, and laughed.

Arnett dropped his head, and shook it. "Wax on, wax off. Well, I guess that proves we're on the right track."

James Roy's eyes flicked between them. "That who you were looking for?"

"Sure, when I was seven and obsessed with karate." When the man's expression didn't change, Jo continued. "It's fake. Pat Morita's a movie star, and so is Ralph Macchio. Both starred in *The Karate Kid*."

"I thought that starred Will Smith's kid?"

Jo opened her mouth to explain, then thought better of it. "When exactly did she stay here?"

James looked back at the computer screen. "Says here they checked in Friday, April 5th. Paid in cash upfront for a week."

"Were you working that day? Do you remember anything about the person who checked in?" Arnett asked.

He squinted at the wall. "Vaguely. I think it was a small dude, in a ski cap. I can't be sure, though."

Jo wasn't surprised—his memory probably hinged completely on how much weed he'd smoked just prior. "And there was just the one person, alone?"

"If I'm thinking of the right guy." He shrugged.

"Can you describe him?" Jo asked.

James tilted his head to the side. "Not really. I just remember the ski cap 'cause it had one of those ridonculous pompoms on the top. Older, I guess?"

"Your dad old, or your grandpa old?" Arnett asked.

"Closer to my dad, I think."

Jo pushed down her frustration at having to pull teeth. "Hair color? Eye color? Mustache, beard?"

"Hair was under the cap, but I feel like the eyebrows were dark? No facial hair. No idea on the eyes."

"Are you even sure it was a man?"

He stared at her vacantly. "Huh. Dunno. Maybe not. Chicks start to look like dudes when they get older, I guess."

Jo struggled to keep her face blank. "When did they check out?"

"They didn't. They just vacated."

Jo exchanged a glance with Arnett. "Is that normal?"

James shrugged. "When people prepay, yeah. They don't have to sign anything, and the cabins don't need keys."

Arnett shot a questioning glance at Jo, who nodded. He turned to James. "So here's the thing. We're actually looking for two missing women, and one was likely the victim of a violent assault, possibly a homicide." Arnett paused and watched James' face go pale. "Which means we're gonna need to take a close look at that cabin."

CHAPTER TWENTY

The Millers weren't at all happy about being removed from their cabin, and still less happy about giving fingerprints and hair samples so they could be ruled out of whatever evidence Marzillo and her team collected—but they were apoplectic about having their belongings catalogued by strangers.

"There was nothing here when we got here, not even a spider in the corner," Todd Miller protested. "Can't we just take our stuff into the other cabin?"

"Think of this like an archaeological dig. We have to carefully go through the things that aren't relevant and rule them out until we know what is." Jo pointed to his pants. "Let's say we find brown fibers in a groove on the floor. We need to know whether they came from you, or from something none of you have in your possession. I promise, we'll be done before you know it."

Marzillo called out from the cabin. "Jo, Bob. Suit up and take a look at this."

Once they were inside, she switched on a black light. A corner of the cabin's floor and walls lit up with glowing blue patches.

"Blood," Jo said, bending in for a closer look.

"A shit-ton of blood," Arnett said. "And from the swipe marks, it looks like someone tried to clean it up?"

"Correct. They didn't leave much in the way of patterns to analyze." She pointed to one of the walls. "From the height of these patches, I'd guess the victim was standing up for at least part of the assault, but I can't be certain. Without any directional evidence, this could have been splashed up from a strike or from some sort of arterial flow."

Jo gestured around the large section on the floor. "But this has to indicate someone bled out, right?"

Marzillo rubbed her forearm across her forehead, careful not to contact the glove on her hand. "Not necessarily. Our perp may have spread the blood around when trying to clean the area, which makes it hard to estimate. It's safe to say there was a fair amount, but not enough to conclude someone bled all the way out. The good news is, we'll be able to take a sample for analysis. The bad news is, I smell bleach, which means the DNA might be too degraded to identify."

Arnett walked around the edge of the stain. "I see three possibilities. Our vic got up and walked away, or was taken somewhere, injured or dead. We checked every hospital in western Mass, and nobody presented with an injury that matches this. So what are the odds someone walked away from this?" Arnett asked.

"Without help? It's possible, but the odds aren't good," Marzillo replied.

"Which means someone either transported our victim seriously injured, or dead, from the scene." Jo pulled out her phone, and tapped into her contacts.

A moment later a voice came over speakerphone. "Ivan Geary."

"Josette Fournier. You helped me and my partner Bob Arnett yesterday?"

"Right, the missing woman running through the woods. How can I help you?"

Jo explained the situation to him.

"You need a cadaver dog. I'll get a team out to you as soon as possible."

*

Amid the dying rays of sunset, Jo, Arnett, and Vince Pepper set off down the right fork in the cabin's path, led by a springer spaniel named Bones. His handler, a man named Garrison Hutter, chatted easily with them despite the brisk pace. "He's following something. You don't know if your victim is dead or alive?"

"No," Jo answered, and gave him the basic facts of the case. "She may have run away of her own accord, the same way Zoë did. But from the amount of blood, our senior medicolegal thinks that's unlikely."

Garrison nodded. "Well, we'll see shortly."

"Shouldn't we be quiet, let the dog concentrate?" Arnett said, struggling to keep from panting.

"Psh. Cannons could go off around him and he'd keep right on after the scent. You need complete quiet to enjoy the smell of your favorite pizza? Same principle."

Evening fell quickly around them, stitching together the long shadows cast by the trees into a blanket of darkness. Everyone pulled out their flashlights, but Jo found it harder by the minute to keep an eye on where her feet were landing as they kept up with the pup. Although they hadn't gone far, any sense of their relative location faded away.

"Thank goodness for GPS, these sorts of searches must have been a nightmare for you in the days before," Jo said.

Garrison laughed. "Not as bad as you'd think, though. Usually I'd have someone out here with me tracking as we went, but we hurried to get out here for you. But I've been finding my way through woods with a compass and a topo map practically since I was in diapers. And technology or not, I always make sure I have 'em with me." He patted one of the pockets on his cargo vest.

"Not a bad skill to have. Makes me wish—" Jo started, but Garrison's hand shot up to cut her off.

"Smell that? We're close," he said.

Seconds later the noxious, cloying odor of rotting meat hit Jo's nose. She'd long since trained herself to tolerate the smell of decaying corpses—it was a point of pride to her, a sign of respect she tried to show the deceased unless there were civilians around to be protected—but as the smell intensified, Pepper wretched. She chastised herself for not having the foresight to bring the jar of Vicks VapoRub she kept in her kit. It was cliché, but it worked.

Then, Bones suddenly stopped.

Four flashlight beams scanned the area in front of him.

"Didn't you say you were looking for a woman?" Garrison asked.

A huge, ghostly cocoon lay on the ground, misshapen by one edge of a blanket pulled back from the rest. The remains of a man stared out at them, a short ruffle of dark hair sprawled out from his caved-in head, face bloated and discolored by shades of black. The visible upper torso seemed to shimmer, the effect of hundreds, maybe thousands, of maggots feasting on his flesh.

Jo bolted away and vomited.

CHAPTER TWENTY-ONE

Jo slept late Tuesday morning, taking advantage of Lieutenant Martinez's instruction to rest while Marzillo finished processing the scene. Jo's embarrassing reaction to the corpse the night before made one thing clear—she couldn't afford to be in denial about her pregnancy any longer if it was going to interfere with her ability to do her job. She needed to make a choice, and no matter what she chose, she needed to talk to a doctor.

She called her general practitioner, who had her drop off a urine sample. Two hours later she received an e-mail from her Commonwealth Care medical account; she clicked through to her test results, which put the kibosh on any remaining hope that the cheap drugstore tests had been mistaken. The doctor included a referral to an ob-gyn and an instruction to make the appointment as soon as possible.

She had no idea how long she'd sat staring at her laptop when her phone jolted her out of her daze. Her sister. "Sophie. Is everything okay?"

"Josie. I don't know. I just got off the phone with Dad's doctor, and he's concerned. Dad's results are coming back all screwy again, and although the doctor said there's no need to worry yet, he wanted to let us know, because Dad rescheduled the appointment he had for today."

"Dammit. I'll call him and talk to him."

"I already did, and he claims he'll go tomorrow, the doctor said he can fit him in. I just wanted to keep you in the loop. I don't think he understands that just because he's feeling better, that doesn't mean the cancer's gone for good. But you know how he is, if we all call him and get on his case, he'll just disappear on some fishing trip for a couple of weeks to show us who's boss."

Jo barked a dry laugh. "That he will. So there's nothing I can do?"

"Not for now. I'll let you know."

For once, she was disappointed to be let off the family hook. "Okay. I'll check in with him tomorrow. Thanks, Soph."

"Oh, and I almost forgot. Ma needs you to call her."

"On it. Thanks." Her sister hung up.

Jo exited out of the screen, then tapped the contact for her mother.

"Josie. Perfect timing. I was just about to call you about Easter."

Jo sighed with relief. Just run-of-the-mill holiday plans—thank goodness. "Don't worry, Ma, I'll bring dessert."

"No, it's not that. It's just that we're going to have to have Easter Sunday tomorrow night."

"Wait, what? You can't just put Easter Sunday on another day, Ma. That's why it's called Easter *Sunday*. Christ hasn't risen yet."

"Yes, very funny, but I don't have time for your jokes or your sacrilege right now, I've been going crazy trying to get this all worked out. Sophie and David are going to his parents' house for Easter, because apparently his mother isn't well. They're leaving Thursday night so they can spend a long weekend in Maine. That means I either don't get to have an Easter celebration with my grandchildren or we do it Wednesday night. We'll do the egg hunt in the evening, the girls will love that, and then we'll have Easter dinner."

"Can't we do it the following weekend?"

"That's too late, it won't have any meaning."

Of course not. A week too late, that made no sense, but celebrating Christ's resurrection before the point in Holy Week where he actually died was the most obvious thing in the world. Fraught with significance.

She immediately chastised herself. Really, did it matter when they celebrated Easter? No, it didn't, and that wasn't what she was really upset about. The real issue was nobody thought to ask what *her* plans were. She was angry that her life simply didn't matter next to Sophie's all-important children.

Jo replied through clenched teeth. "I'm not sure I'll be able to be there, Ma. We've got a woman who lost her memory, and now she's missing and most likely in danger. Hopefully we'll find her before then, but—"

Her mother sighed. "Please try, Josette. Your nieces won't be young forever, you know. There are only a few more years before they'll be off to college and we'll never see them again. And since *you* don't have kids, you need to keep up good relationships with them. Otherwise who's going to take care of you when you're old?"

Jo squeezed her eyes against the tears that instantly sprung up, and forced her voice to come out normally. "Stop exaggerating, Ma. They're six and eight."

"That time will pass before you know it. I swear I was taking you to ballerina classes just yesterday, and now you're on the verge of menopause."

The word hit Jo in the stomach. "Ma!"

"You know I'm right, Josette. All of the women on my side went through it early. I started at forty-five, and Aunt Isabelle was only forty-three."

Jo's empty hand squeezed into a fist and pounded her leg as she forced herself not to take the bait. "I promise I'll do my best to be there."

"Thank you, honey, I appreciate it. We'll see you tomorrow night, then."

They said goodbyes and she hung up, still in shock. This was a new tactic from her mother, and she wasn't prepared for it. She'd built up a thick skin against her mother's usual poking and prodding Jo to have kids, even if it meant artificial insemination. But *this* was like she'd given up. Like rather than fighting Jo's status as a *childless spinster* she'd embraced it, and was using it to manipulate Jo into kowtowing to the important members of the family, the next generation and the sister who had produced it. To bring up menopause—that was an all-time low, and it felt like someone shot a hole through her chest with a cannon.

She bolted up out of her chair. She had to do something, she couldn't just sit with this feeling. She marched to her bedroom, put on leggings and a T-shirt, grabbed her earbuds and started the treadmill.

But she couldn't get the conversation out of her mind. Why had it upset her so much? Her therapist had always told her that *people* don't make you feel a certain way, you make *yourself* feel that way. If someone came up to you and called you a child-beating embezzler, you wouldn't take that personally, you'd realize the other person was crazy or had mistaken your identity. You wouldn't be up all night asking yourself if you really were a child-beating embezzler, because you'd know you weren't. So if something someone says upsets you, it's because it triggers something in *you*. Some fear. Some worry.

It didn't take much of a leap for Jo to identify her something—her mother wasn't far off the truth. Jo was in her very early forties, that was true, and the women in her family *did* start menopause early. Which was a natural part of life, right? It shouldn't be a big issue.

But there was something about that word. Something about the idea that her choices were being taken away from her. And that she was about to become *less than*. Which was ridiculous. She had never once, not for a day, wanted to have children. She loved her nieces and her cousins, and she enjoyed being around children, but she had absolutely no desire to have her own.

But you always had the option to change your mind.

The thought came unbidden, and she instantly pushed back against it. What use was the option to change your mind if you knew you didn't want to change it?

And yet, it mattered. She could argue the logic of it with herself until her brain seized up, but that wouldn't change the fact. And if it really did make a difference to her on some sort of deep level, now was the time for her to come to terms with that. Menopause or no, getting pregnant at forty-two wasn't an everyday occurrence. The stories were in the news all the time about how women who put off having children until later in life were discovering they'd waited too long.

This was very possibly her last chance.

She turned up the speed on the treadmill and tried her best to outrun the years that were overtaking her.

CHAPTER TWENTY-TWO

When Jo got out of the shower an hour later, she found a text from Marzillo letting her and Arnett know she was ready to meet with them.

Jo stopped to pick up coffee for everyone, then grabbed Arnett and hurried in to the lab. Lopez looked up from her computer and called to Marzillo, who emerged from the depths of the lab, expression grim. Which wasn't surprising, considering she hadn't slept and the smell of the corpse was still clinging to her.

"I spent the morning with the ME on this one, helping as best I could." Marzillo shook her head, and pulled up two diagrams, anterior and posterior, detailing the man's injuries. "Not fun, I promise you. First things first, the time of death matches approximately with the timing of Zoë's appearance; the stage of decomposition and insect activity lines right up within a day of when Zoë found herself running through the forest. We've sent out samples for a DNA profile, but since I've already called in all of my favors, I'm not sure how soon we'll get it back. And before you ask, yes, he is a biological male, and no, his blood type does not match the blood found on Zoë's clothes, so we're not looking at some rare sex chromosome anomaly."

Arnett leaned forward in his chair. "So we're searching for a female who lost a considerable amount of blood, and instead find a *male* corpse that was murdered the same day. That just can't be a coincidence." He pointed to the pictures. "I'm assuming there's no way that's accidental."

Marzillo followed his gaze. "No. He died of blunt-force trauma to the head. He was repeatedly bludgeoned with a long object of some sort. After he was dead, he was wrapped in the blanket, probably to contain the blood."

"Like some sort of billy club?" Arnett asked.

"Possibly. But it's hard to say, since there's so much damage. Only this spot here and this spot here give me an indication that we're looking at something long, and maybe an inch wide." Marzillo's finger circled the areas as she spoke.

Jo examined the victim's head. "Quite a beating—I could see the dent in his skull from several feet away at the crime scene."

"It's considerable, yes. But there are also several other points of impact on the left temple, toward the front of his head. My guess is that his attacker was facing him at the time of the first hit, but then the victim either turned away or fell, and the attacker continued to strike."

"Overkill? So some sort of strong emotion behind it?"

Marzillo considered the wound. "Possibly. But blows to the skull can be strange—it can be difficult to tell how much damage has been done when you hit someone, so he may have just been hedging his bets, simply making sure the victim was dead."

"Charming," Arnett said.

"Is this head wound consistent with the blood we saw in the cabin?" Jo asked.

Marzillo tilted her head to one side and took a deep breath while she considered. "I can't say for sure he's the one who was attacked in the cabin, but he certainly could be. If he was standing up when the first blow or two hit, there could have been blood spatter on the walls. More likely cast-off if he was beaten while lying on the floor, too."

Jo fingered the diamond at her neck. "Is there any way his blood might be on Zoë's clothes, too, and we just missed it?"

Marzillo took another deep breath, and nodded. "I can't rule that out. I always take six cuttings from a sample if I'm able, for just that reason, but there was so much surface area covered on her clothes, it's possible I missed something. I'll send in a few more to be sure."

"I see where you're going," Arnett said to Jo. "Maybe he attacked Zoë and her daughter, and got more than he bargained for?"

"Or that Zoë attacked him for some reason," Jo answered.

Lopez took over. "The good news is, we don't need to wait for his DNA to figure out who he is, because he had identification on him, and a phone. He's Logan Tremblay, thirty-five, from Montreal."

"I don't suppose we can tell if it's his blood or Zoë's daughter's blood we found in the cabin?" Jo asked.

"No. Whoever cleaned up the blood used bleach, so I can't get a DNA profile from it."

Lopez waved a finger. "That reeks of premeditation. The only reason to bring bleach on a camping trip is if you're OCD about germs, in which case you wouldn't go on a camping trip in the first place, or you're planning to clean up blood. Maybe little Logan here is a serial killer."

Arnett's eyebrows shot up. "So how does he end up dead if he did the cleanup? Seems more likely someone else killed him, then cleaned up after it."

Jo's brow furrowed. "True. In that case, we need a motive for why Zoë or her daughter would want Logan dead—we'll need to look for any connections between them all asap. But it still could be possible that Logan was some sort of killer. Maybe Zoë was out for a hike, and Logan killed her daughter while she was gone, then she returned after he'd cleaned up the cabin? Maybe she met him on the path carrying her daughter, and attacked when she realized what was happening?" She turned back to Marzillo. "I'm guessing with the advanced state of decomposition, we can't really tell if he had any defensive wounds, anything like that to narrow down if he was a victim or an aggressor?"

"Correct," Marzillo said. "That's about all we can tell from the autopsy. Then there's the rest of the scene back at the cabin. All the prints we found in and around the cabin belonged to the Millers, so most likely our killer wiped everything down before he left. The cabin's small enough that wouldn't be hard. We did find a few interesting things outside, however." She clicked several new pictures up onto her large monitor. "We found these tiny scraps of fabric in the fire pit. Since Logan was wrapped in a blanket in the woods, my guess is these are either from the cloth our killer used to clean up the blood, or the clothes he was wearing during the attack, or both. We'll see if we can figure out more microscopically. Maybe we'll get lucky and the fibers will be some strange polymer blend made by only one manufacturer in the world."

"But you doubt it," Arnett said.

"Based on the widely-available Target blanket Logan was wrapped in, I do."

Arnett stared at the pictures, head shaking. "So, here's the big question—where's Zoë's daughter?"

Lopez tapped her pen on her desk. "No way I buy that two people ended up losing a significant amount of blood in the same area at the same general time coincidentally. Maybe Logan killed her, or maybe someone else killed them both. But she's out there somewhere, dead or in danger."

Jo nodded. "Which means we need to find out as much as possible about Logan Tremblay and hope that leads us to her."

*

Finding information about Logan Tremblay turned out to be unexpectedly easy. He was a single, high-powered, high-profile software developer who owned his own company, and who, according to his sister and brother, took an extended hiking vacation once a year to unwind. Part of that was going completely dark—he carried a phone with him, but kept it turned off so he could completely disconnect from work. Last year he'd gone to Alaska, and the year before to the Adirondacks. This time he was RVing and hiking through the Berkshires, alone, and his family hadn't expected to hear from him for at least another few days.

James Roy confirmed that Logan Tremblay had been staying in Aspen Ranch's RV section. When he checked, he found Logan's rented RV still parked in its allocated spot. None of the current neighbors could remember seeing him, but none of them had been at the campgrounds the week of his death.

After half an hour searching his phone and social media accounts, Jo shoved her chair away from her desk. "They weren't kidding about him going dark. Lopez said his last tower ping was before he left Canada, and when she turned the phone back on, it went nuts with notifications. As far as I can tell, the few Americans he knows live in upstate New York, or out in Silicon Valley."

"But until we find out who Zoë is, we can't find out how any of this is connected, anyway. How do we even know where she's actually from? She has a western Mass accent, but she might be living anywhere now. She could be back on vacation from her new home in South Africa for all we know. And if so, maybe nobody'll ever recognize her from our local broadcasts."

"Excellent point. We need to go wider with her picture and vitals. News outlets, but maybe also social media?"

Jo's phone rang. "Lopez, what's up?"

"Can you guys come in here for a minute?" Her voice had an excited edge.

"On our way."

They had to search deep into the bowels of the lab before they found her staked out at a different computer. "There you are," Jo said.

"Oh, sorry, I should have told you where I was. This computer has a much faster processor than mine. Grab a chair." She called out to Marzillo, who did the same.

"You got results already?" Marzillo asked.

"Don't ruin my story," Lopez said, gleam back in her eyes, and gathered some papers from the printer next to her. "So, Marzillo got the DNA profile back in the right format so we could upload it to GEDmatch. Which is what I just did."

She handed everyone a sheet, and they all looked down at it. Marzillo let out a sharp whistle.

"That's right, ladies and gentleman. We have a definitive match."

PART TWO

Saturday, April 13th – Tuesday, April 16th

Zoë

CHAPTER TWENTY-THREE

As soon as the man showed up at Sunset Gardens on Saturday, Zoë had known she had to run. Luckily, she'd already been preparing to do just that.

She'd been afraid enough after she remembered running from someone through the woods, but then to find out her daughter had been attacked, too? No way she was going to sit in a chair drinking tea when her daughter could be tied up in someone's cellar, being beaten or raped or God only knew what. Maybe under normal circumstances the police were better equipped than she was to find her daughter, but she'd given them a chance and they'd come up short. They couldn't figure out who *she* was, let alone who her daughter was or what happened to them both. And she'd trusted them after she pointed out how flimsy the security was and they'd metaphorically patted her on the head—no way she was going to make the same mistake twice.

Because whoever the man was who'd tried to get to her? Now he'd know the layout and how lame the security actually was. He wouldn't fail a second time. And how had he known where to find her, anyway? There was something they weren't telling her. She couldn't trust them.

Especially because—call a spade a spade—they didn't trust her. When you're covered in someone else's blood and nobody knows why, you're a suspect. Maybe not the primary suspect, but a suspect nonetheless. Hell, it was one of the first horrifying possibilities that flashed through her *own* mind when they told her about her daughter, how could it not have flashed through theirs? She might not be able to remember, but she wasn't stupid, and even if she had been, all the crime shows she'd binged over the past week would have opened her eyes: part of the reason they were keeping her in a 'safe' place was so they could keep an eye on her. And that meant whenever they felt like it, they could take her into *police* custody, and then she'd have no chance of getting away. All while the clock was ticking, and her daughter was possibly dying.

That's why the moment they told her about her daughter, she'd started putting together a plan so she could run if she needed to.

If familiar things could trigger her memory, then she'd find familiar things. She knew the name of the town where she'd stumbled out of the woods, and she knew the direction she'd walked to get there. She'd been watching TV anyway trying to trigger herself, but she watched more. She watched as many episodes of *Survivorman* as she could, jotting down notes as she did. He tracked his own location in part with topographical maps, which, he said, were available online. So once she found the creek she'd followed, she'd be able to use one to estimate her starting point, then work backwards until something triggered a memory.

But she had no money, no car, and nobody to help her. She needed to figure out a way to get herself to Taltingham—without the police catching her and dragging her to jail.

So when *Survivorman* wasn't on, she watched *The First 48* and *Forensic Files*, one of which was always on some channel called HLN. They were gold mines of information about how criminals got caught—and by implication, how *not* to get caught. Most useful of all was the information they gave her about how police tracked people: phone records and GPS signals. License plates. Money trails. The cops on the shows even said it themselves—most criminals got caught because they made stupid mistakes. Burner phones purchased with credit cards, so the numbers could be tracked. License plate sightings at gas stations. CCTVs. But she wasn't stupid, and she didn't need to disappear forever. She just had to stay one step ahead of them until she could find out who she was.

In addition to transportation and money, she needed as big a head start as possible. So she familiarized herself with the Sunset Gardens complex, the staff, and everyone's routines, especially the night staff's. She honed in particularly on Dolores, who had the same color hair and eyes she did—and whose ID could pass for her own. And Julie, who, despite being sweet and quick to laughter, routinely forgot passwords and took shortcuts around standard procedures because she was forever locking keys into cabinets or forgetting to lock them at all. Zoë pretended to be starved for conversation, and pulled out of them the sort of personal details that were often—according to the true crime shows—used for passwords and PIN numbers.

So when 'Oscar Snow' showed up, after the detectives left, she pretended to go to sleep as normal. Then, late Saturday night when Dolores and Julie went on the break they weren't supposed to take together, she put her clothes back on and snuck out. She grabbed the purses out of the cabinet they never locked, aware they wouldn't be missed until morning. She chose Dolores' Suburban as the more useful of their two vehicles, then dropped Julie's keys by her smaller economy car because she wasn't looking to harm or inconvenience anyone—she just wanted to find her daughter.

She used Dolores' GPS to locate the nearest Walmart. After buying most of what she needed, including a hoodie to hide her face from the cameras, she hit the ATM with Dolores' and Julie's cards, promising herself she'd pay back every penny once she knew who she was. Then she returned to the store and purchased a burner phone with cash—even if they thought to keep watching the security cameras after her first check out, they'd have no record of the phone's identifying codes.

At just past midnight she hit the ATM again, made a pit stop at the gas station, filled the cans, and removed the license plates from the Suburban. She dumped the cell phones off the Pike, hoping that and the gas-station stop would lead the police in the wrong direction for at least a little while. Then she drove to Taltingham and backtracked from the antiques store out to her creek, hoping she'd be able to find it in the dark. Once she found it, she used an online topo map to calculate the most likely possible starting point radius. She drove out to Pelhaven, the farthest of her possible starting points, and thus, she hoped, the least likely place the police would begin their search for her.

After tracking down a place to hide the vehicle off-road, she climbed in the back of the Suburban to sleep until she could begin her search at morning's first light—she'd never recognize anything more in the dark. Dolores and Julie would find their purses gone around six the following morning, and the fastest the police would put everything together and make it out to Taltingham was seven. If she woke at sunrise, she'd still have a two-and-a-half hour head start.

*

Luck was with her the next day—she recognized the third campsite she checked radiating out from Pelhaven.

The sign for Aspen Ranch was, oddly enough, shaped like a huge pine tree and painted green, like a giant Christmas tree overlooking the road. At the sight of it, a quick memory flashed through her head: staring at the sign from the side window of a car as it turned into the campground. She drove around, following flashes of familiarity, then got out to explore a cabin that felt right—and almost instantly ran into an overly friendly family. She bluffed her way through it as quickly as she could, then bolted as soon as they were out of sight, heart pounding out of her chest.

Then, as she drove toward the exit, she recognized the RV sign.

She jerked the car around and followed the curving road to a group of RV lots arranged in a large, misshapen blossom. As she scanned the variety of RVs—small, medium, and large, some attached to pickup trucks, some self-contained—she recognized several models. Somehow, she knew their internal layouts, and what special features they had. *That* model had an awning you could extend to create a patio. *That* huge one had a deck up on top.

But one in particular spoke out to her. A medium-sized vehicle that wasn't quite right, but called up a childhood memory of a similar model.

The RV she remembered had pull-down steps in the entryway; she'd tried to jump into the opening without pulling them down, and had missed. She remembered someone's laugh ring out behind her as she landed on her knees and smacked her chin on the step—but someone else ran up beside her to see if she was alright. Her aunt.

She had an aunt. And she'd been camping with her aunt in this very park when she was a child.

She stopped the Suburban and stared at the RV—something else about it was tugging at her. Something about the door of her aunt's RV, something they'd added to personalize it. Something cheesy, that her parents made fun of behind her aunt and uncle's backs. What was it?

She closed her eyes and tried to picture it. A sticker? Yes, of a stylized yacht. With the name "*U.S.S. Huggusi*" written under it in a 1980s font.

Her eyes flew open as she remembered. Her uncle had the design custom-made and put it on the door of the RV because Huggusi was his last name. And the reason her parents made fun of it mercilessly behind his back was because of the unfortunate rhyme her aunt's married name had become.

Lucy Huggusi.

She snapped a picture of the RV and stepped on the gas—she'd been staring too long as it was, someone was bound to notice. She drove out of the campsite, then found a spot off-road where she wouldn't be visible so she could park and think.

She grabbed a protein bar and a packet of beef jerky, then settled in to search the internet. She had no problem finding Lucy Huggusi, since she was the only Huggusi listed in New England, but the internet only showed her city of residence, Worcester. Several sites popped up offering to search her phone number or specific address for a fee, but Dolores' and Julie's credit cards must have already been reported stolen, and would instantly alert the police to the name and address she was searching, besides.

She tried a few more searches, plugging in random search terms she thought might help: *Huggusi, Worcester, RV.* Then *Huggusi* and *obituary*, since her aunt was the only Huggusi listed, so her uncle had either died or left the state. She tried searching the years her aunt most plausibly might have gotten married along with *wedding*, then *married*. All returned nothing.

"Dammit!" She threw the phone down on the passenger seat in frustration, and it bounced to the floor. She dropped her head and banged her forehead on the steering wheel. Apparently you couldn't find everything on the internet, and she had no idea how to find what she needed any other way.

She sat upright, and laughed, then reached over to grab the phone. If the internet couldn't tell her the address, maybe it could tell her *how to find* the address.

She typed in exactly that. After scanning a few sites, she found a blog post by an ex-private investigator that outlined several methods for locating a person's address. Most of them required databases she couldn't access, or other methods that weren't practical for her. But, when all else failed, the article said, deeds were a matter of public record. That meant if you found the right records office, you just had to go request the information. A first and last name should be enough. That meant the next step was to find out where the Worcester records office was located, so she plugged the relevant words into the browser—then stared unbelieving at the results.

The records were accessible, twenty-four-seven, *online*.

She typed in her aunt's name. A general entry popped up, but it didn't contain the address. She clicked on several fields that gave no further information, finally making her way to a book icon.

The full entry included her uncle's name—Kevin, of course it had been Kevin!—and the street address.

Ninety-two Peony Lane.

Tears of relief streamed down her face, and she exhaled a breath she hadn't realized she'd been holding. Everything was going to be okay—her aunt and her uncle would know who she was. They'd help her, and she'd be able to figure out what happened to her daughter.

CHAPTER TWENTY-FOUR

Worcester was at least an hour and a half away, and Zoë would certainly be noticed by the police if she drove main, well-populated roads without license plates—she needed to change that before she drove any real distance. She had an idea how to fix the problem, but to be safe she needed to wait to do even that until dark. She pulled up the area map and pored over the area campsites, gauging how long she could afford to delay.

The police were methodical; they'd have started close and worked their way out. They'd only been at it for a few hours, and they wouldn't have the advantage she had—they'd have to stop and talk to multiple people at each town and campsite. And even if they found the family that could identify her, what did it tell them? They couldn't know what she remembered, or where to go from there. They had no way of knowing she had an aunt, let alone what her aunt's name was. There was no way they could know where she was headed—but odds were high that some nosy cop would pull her over for driving without plates before she could find replacements. The smartest thing to do would be to wait.

As she waited, she searched the local news sites to see if she'd been reported missing. She had—several articles showed her picture and said she'd disappeared from 'a care facility' early that morning, and had possibly been abducted. She laughed out loud—she hadn't considered that, but of course they'd assume Oscar had come back for her. Were they even out here looking for her at all? No, she couldn't afford to assume otherwise. But regardless, they hadn't mentioned she might be in Berkshire County rather than Oakhurst County. They were smart enough to keep that information out of the hands of the killer, at least, and it meant regular citizens wouldn't be looking for her here.

When darkness set in, she slipped onto the back roads and backtracked to a nearby roadhouse-and-motel complex she'd spotted earlier. The L-shaped motel formed a rough horseshoe with the Rustic Ridge Roadhouse, and while parking ringed the entire complex, the rooms all opened to the inside of the U.

To be safe, she needed to kill another hour or two, to be sure most of the motel guests were settled in for the night. She parked behind the building, out of sight of the road. She tucked her hair back up under the ski cap, then checked her reflection from several angles. Perfect—in these clothes, with no make-up, she looked like a scrawny man. Even if someone out here had seen the news alerts on her, they'd never recognize her like this. She locked the car behind her and strolled into the restaurant.

The roadhouse, a blue clapboard rectangle with white trim and a covered entryway, looked like it'd be more at home out on the coast than set this far into western Mass. She pushed open the door and stood next to the hostess booth, checking out the interior as she waited. She'd expected an open space, but dividing walls sectioned out tables and booths.

"Just one?" the middle-aged blonde with a too-long ponytail and too much make-up asked, with a faux-sympathetic tilt to her head.

Zoë bristled. "Just one."

The woman led her to a small table in the far corner of the furthest-back room, past empty table after empty table. Annoyed at the slight, Zoë opened her mouth to object, but then clamped it shut again. The last thing she needed was to draw attention to herself.

The clam chowder called to her—she'd been freezing cold all day—and she followed it up with a large T-bone and a baked potato. She ate slowly, savoring the warmth of the food, and finished up with a cup of coffee that tasted far better than it should. The fugitive lifestyle didn't agree with her—she'd been on the run for less than a day, and already she was missing creature comforts.

She paid cash when she finished, then strolled casually back to the car. At just past nine, most of the lights were out in the motel windows—either the guests had decided Sunday night was for turning in early, or they hadn't returned yet.

Behind the building, she located two cars parked next to one another. She backed the Suburban into the spot next to them, then pulled her flashlight and Swiss army knife out. She crouched between the vehicles and the shrubs that bordered the property, unscrewed the front license plate from the closest car, then screwed it onto the back of the Suburban.

Just as she finished, a car turned the corner of the motel.

Heart pounding in her chest, she ducked down, hiding herself as the lights swept past. The car parked several spots away in the wrong direction—they'd have to walk past her to get to the hotel.

A moment later they came into view, hands all over each other, gushing and slurring about how horny they were, stumbling and laughing just a bit louder than they should. Zoë froze and held her breath.

They passed without a glance at their surroundings, single-mindedly about getting to their hotel bed as quickly as possible.

Once their footsteps faded around the corner, she flipped the Suburban around. With trembling fingers, she removed the front plate from the second car, then attached it to the Suburban's front end.

She climbed into the car and turned the engine over, trying to calm her breathing. She was fine, she told herself, and everything was good. Most likely the two cars wouldn't even notice their missing front plate for days, probably not until a cop pulled them over. Until then, she had legit plates that wouldn't flag traffic cameras.

She pulled out of the lot, and headed toward Worcester.

CHAPTER TWENTY-FIVE

The man paced the length of his tiny hotel room.

The visit to Sunset Gardens had been a Hail Mary play, he'd known that at the time, but figured he might as well check the place out regardless. He couldn't think of anything he'd done *wrong* exactly, but couldn't help feeling he'd played his cards too early.

As soon as the nurse left to get her, he'd ducked behind the counter to search for info about her. The computers were password protected, and there was no convenient sheet lying out with room assignments set out nice and pretty. But he found a map of the grounds and buildings, and learned that the rooms where the nurse had turned were all marked with a B—rooms 1–10B.

As soon as the solitary set of footsteps returned down the hall, he'd taken off, but he hadn't gone far. Hidden in a dark spot two blocks down, he watched the entrance. As he feared, less than half an hour later, the detectives working her case pulled up to the gate in the unmarked Chevy Cruze that wasn't fooling anybody.

He drove back to the hotel as calmly as he was able. He needed to wait for things to cool down, and he needed to work out his next move. The staff would be different during the morning weekday shifts; he could call back then and pretend to be from the police. Maybe ask to talk to her, say there'd been an important break in the case, and say they needed to talk to her immediately while the other detectives were out on another case. He'd casually verify her room number: *You're in 9B, right?* If he happened to guess right, she'd say yes, and if he guessed wrong, she'd correct him. That's all people needed, just a little bit of something that made you sound like you knew what you were supposed to know. Then they'd tell you anything. He'd call back and tell her it was a false alarm so she wouldn't be concerned when he didn't show up. Then he'd wait until dark, scale the wall, break into whichever of the very large picture windows was hers, and escort her off the property at gunpoint.

Having a plan worked out allowed him some peace of mind, and since he'd have to wait for the weekday shift, he figured he might as well relax and conserve his energy. He spent the rest of Saturday evening and most of Sunday vegging out in front of the free HBO movies.

Which turned out to be a huge mistake.

Late Sunday, he checked the late news to see if the police had released more information about her. Sure enough, there was a segment on her—but as her picture filled the screen, the anchors announced the police were *searching* for her. She'd been discovered missing that morning, and had possibly been kidnapped.

His guts instantly turned to liquid. *Fuck, fuck, fuck.* He hadn't considered that his visit might scare her enough to bolt, and he didn't have a plan for how to deal with that. And now they'd be looking specifically for *him*.

He sprung up and paced the room. He needed to think out all the possibilities, and that was never easy when his mind was running a hundred miles an hour. He grabbed the pad and pen by the hotel phone, and drew two columns: *memory, no memory.* If she still couldn't remember, she was running blind, and there was no way to trace her. In that case he might as well head for Mexico right now, because he'd be on the run for the rest of his life.

If she did remember, she'd know exactly what happened, and she'd have two choices: go to the police, or run to keep herself safe. Since she was running, she hadn't gone to the police. And she'd go to predictable places, so there was a good chance he could find her.

But then again—maybe she *had* gone to the police. Maybe the whole broadcast was a stunt designed to flush him out, and—

He slammed his palm onto the table. No, that was paranoid thinking, and once he started down that road there was no coming back. No, she hadn't gone to the police. So what would she do next? What would he do if he were her?

She'd need to get the pictures, wherever she'd stashed them. And he couldn't let that happen.

CHAPTER TWENTY-SIX

Late Sunday, Zoë parked the Suburban around the corner from 92 Peony Lane and walked the rest of the way. As she approached, she took a long moment to study the house, trying to bring up any sense of familiarity. Small enough to be called a cottage, with a red-brown brick exterior on the single story and red wood planks under the high gables, it didn't spark any memories. Which confused her—why would a similar RV bring back memories, but not her aunt's house?

She hurried up the path and rapped quickly on the door.

Just as she was about to knock a second time, the door opened. The woman in front of her was a few inches taller than she was and had quite a few more pounds on her, but the shape of her figure was similar. She had brown eyes, a short blonde bob, and her face was arranged into a suspicious scowl.

The woman looked her up and down. "Marissa. What are you doing here?"

Marissa? That was her name? A strange combination of relief and disappointment washed over her to finally know it—*Zoë* was so much prettier. "Aunt Lucy?"

The woman didn't move forward to embrace her, or even step aside to let her in. "I didn't realize you had this address."

Prickles of fear doused Marissa's relief. What was going on? "I need your help. Can I come in?"

Aunt Lucy looked past her out into the darkness. "Is this some sort of trick?"

Marissa paused, unsure what to say. "A trick? No. I was in an accident, and I can't remember anything. Didn't you see me on the news? I can't even remember my name. But today I saw an RV that reminded me of camping with you, and I remembered your name. I searched for you."

"An accident?" The suspicion stayed in Lucy's eyes, but she stepped back. "I don't watch the news, it's too depressing. Come in. Are you okay?"

"I'm okay now. I had a bad head injury, but I was in the hospital, and they took care of me."

Aunt Lucy waved her into the living room. "Sit down and tell me what happened."

Marissa's mind raced as she settled into the sofa and gave Aunt Lucy a quick recap. This wasn't right. No hug, no kiss, and barely any concern—in fact, her own aunt seemed angry and hostile. Why? Until she knew, it would probably be best to keep some of the story to herself, especially if Aunt Lucy didn't watch the news.

"They let you out of the hospital when you didn't even know your name?"

"They couldn't keep me indefinitely. I didn't have an ID or anything, so they don't even know if I have insurance," the half-truth flowed. "What's my last name?"

Aunt Lucy searched her face. "Your maiden name was Pesaro. When you married Miguel, it changed to Navarro. I'm fairly certain you changed that to Stasuk when you married Bruce."

Marissa's head spun. She'd been married twice? "Bruce Stasuk? Am I still married to him?"

Aunt Lucy leaned back in her armchair, and hesitated a long moment before answering. "As far as I know, Marissa. Since your mother died, we've only spoken to each other when we have to." Her eyes raked Marissa's face as she continued. "Ten years ago."

Marissa rubbed her eyes as she struggled to make sense of the information. Ten years? She tried to picture her mother, or the funeral, or any sort of fight with her aunt, but nothing came. "Why aren't we on good terms?"

Aunt Lucy took a deep breath and exhaled slowly before responding. "Why are you here, Marissa?"

Tears of frustration formed in her eyes, and she forced herself to be patient. "I need to find out who I am. I need—I need to find something to trigger my memory. But I don't recognize anything, not your house, not you, nothing." She rubbed her eyes to hide the expression on her face—she'd almost blurted out *I need to find my daughter*, and stopped herself just in the nick of time. Until she knew why Aunt Lucy was being so hostile, she had no choice but to assume she couldn't trust her.

Her aunt shook her head. "No, you wouldn't recognize the house, you've never been here before. I had to move after Uncle Kevin died, I couldn't bear to be in that house without him, and I wanted something smaller. And I suppose I look pretty different than the last time you saw me. I used to have black hair and I've put on a lot of weight. It goes straight to my face." Aunt Lucy stood up and pulled down a photo album from the bookcase. She opened it, and brought it back to Marissa. "Here."

Marissa recognized the picture immediately. Her aunt, but also her uncle, and her mother and father standing next to them. She vaguely remembered the occasion of the picture, one of the adults' birthdays—but the hazy memory wasn't due to the complete blackout of amnesia, but rather the gentle fading of time and childhood. The quartet stood in the living room of her childhood home, so instantly familiar she now couldn't imagine *not* remembering it. She closed her eyes and pictured the exterior of the house, and the street they'd lived on. She could even remember the route she'd walked to her high school. They'd lived somewhere else when she was in grammar school, a duplex. But she couldn't remember anything after her high-school years. She pressed her palm into her eyes, but those answers wouldn't come.

She told her aunt as much. "And I don't remember Ma dying." Her finger ran over her father's picture. "Is Dad still alive?"

Aunt Lucy sat back down, still watching her carefully. "No. He died a few years before your mother. Heart attack. She was never really the same after he passed."

Marissa nodded, tears falling down her cheeks now, feeling like she'd just remembered them only to lose them again. She lifted the next page slightly. "May I?"

Aunt Lucy nodded, and Marissa slowly flipped through the pages. Birthdays. Summer parties. Christmases. Her basic needs were taken care of, with a few extras here and there, but they'd been poor. The only vacations they'd been able to afford were camping trips in the RV, and she never had the toys and clothes that the other children had as her parents struggled, and many months failed, to pay the mortgage. An old emotion resurfaced—the constant frustration of never quite fitting. Not in with other kids, and not in with her family—her mother had never been pleased with who Marissa was. "I don't see any siblings here, and I don't remember any?"

"No, no siblings."

"And I can't recall any other aunts or uncles."

She shook her head. "I'm your mother's only sibling, and your father was an only child."

Marissa nodded. So far everything Aunt Lucy told her meshed with the memories that had returned. But she hadn't answered Marissa's question about the falling-out. Why? And what else was she leaving out? And surely whatever fight they'd had was trumped by her injury and memory loss?

A thought sent a chill through her. Did Aunt Lucy know something about what happened out in the forest? Was she involved?

Marissa kept her head down, staring at the pictures, while she processed the possibility. She needed to be careful, and she needed to know how forthcoming Aunt Lucy was really being.

"Do I have any children?" she asked.

Her aunt was silent. Marissa's head snapped up to meet her eyes.

Aunt Lucy cleared her throat. "You have a daughter. Sara. From your first marriage."

The chill intensified. Why had she hesitated? What possible reason could she have for being cagey about something like that?

"I don't remember her. I don't suppose you have any pictures of her, too?"

Aunt Lucy stiffened, but reached to the table next to her and grabbed her phone. She tapped and scrolled, and finally held out a picture of a woman who looked remarkably like Marissa, standing next to a tall young man with short black hair and striking blue eyes.

Marissa stared at the picture for a long moment, trying to remember her. "Is this recent?"

"Taken about a month ago."

Marissa chewed at her lip. "Who's this standing next to her?"

After another hesitation, this one almost imperceptible, Aunt Lucy cleared her throat again. "That's her boyfriend, Hunter Malloy. Well, fiancé, now."

"Do you have her address or phone number? Or his? I need to find her."

Aunt Lucy blinked several times, and shook her head. "I don't, I'm sorry."

She didn't have her address or phone number, but she had a recent picture? Why was she lying?

She met her aunt's gaze again. "Aunty, I can tell you're not happy to see me. I don't know why, so I can't apologize, but I am sincerely upset to find out there's a problem between us."

Aunt Lucy looked at her for a long moment, then nodded. "What are you going to do now?"

Marissa's fear flared into anger. She'd just extended an olive branch, and *that* was her aunt's only response? *That's* all she had to say to her only niece? No offer of a meal or something to drink, maybe a place to stay? Not that Marissa would accept, because if the police figured out who she was they'd certainly look here.

No, she wasn't safe with this woman. And until she knew why, she was going to protect herself.

She kept her face neutral and sighed. "I have a home somewhere. I was hoping you'd know where it is."

"I'm sorry, I don't. The last time I was invited to your house, you still lived with Miguel, but I know you moved out after the divorce." Her eyes narrowed. "But you managed to find my house. How did you do that?"

Marissa's brows shot up with realization. She explained, leaving out mention of her burner phone. "I should be able to do the same with my name. Do you have a laptop I could use, by chance?"

Aunt Lucy shook her head, but picked up her phone again. Marissa directed her what to search, and they located the right site. They tried Worcester with no luck, then tried Oakhurst County, and her name popped up. "Now click on that book icon."

The address appeared: 756 Crabtree Lane, Wortham.

"Hold on." Aunt Lucy reached into a drawer on the end table, and pulled out a pencil and a Post-it note. She jotted down the address and handed the note to Marissa.

"Thank you." Marissa stood up. "I really appreciate your help. I'll get out of your hair."

Aunt Lucy stood up, too, brows knit. "How will you get there? How did you get *here*? Do you need a ride?"

Marissa plastered on a grateful smile. "No, I'm fine. The nurse at the hospital was worried about me and offered to bring me here at the end of her shift. That's why I came so late. I told her I wanted privacy and she said to meet me at the 7-Eleven when I was done and she'd take me to my house."

"That was kind of her." She didn't move out of the room. "But I'm worried about you. Is there some way I can reach you if I need to? I'll make some calls and see if I can get a current address for Sara."

Calls to who? Did this woman think she was stupid? But no matter—if she decided to give up the information, Marissa wanted to get it. But how? No way was she giving Lucy her burner phone number and risk having her trace it somehow. "I know. Give me your phone number and I'll call you as soon as I know my own number."

Her aunt nodded, and took back the Post-it long enough to write a number on it.

"Thank you again, Aunty. I'll give you a call as soon as I can."

CHAPTER TWENTY-SEVEN

Marissa drove by 756 Crabtree Lane twice, searching for anyone who might be watching the house, glad for the cover of darkness. Luckily, Wortham leaned toward the less-populated side of suburban; the houses sat on large lots with trees and shrubbery in between, set back from roads that had no sidewalks. She wouldn't be noticed driving by unless she was stupid about it, but the downside was this type of neighborhood didn't routinely have many cars parked on the streets. She'd have to risk it, and hope that since the neighboring houses were dark, most everyone was already asleep for the night.

She parked around the block and slipped the bear spray into the waistband of her pants. She shoved the flashlight and a shirt into the backpack. She double-checked everything, and examined the house as she walked around the corner: a two-story Cape Cod whose paint appeared gray in the dim street lighting, although it might have been a slate blue. Whatever the color, she didn't recognize it, or the red Chevy Malibu in the driveway, and frustration filled her. How had she recognized the photos and remembered her childhood, but couldn't remember anything since?

She trotted up the front stairs to the door as though she had a reason to be there, because the best way to avoid suspicion was to act like you belonged. Except, she realized with a laugh, she *did* belong here. This was *her* house. She just didn't have a key.

Hoping to find one underneath, she lifted the mat and the potted plant by the door, but she and her husband apparently weren't that sort of people. She tried the door on the off-chance, but it was locked. She slipped around the back of the house and did a cursory search for other hiding places, but again found nothing. The back door was also locked, with no convenient pet door she could squeeze through.

That left only the window. For all she knew, someone could be lying in wait—but she had no other options.

She wrapped the shirt twice around the flashlight, punched the end through the window next to the back door, then knocked out the remaining shards of glass. With as much caution as her shaking hand would allow, she reached through the window, unlocked the back door, and opened it carefully.

The flashlight beam revealed a small-ish kitchen with a white-and green decorating scheme. Several dishes languished in the sink, and a smattering of items littered the counter. But she'd been neat without trying back at Sunset Gardens. Possibly her husband wasn't?

Two doors led off the kitchen. The first opened into a garage lined with stacks of boxes, some labeled as household goods and files, and others labeled *memorabilia*. Probably not much there to shed light on what happened, but she'd return to it—maybe it would trigger more memories.

She retreated back inside and searched the house quickly, heart pounding as she checked each room, half expecting someone to jump out at any moment. Nobody did—the house was empty.

She stopped for a moment in the upstairs master bedroom to let her heartbeat return to normal. The room answered one of her pressing questions—she was definitely still married. Men's clothes hung in the closet, and both sides of the bed had end tables dotted with personal possessions. Which left a bigger question in its place: where was her husband? It was the middle of the night and he wasn't home. And, he hadn't filed a missing persons report about her, which meant he either didn't want her to be found, or he was missing himself.

No longer worried about keeping quiet, she hurried back downstairs to the key hooks she'd noticed by the kitchen door. She clicked the remotes. The Chevy's lights flashed; she dashed outside, opened the glove compartment, and checked the registration. The car belonged to Bruce Stasuk and Marissa Stasuk. The trunk was empty except for a roadside emergency kit.

Back in the master bedroom, she turned on the light and searched the nightstands. Several magazines covered the top of hers—*Mother Earth News, Outdoor Life, Better Homes and Gardens*. She yanked open the nearly empty drawer to find a pad of paper, several pens, and earplugs—Bruce must snore. The second nightstand contained a similar assortment of nondescript items. She slid her hand around all of the clothes in the bureau and rummaged through the jewelry box, but found nothing interesting or of value.

She checked the medicine cabinet in the master bath for prescriptions, but found none. But then, if she or Bruce had any, they would have taken them on the camping trip, wouldn't they?

The second bedroom had been turned into some sort of combination office and craft room. She flipped through the few personal records she could find—she and Bruce must have done most of their banking online—and found the original paperwork for their cell phones. She jotted down the mobile numbers, unsure which was hers and which was Bruce's. She picked up the landline extension and called both numbers in turn—both went immediately to voicemail.

Once she finished with the upstairs, she returned to the boxes in the garage. She peeked into several, then pulled out the memorabilia. Inside she found photo albums and manila envelopes filled with ticket stubs, letters, matchbooks, and other paper-based scraps, all labeled by time frame. She started with the most recent and worked her way back to the final one, labeled 1998–2000. Not a single item in the envelopes sparked a memory, not even her divorce papers. Only the photo albums from her high school

years and before brought back floods of memories: hanging out
with a small group of friends, teachers she liked and others she
hated, romantic dates with old boyfriends, the desperation to be
finished with high school and out building an actual life. Even
Sara's baby book could have belonged to a stranger.

As she closed the boxes and restacked them, she noticed a fire
safe in the far corner. She pulled out the boxes that were on top
of it, and lifted the lid. A laptop. A small jewelry box. A plastic
document holder. She shoved the first two into her backpack,
and opened the third. Her original mortgage paperwork, along
with a refinance signed just over a year before. Her and Bruce's
birth certificates. She was born May 15th, 1975, and Bruce was
several years younger than her, born in 1984. She smiled. Not
bad—a younger man.

Back in the living room, she flipped on the light. A trio of
lighthouse paintings jarred her—ugly as sin, she couldn't imagine
having agreed to put them up. Objects littered every surface,
giving a disheveled feel that some might charitably call lived-in,
but that made her feel anxious. She methodically sorted through
it all, gathering everything into a single pile to be sure she didn't
miss anything, and paused when she came to a white envelope
that contained several printed photos inside.

They were embarrassingly intimate—a couple laughing and
flirting, and finally passionately kissing, his hand on her breast.
Marissa recognized Sara, her eyes sparkling and her skin flushed.

But the man kissing her was not her fiancé, Hunter Malloy.

*

Marissa stared at the pictures, chest constricted. Aunt Lucy said
Sara was engaged to Hunter, and the photo she'd shown Marissa
had been taken only a month previous. But according to the date
printed on the pictures, Sara had been cavorting with a blond-

haired, blue-eyed someone who wasn't Hunter at about the same time. Maybe she and Hunter had broken up, and Aunt Lucy was mistaken about when the photo had been taken?

But she knew that was wishful thinking. The angle of the pictures, and the graininess—these had been taken from a distance, with both Sara and the man unaware. And nobody printed out pictures anymore, she'd seen the proliferation of digital in every TV show she'd watched, and even Aunt Lucy's picture of Sara had been on her phone. Plus, each photo had a time and date stamp: February 14th, 2019, 9:53 p.m., 9:55 p.m., etc. So why would someone take pictures of Sara with someone who wasn't Hunter and print them out, complete with incriminating dates and times?

There was only one answer. Sara had been cheating on Hunter, and someone found out. And that person must have been black-mailing Sara.

As soon as she thought the word, an image flashed through her mind. Sara, standing in front of her, face screwed up in anger. "Don't you get it?" she'd said. "I'm not going to be a slave to blackmail my whole life. I'm not paying a penny. I'll tell Hunter myself."

Marissa squeezed her eyes shut and pressed her palm against them, trying to remember more. But the harder she tried the farther Sara slipped from her, and even the flash she'd remembered became fuzzy. But she'd seen enough. If Sara had refused to pay, maybe even threatened to go to the police, the blackmailer might well have decided to shut her up. And if Marissa had gone with Sara to face the blackmailer, he would have tried to attack her, too.

But she gasped as another thought occurred to her. Maybe Sara had gone to Hunter first and confessed the affair. Maybe he'd been so enraged he killed Sara, and tried to kill Marissa. Or maybe Sara had broken off the affair first, and the mystery man had refused to take no for an answer? Maybe he had her tied up somewhere, determined that if he couldn't have her, nobody could?

"Dammit!" Marissa threw the envelope across the room. It bounced off the wall and pictures scattered across the floor. She took a deep breath and tried to focus herself. She gathered the pictures and shoved them into the envelope, then slipped it into her backpack.

She should take the pictures to the police and tell them what she'd learned, right now.

But the instant she had the thought, her panic returned. What if she was wrong? What if the blackmail was completely coincidental? She wasn't stupid enough to go confront a blackmailer out in the woods, and she doubted any daughter of hers was that stupid, either. And if Sara was being held somewhere by some psychopath, Marissa couldn't be sure the police would take her seriously, especially now that she was a fugitive. No, she couldn't go to the police until she knew for sure what had happened, and who had done it. That was the whole reason she'd run, and she wasn't going to stop until she'd found Sara.

She forced herself to think. So what was the next step? She'd located her own life, and her memory still hadn't come flooding back. If she couldn't figure it out that way, she needed to go where Sara should be. *Her* house, her job, talk to the people who knew her. Maybe she'd regained consciousness when the attacker was chasing Marissa, and managed to get away? The detective said they'd searched local hospitals and morgues for anyone that matched up with profusely bleeding injuries, but they hadn't known her identity, so they hadn't been able to look for her specifically. Maybe they just missed whatever her injury was. Maybe Sara was home now, recuperating, desperate to know where Marissa was, but not well enough to file a missing persons report yet. She needed to know for sure.

Marissa grabbed her phone to search for Sara's address, but stopped. She couldn't use the same trick she'd used to find Aunt

Lucy's house and her own—Sara was young, she couldn't possibly own her own home yet.

She snatched the laptop out of her backpack—surely Sara's contact information would be somewhere on it. She ran her nails across the table as it booted up, until finally the welcome screen appeared.

Shit—she needed a PIN.

She tried *password*, 1234, 12345, and so on, all the tricks she'd learned from the true-crime shows. Her name, Bruce's name, Sara's name. She grabbed the baby book out of the garage and tried Sara's date of birth, then checked Bruce's birth certificate in the fire safe and tried his. She tried combinations. Nothing worked.

"Fuck!" She slammed her fist on the table. The shock of the blow slashed up her arm, and toppled her carefully stacked pile of detritus. She rubbed her wrist and laughed a dry, sarcastic laugh. "I can figure out the two idiot nurses' passwords, but I can't figure out my own. You *have* to be kidding me."

How the hell could she find *nothing* current in her house about her daughter? Probably because all her important information was on her cell phone, and God only knew where *that* was. Cell phones sounded good in theory, but what did you do when you lost them? Having everything in cyberspace wasn't as awesome as it appeared to be on TV when all you had to do was tap a button to call anybody or anywhere in the world.

She started gathering the papers from where she'd knocked them over, and ran across the divorce papers she'd pulled with everything else out of the fire safe. Miguel's name jumped out at her.

Of course, why hadn't she thought of that before? Surely Sara's father would know how to find her.

She did a quick search to see if she could find his phone number online. It returned a slew of Miguel Navarros, and she had no way of narrowing the list down. She'd have to go to his house and speak to him in person. But did he still live at the same address he'd had at the time of the divorce? She couldn't risk showing up to a stranger's house in the middle of the night and have them report her to the police.

She tapped the address listed on the divorce into the land records website to be sure he still lived there.

He didn't.

The current owner was listed as Sara Navarro.

CHAPTER TWENTY-EIGHT

The man was careful not to slow down as he drove past the house. No lights on, no drapes open, no unidentified car in the driveway. But then, she wouldn't be stupid enough to do any of those things, being on the run and all, so he couldn't be sure.

He parked the car two streets over, on the side of a corner lot largely masked with bushes. He stuck in earbuds, then pulled on a trooper hat that matched his outdoor running gear, careful to cover as much of his face as possible with the flaps. He locked the car, pulled on his gloves, and did his best impression of a jogger out for a late-night run.

He kept his speed low and even, then, as he passed the largest of the bushes on the lot he veered abruptly in toward the house. In a moment he was around the side and up on the back porch, scanning the house for any sign of habitation or disturbance.

A wide grin spread across his face when he saw the window next to the back door had been carefully smashed—no chance a random burglar happened to pick now to break in. He reached through and opened the door.

He stood for a moment, listening. Then he pulled out his flashlight and crept as silently as he could through the dark kitchen.

She wasn't in the living room. He turned down the hall, and checked the first-floor bedroom. Nothing.

He climbed the steps, careful not to make them creak. But each room at the top was empty.

He flew back downstairs, and into the garage. She wasn't there.

"Dammit!" She must have been there—burglars didn't leave valuables and close the door behind themselves. But she was gone.

He went back through the house, faster this time, ransacking drawers and the personal papers in the office, everywhere he could think that she might have shoved an envelope of pictures. He ended in the living room, where a big pile of crap poured over the coffee table onto the floor—magazines, circulars, shipping envelopes from Amazon, receipts, half-used notepads. He sorted through it all on the off-chance, but didn't find any pictures.

He kicked at the pile in frustration, scattering more of the contents onto the floor. What the hell was he supposed to do now? Whatever that was, he needed to get the hell out of here, immediately. If she hadn't gone to the police, they could be here looking for her any minute.

He turned and slipped back out of the house, then jogged back to the car, forcing himself to keep a steady pace. If he just calmed down and figured this out, he could find her and play out the rest of the plan, and everything would turn out just fine.

If he were Marissa, what would he do? There were really only two possibilities. She'd either go to the police, or she'd go looking for Sara. Which made his choice easy, because he couldn't very well go wait for her at the police station.

CHAPTER TWENTY-NINE

Marissa recognized her house, now Sara's, as soon as she turned the corner.

As with the pictures of her childhood, there was no struggling with a flash of memory, no Picasso-esque fragmentation of parts and pieces of person, place, and context like when she remembered running through the woods. She just knew, in a way she couldn't imagine not knowing, that this was the house she'd purchased with her husband shortly after their wedding. She remembered the neighborhood and the house-hunting, a process she'd found annoying and endless, and she remembered the relief when their bid was accepted after losing two other houses to competing offers. She remembered living with Miguel's parents for six months before they found the house, two of those months before the wedding, because her mother made it clear she wasn't welcome to live at home anymore. She hadn't said it—that would have made her look like a bad person to her new in-laws and to her sister—but she made it clear. The tension had become nearly unbearable, and her mother would hardly stay in a room with her for more than a few minutes by the time Marissa moved out.

And along with the house, she now remembered Miguel Navarro. He'd been her knight in shining armor, her ticket out of everything. Out of her poor childhood and away from parents who'd never be more than they were. Because unlike them, *she* wanted to be more. Miguel adored her, showered her with presents and compliments, wanted nothing more than to make her happy.

When she decided to take college courses, he paid for them and even cooked dinner after he came home from work so she'd have time to study. When she decided the endless list of pointless classes needed to get a degree that wouldn't really help her anyway was a waste of time, he gave her the money to start her own soap-making business. When she realized how sensitive she was to the scents, he never made her feel bad for one minute when she switched gears to making cupcakes. And when it became clear that she'd chosen the exact wrong time amid a sudden explosion of cupcake shops, he was fine with her abandoning that, too. As an engineer, he made enough to support them, and just wanted her to be happy.

But her memory after the cupcakes stopped like an abandoned railroad track bisected by a brick wall. She was sure Miguel had supported whatever else mattered to her after that, but she couldn't remember what it was.

Miguel had been a huge source of tension with her mother. Not Miguel exactly, though, that wasn't the right way to put it. Marissa had never been good enough for her mother—she treated Marissa's goals like silly fantasies, and even called them 'little hobbies'—so Marissa knew if she loved Miguel, her mother would be opposed to him. But not because she didn't like him, that was the ironic part. Because *Marissa* wasn't good enough for *him*. The same way her mother said Marissa failed at everything because she didn't care enough and didn't put in enough effort, she said Marissa didn't really understand love, and didn't really love Miguel.

The anger flared through Marissa all over again as she remembered her mother's words. How dare she presume to know what was in Marissa's heart? Miguel made her feel loved, made her feel special. Believed in her. That was more than anyone else had done, by far, ever. And he took care of her.

But the last straw was that she accused Marissa of *using* Miguel. How was *that* supposed to work, exactly? You weren't supposed to take gifts from your boyfriend? You weren't supposed to let him help you? Isn't that what partners were supposed to do, help one another and support each other's dreams?

Headlights flashed in the distance as a car drove down a cross street, pulling her back to the present. She scanned her surroundings. The neighbors were settled in for the night, lights out and nobody peeking out from windows. She drove past the house, noting the Tesla in the driveway. Then she drove to a McDonald's around the corner, ordered a quarter-pounder meal, and ate it while she figured out a plan of attack.

This neighborhood was more compact than her new one, with smaller lots and houses within earshot of each other. But she'd made sure her house, now Sara's house, was separated from its neighbors by tall hedges and trees, believing firmly in the principle that good fences made good neighbors. So now, once she parked in the driveway, only the neighbor directly across the street would be able to see the car. If someone happened to look out the window, they'd see her pull in, and possibly be puzzled by the strange car. But that was a far smaller risk than parking for any period of time in front of anyone else's home.

After finishing her French fries, she drove back to the house. She slipped out of the car and pulled up on the hidden cord to release the side gate, then trotted around to the back door. She knocked, then put her ear to the door and listened. No footsteps, no talking, nothing except the ticking of the horrible grandfather clock Miguel's parents had given them as a wedding present.

After a second knock to be sure, she crossed to the window. The house had been painted a different color, but the window frames underneath were the same as when she owned the house—and she knew of a little peccadillo she'd never told anyone about. She trotted around to the side of the house, and ran her fingers around the edges of the glass. She pulled at the gray weatherstripping while shifting the pane—it slipped out into her hand, and she gave a silent whoop of joy.

The air inside had a stale, stuffy smell. She hurried through each room calling Sara's name, hoping to find her injured but recuperating, too soundly asleep due to some painkiller to hear Marissa's knocking.

The rooms, covered in dust, were a confusing pastiche of furniture she remembered from when she lived there and pieces that were completely foreign to her, giving her a disconcerting sense that she'd slipped into some sort of parallel dimension. A brand-new couch kissed Miguel's old armchairs, its blue-and-white Moroccan pattern clashing with their earthy sage.

She ended in the master bedroom. Men's clothes hung in the closet, and an abandoned pair of men's boxer briefs lay crumpled on the floor. One half of the bed was meticulously made, and the other mussed from a night's sleep—the side where men's dress shoes peeked out from under the dust ruffle.

She jogged back down into the kitchen and pulled open the refrigerator. The expiration date on the milk was five days previous. Green mold dotted the loaf of bread and a container of leftover spaghetti and meatballs.

Despair pressed down onto her chest. Not only hadn't Sara returned home to recover from her injury, nobody had been home in at least a week. Not Sara, and not Hunter.

She dropped to her knees on the tan linoleum floor, fighting back tears. She *would not* let herself believe Sara was dead. She couldn't deal with that grief on top of everything else she was trying to cope with, she just couldn't. And she couldn't afford to break down now, she had to find a way to be strong—her daughter needed her. She had to focus.

What was her next step?

Information—she needed information. Paperwork, to start with.

She crossed through the house to the downstairs bedroom. Miguel had always used it as an office, and Sara had adopted it for the same purpose. She went through the desk drawers systematically, gathering what little she could. Sara's place of employment—a bank—and Hunter's—some sort of PR firm. Insurance records that confirmed the Tesla Model S was registered to her, in her name only. A few credit card statements that showed the same sort of banal purchases you could find on anyone's—trips to the grocery store, to Target, a couple of dinners out. The deed to the house, along with transfer paperwork because Miguel had passed—

Miguel was dead? But he was so young; he'd only have been, what, fifty-five years old. His father had died young of a heart attack, had the same thing happened to him?

She wiped the tears from her eyes with the back of her hand, and shook herself. She could grieve for him later. For now, she had to stay focused. At least now she knew why Sara's name was on the house rather than Miguel's—she'd inherited the house, along with an insurance settlement. Part of which had paid for the Tesla, based on the timing involved, while most of the rest went into her 401K, according to the statements. Pride washed through her—her daughter was smart to be thinking of retirement so early. She must have a solid head on her shoulders.

Marissa scanned the rest of the house. Lots of bookshelves—someone loved to read. Sara must enjoy knitting, because the other spare bedroom was filled with skeins of yarn and several half-finished sweaters. Hunter apparently liked drones, because she found three of various complexity on a different table in the same room. Or, for all she knew, the drones were Sara's and Hunter enjoyed the knitting.

As she crept back down the hall, she studied the pictures that lined the walls. One of Sara and Miguel. Another of Sara in a graduation gown. A third with Sara and Hunter. She leaned in to verify—yep, he was the same man she'd seen in Aunt Lucy's picture, and most definitely *not* the man in the pictures she'd found.

As she passed the living room, a flash of brown leather next to the couch caught her eye. A purse, tucked under the end table.

She grabbed it and rifled through. Several lipsticks, a mascara, a folding mirror, and a small datebook, but no wallet and no keys. Sara must have taken the essentials when she packed for the camping trip, and left what she didn't need here, waiting for her return. Marissa flipped through the book to the pages for April, and found a segment marked off: *Camping with Mom.*

So they'd gone camping together. But the phrasing was ambiguous—did it mean just she and Sara had gone, or had both couples gone?

Marissa dropped her head into her hands and tried to think. Sara wasn't here, but her car was, and a red Malibu had been parked in Marissa's driveway. The Malibu might have been the car Bruce drove, but she doubted it—during the parts of her life she remembered, she drove red cars, because it was her favorite color. So who'd driven them out to the Berkshires? And where was Hunter? Like Bruce, both he and his car were missing. Had they all been murdered out in the woods, and only Marissa had managed to get away?

Except—Sara's bed was half-made. The last time it was slept in, Hunter slept in it without Sara. But maybe he left the following Monday for some business trip? PR people did that, right? Bruce was a different story; according to the paperwork she found, he worked in construction. But maybe he had to work a site out of town? Maybe that's why she and Sara had decided to go away when they did, because Bruce and Hunter were going to be away, anyway?

She shook her head. No, none of that made sense. Even if one or both were out of town, they'd expect to have heard from Marissa and Sara by now. Someone would have filed a missing persons report, wouldn't they?

But maybe not. It had only been a week and a day since she stumbled into Taltingham. If that had been the first night of their trip, nobody would have expected them home until Friday, and they might have assumed cell service was bad when they didn't get a call. Any police report wouldn't have been filed yet when the detectives were looking for it.

So what did that leave her with? The only other place she knew to look for any of them was their jobs—but she couldn't do that until morning.

Her eyes darted to the darkness outside. Which meant another desperate night hiding from the person hunting her.

CHAPTER THIRTY

The man drove the shortest route to the house, but hit every light red. He fidgeted in his seat, waiting for them to change, fuming as he pictured Marissa slipping into the darkness again, this time forever.

By the time he made it to the right neighborhood, he'd wound himself up so tight he had to force himself not to race through the turns.

As he pulled onto the right street, he spotted a large SUV pulling out of a driveway midway down the street.

He tried to calm the rush of adrenaline. Was that the right driveway? He couldn't tell for certain because the dark was messing with his depth perception. Could it still be her, after it took him so long to get here? It couldn't be her, could it? He maintained his pace and kept an eagle eye on the driveway until he pulled close enough to be sure.

It was the right driveway. It had to be her.

He pulled over to the side of the road, pretending to park, hoping the SUV hadn't noticed him.

CHAPTER THIRTY-ONE

Marissa did a double take when the headlights appeared around the corner.

Dammit! Just when she was almost gone! What were the odds that someone would show up right as she was pulling out?

But—that wasn't automatically a problem. Maybe this particular neighbor wasn't all that observant. Or maybe they'd had a horribly bad day at work and just wanted to get home to bed, and didn't have an extra thought to give the strange vehicle pulling out of the neighbors' driveway. After all, she could just be a harmless visitor. Unless they noticed the house was completely dark. And how late it was.

She kept her speed steady and her eyes on the headlights in the rearview mirror. The car pulled over to the sidewalk—and she breathed a sigh of relief. She'd been overreacting, anyway. Even if they called the police, what did it matter? The police didn't know her true identity, or Sara's. And the neighbor hadn't had time to jot down her license plate number. She was fine.

So why did she feel so uneasy?

CHAPTER THIRTY-TWO

He watched the SUV approach the corner.

Should he follow? Was there any real possibility it wasn't Marissa? Sara didn't have friends who just dropped over unannounced; in fact, she didn't really have any close friends at all. And she'd only just be due back at work, so nobody would come around looking for her this soon; the police wouldn't even have taken a missing persons report seriously for twenty-four hours after she should have shown up for work. The only other person he could think of was Aunt Lucy, and she drove an ancient, beat-up Caddy. But if he were wrong, he might blow his only chance to catch Marissa when she did show up.

The car would be gone in a moment, he had to decide, *now*. And his instinct told him she was in that car.

He pulled away from the curb and turned at the same corner she had. The high red taillights were visible in the distance, stopped at the traffic light, signaling her intention to turn left. Which would put her on Elm, the main road through town, and he'd be able to follow her from a safe distance.

He maintained his speed, slowly closing the distance between them as she waited for the light to change.

When it did, she rolled through the intersection. He sped up, but couldn't make it through in time.

He watched as she pulled away, hoping he'd have a chance to catch up before he lost track of which taillights were hers. "Stay on the road, stay on the road," he chanted. Two cars passed by, adding two additional sets of red dots in the distance. He swore.

Then the traffic light in front of her changed, forcing her to stop.

After an eternity, *his* light turned green. He accelerated onto Elm until he reached thirty-five, the speed limit, then forced himself to maintain. By the time her light turned green, he was about a block away from her, nestled behind the cover of the other cars.

He relaxed and settled in, enough to enjoy guessing where they were going.

CHAPTER THIRTY-THREE

Fear constricted Marissa's chest when headlights turned from the street she'd just left. No way that was a coincidence—it was too late for another car to be out on the same sleepy street.

The car stayed a few lengths back. She changed lanes to see if it would follow—it didn't. She picked up her speed, and it fell behind.

Maybe she was wrong. Maybe this was just a really odd coincidence. It was possible, even if it wasn't likely.

But she couldn't afford to take the chance.

She'd originally planned to turn right off Elm to Dwight, which would take her to the highway. But that was another of the town's main arteries, and the most likely path for *any* car on the road to take—if the car followed, she still wouldn't be certain why. So she drove past Dwight.

The car did the same.

She turned right onto Blanquette, which led back to the sleepy neighborhoods.

The car followed, now keeping less distance between them.

Her heart pounded in her chest. There was no doubt now. Whoever it was knew what she was doing, and now wasn't afraid of being detected. Which meant she needed to lose them, fast.

She searched what she'd recovered of her memory for any strange anomaly that would allow her to slip away and double back. Surely there was something—

She accelerated into the next turn, praying as her tires squealed.

CHAPTER THIRTY-FOUR

The moment she turned back toward the neighborhood, he knew she knew.

He sped up, but just a couple of miles over the speed limit. If the cops pulled him over, he might as well come up with a prison nickname right now.

Suddenly she increased her speed as well, and turned back out of the neighborhood. He fought the urge to floor it and catch up to her. What was he going to do, run her off the road right in the middle of the city? She'd only go so fast—if she really was a fugitive, she didn't want to be stopped by the police any more than he did.

She must be trying to get away. But how? He scanned his mental map of the area. What would he do if he were trying to get away from someone here?

She made another right turn, then a left onto the Columbus Community College campus. Then down a long street that led to a large, two-block-long central administrative building.

He smiled to himself—she was panicking. Running blind into a net of limited space, with even more restrictive speed limits, straight toward the lake on the far end of campus. Perfect for him—he'd herd her toward that more rural area and run her off the road there.

The signal light where the street dead-ended at the administrative building turned yellow—she floored it, tires squealing around the sharp turn behind the back of the building. He sped up, but couldn't make up the distance before the light turned red.

He gripped the steering wheel, shouting at the light to turn. Thirty seconds later it did, and he threw the car around the bend.

She was gone.

His eyes darted around like a trapped animal—the road ringed the building in a squashed oval, with a different road radiating off every few yards like the spokes of a wheel on the flattened sides. In the thirty seconds she was out of sight behind the building, she could have taken just about any one of them.

"Motherfuck!" He slammed his hands on the dash.

He circled around the ring, hoping to spot her. But this was a college campus, and despite the late hour, taillights dotted every street.

Then—miracle of miracles—he spotted a pair higher than the rest. He screeched onto the street in question and jammed his foot onto the gas, determined to catch up before she disappeared around another corner, police be damned.

He pulled up behind the SUV—and screamed with frustration.

It wasn't a Suburban. She was gone.

CHAPTER THIRTY-FIVE

After turning up the first street behind the Columbus Community Administration building, Marissa took the next right immediately, and backtracked toward the edge of campus nearest the highway. After a few more zigzagging turns, she pulled into the student union parking lot, then sandwiched herself by the edge of the structure where she could watch cars passing by on the road.

Then, heart pounding so loud she could hear the rushing blood in her ears, she waited.

She didn't recognize any of the cars that turned into the lot, but that meant nothing. She hadn't been able to tell much about the vehicle through the rearview mirror, staring into the headlights. It was dark, maybe blue or black, and it was an economy-ish sized car, not a sedan or truck or SUV. More than that she couldn't tell. But none of the cars that pulled into the union gave her a second glance.

Her pulse refused to slow. If she'd had any doubt after 'Oscar Snow's' appearance, it was gone now. Whoever had hurt her and Sara was after her. And, they knew her well enough that they'd been able to guess where she'd show up. Did they know her personally, or did they just have Sara's ID? Either way, she didn't have the luxury of casually visiting everyone's workplaces tomorrow. She desperately needed time, and a place, to think.

After half an hour with no sign of the car, she drove off campus, eyes glued to her rearview mirror. She used back roads to move unpredictably through the next two towns, then checked into the first motel that took cash and didn't ask questions.

CHAPTER THIRTY-SIX

Marissa jolted awake and sprung upright, terrified that she didn't recognize her surroundings—was her memory gone again?

As she took in the dark carpet on the floor and the dirty walls with their simple warped pattern, recognition kicked in. This was just the cheap motel she'd picked out the night before. Once holed up inside she felt safe enough that the adrenaline from the car chase had worn off, and sleep deprivation hit her hard. Past the point of resting easy, she'd tossed and turned until she slipped into a dreamless sleep.

She glanced at the clock on her nightstand—eight in the morning. She'd only been asleep for five hours, but she was wide-awake now. What day was it? She checked her phone. Monday, April 15th. How had she only been gone from Sunset Gardens for a day? So much had happened it felt like a lifetime.

She got up, set the tiny coffee pot to brewing, and stepped into the tiny bathroom. A warm shower would help her think. She turned the knob and ice-cold water blasted out—she jumped back and shrieked, annoyed with herself for not testing it first, and cranked up the warm water.

She forced herself to think. Visiting the job sites wasn't an option anymore, so what could she do now? Could she call them and find out? But would they be willing to give information to a stranger over the phone? She could just ask to speak with them, and see if the employers put her through. But what would it really tell her if they just asked to take a message? Nothing, and she didn't have a call-back number she could give. If she could find a phone that wouldn't trace back to her it might be worth a shot, but that was a big *if.*

Was there another way? She couldn't think of one. The only other person she could remember that was alive was Aunt Lucy. She couldn't get into her own computer, and Sara's tiny date book hadn't contained any personal information—her friends and family were most likely all located in her phone and computer, too. But it probably wasn't smart to turn to someone in their circle, anyway. Those episodes of true-crime TV said over and over that the people closest to the victim were always the most likely suspects, and the photos she'd found indicated a strong motive for why that might be right.

Marissa chewed at her lip. Maybe she was shutting the door on Lucy too fast. Maybe she just had to be smart about it. If Aunt Lucy had nothing to do with Sara's disappearance, surely she'd want to help find Sara. And if she *did* have something to do with it, but didn't realize Marissa remembered anything about the blackmail, didn't that give Marissa the upper hand? There had to be a way to use that to her advantage. And she should keep the channels of communication open until she figured out how.

She got out of the shower, dressed, poured her coffee into a mug, then settled in at the rickety table with her phone to do some research.

*

An hour later, she walked through the sliding doors of the Woodland Public Library, far enough away from Wortham to feel comfortable. She stepped up to the information counter, currently manned by a young goth employee with a disturbingly large hoop through her nose.

"Hi, I'd like to use one of your computers," Marissa asked.

The girl barely made eye contact. "Just log in using your library account number."

"I don't have one."

The girl slipped out a form from a hidden shelf under the counter. "You'll have to apply for one. Fill this out. We need two forms of ID, driver's license or something else with your address on it, and one other item. Piece of mail, credit card, state ID, passport."

Marissa took the form and a pen decorated to look like a flower out of a little pot on the counter. She fished Dolores' driver's license and credit card out of her purse, and filled out the form with all the relevant information. She waited for Goth Girl to finish helping someone else, then slid everything over to her.

"Just a minute," she said, and stepped over to a nearby computer terminal. Marissa watched as she typed in the information as though she had a vendetta against the keyboard, then disappeared through a door. She returned five minutes later with a small piece of plastic and punched out a full-sized library card, then a smaller version with a hole in it meant to hang from a keychain. "Take this back to our computer room, over there." The girl stopped to point, then continued on in a monotone. "When you log on to the computer, a one-hour session will automatically start. When your time runs out, if nobody's waiting, you can start another session on another computer, and so on." The girl continued on with what felt like an endless explanation of the library's lending privileges. "Any questions?"

"No, thank you so much." Marissa smiled, but Goth Girl had already turned away.

Marissa crossed to the computer lab, and selected one of the dilapidated computers. Then she followed the directions she'd googled for creating a free e-mail account, again using Dolores' address, making up the other information as she went. The website had assured her she could skip the phone-number verification step, and, thankfully, it turned out to be right. The longest part of the process was choosing an e-mail address.

She played around for another fifteen minutes or so, waiting for the older, responsible-looking man behind the computer lab counter to make another of his periodic trips out of the room, leaving the teenaged intern alone. Then she made a show of searching through her pockets and her purse for something she couldn't find, and after an increasingly agitated minute, went up to the counter.

"I'm so sorry to bother you. I just realized I left my cell phone at home. I'm supposed to pick up my daughter in ten minutes and there's no way I'm going to make it." She pointed at the phone near the computer. "Can I use yours?"

The girl's eyes widened. "Oh. Um. I'm not supposed to let anybody use the phone."

Marissa amped up the worried expression on her face. "It's in the area code, I promise. Please, I don't want her standing out in front of the school like a prime target for some sicko."

"It's okay, Kaitlyn. The quality of mercy is not strained. We can make an exception for something like this."

Marissa jumped as the older man spoke from behind her, then circled the counter. He pointed to a phone at the far end. "Use that one. Dial nine to get an outside number." He smiled and winked at her, then turned back to Kaitlyn.

Marissa tried to calm her heart as she dialed nine, then her aunt's phone number. She turned her back and lowered her voice, hoping he and Kaitlyn wouldn't be able to hear her. Aunt Lucy's phone rang, then went to voicemail as Marissa had hoped. She'd gambled that Aunt Lucy would be hesitant to pick up a call from a number she didn't recognize, and this way Marissa didn't have to answer any awkward questions.

"Hi, Aunt Lucy, it's me, Marissa. I'm using a public phone because I still don't have a number where you can reach me, but

I did manage to create an e-mail address." She spelled it out twice. "If you could send me an e-mail so I have your e-mail address, too, that would be great. I'll try to check it as often as I can. I love you and hope to hear from you soon."

She disconnected the call with a finger on the cradle, still talking into the handset as she dialed the number for Sara's work, which she'd jotted on the Post-it her aunt had given her.

A woman with a bright, busy-sounding voice answered. "Wynassett Mutual Bank, how may I help you?"

"I'd like to speak with Sara Navarro, please," Marissa said.

"I'm sorry, Sara's not at her desk right now. Can I take a message?"

"No, thank you." As Marissa's finger again depressed the cradle, she noticed movement from the corner of her eye—Kaitlyn was watching her.

She replaced the handset and turned back around. She waived to the librarian and raised her voice. "Thank you so much, I really appreciate it!"

He waved back and she turned to go. *Stupid*, she told herself. She should have known they'd never tell her anything. She realized she was shaking her head, and forced herself to stop, keeping a casual pace as she trotted out to the Suburban.

CHAPTER THIRTY-SEVEN

After losing Marissa the night before, the man had ringed the campus in widening circles, hoping to cross paths with her again. When that hadn't worked, he hurried back to the highway entrance, hoping to intercept her as she left town. Then he drove to both houses again, even though he knew she wasn't stupid enough to return to either so soon. Or likely ever.

So he was back to square one. Actually, behind step one, because now Marissa knew someone was chasing her, and two of the ways to intercept her were now useless.

He picked another seedy motel and spent the night trying to decide whether or not to throw in the towel. It was only a matter of time before the police figured out Marissa's real identity, and as soon as they did, everything would get real complicated real quick.

But once he ran, there was no turning back, and he'd never have a normal life again. He'd have to leave the U.S. and never come back. He could go to the Caribbean, but that was so expensive, or maybe Canada if he could stand the cold, which he just couldn't. He hated New England winters as it was. So, Mexico, probably. So he needed to hold strong and pull this crap storm out of the drain before it swirled down with the rest of his life.

He spent a good chunk of the night going over everything he thought he knew, running every scenario over in his head, trying to come up with something he'd overlooked. And he couldn't shake the feeling that he was forgetting something important.

"Dammit!" The man slammed his burner phone onto the cheap hotel room carpet. A piece of plastic flew up and cut his face; he swiped the blood away as he knelt to gather the pieces, and snapped them back into place as best he could. Thankfully, the phone booted back up because he really didn't want to go buy another one. He was running through his stash of cash as it was, and couldn't face any more subterfuge at the moment.

He forced himself to lie down on the bed, at least. Pacing the floor of the damn hotel room like a caged animal wasn't helping. At some point while his brain chased itself in circles, he nodded off.

When he woke a second time in the middle of the night, he remembered the crucial thing he'd forgotten.

CHAPTER THIRTY-EIGHT

After creating the e-mail address, Marissa returned to the motel to wait for a response from Aunt Lucy and plan her next move. She spent the afternoon and evening googling everything she could think of, including both Sara and Hunter. She found Facebook and LinkedIn pages, but nothing that gave any information she didn't already have. She created a Facebook profile under a pseudonym, but both their profiles were private. She also discovered during her searches that her trip to the library had been a waste of time—she could have just used a proxy service on her phone and kept her IP address private, and not had to worry about security cameras and records. Well, she couldn't see how the police would track her with any of that anyway—all it did was place her somewhere she'd never be again. And at least she knew now, and could use the information going forward.

Close to midnight, she climbed into bed for a quick search of the local news sites before she went to sleep.

Almost instantly she bolted back up; the police had discovered a corpse in the forest near Aspen Ranch campgrounds.

They were still processing the scene, so no name had been released—but the report claimed they'd found a *man*. Fear and relief battled in her chest. Thank God it wasn't Sara—but what the hell was going on? Was the man they found the one who'd attacked her? But if so, who was chasing her? Could there have been a pair of killers working together? She'd seen a case like that on *Forensic Files*, about two men who abducted women together.

And the mystery man's death had to be related *somehow*, anything else would be too strange a coincidence.

The police would surely feel the same, she realized, and would be seriously considering that either she or Sara killed him. Which meant *two* counties' detective units were now trying to bring Marissa in—not just for auto theft, but for murder. If she went to the police now, they'd instantly take her into custody.

Marissa forced herself to lie down, and told herself it didn't make any difference—she wasn't going to stop until she found Sara anyway, and once she did, she'd be able to clear everything up. But her mind wouldn't rest—visions of headlights chasing her through the streets and police handcuffing her kept her tossing and turning, half through the night. She finally calmed herself by repeating the reassuring portion of the news over and over to herself: the body they'd found hadn't been Sara's. Someone *else* had died at the campsite. There was a chance Sara was okay. And with that filling her mind, she finally drifted off to sleep.

Until the slam of a car door under her window jolted her awake.

Heart instantly pounding, barely able to breathe, she grabbed the bear spray and slipped silently toward the door. She forced herself to slip a finger between the blackout curtains, opening them a tiny crack.

Right next to the Suburban, a vehicle's lights flashed, then went out.

The car was small and dark, but was it the same one that had been following her? She wasn't sure. She couldn't see the driver, he'd disappeared behind the Suburban. She needed to get closer to the window for a downward angle, but couldn't risk it.

She listened for his footsteps.

He appeared again from behind the Suburban. Tall, but not too tall. Neither skinny nor fat. Dark hair, light skin, sleek leather jacket over jeans and black loafers. She didn't recognize him—but what did that mean when she still couldn't even recognize her own daughter? And it was impossible in the dark to tell if he matched any of the photos she'd seen.

He climbed the staircase up to the second floor, and glanced toward her room. She shrank back involuntarily, now only able to see his legs.

They turned toward her, down the external hallway. She slipped her index finger under the safety lip of the bear spray, trying to control her shaking hand.

He paused, inches away from her room.

Then he knocked on the door next to hers.

She risked leaning forward again. A woman with purple hair appeared from inside the next room and flung her arms around him. He stepped inside as he kissed her, and the door slid shut behind them.

She gasped with relief and dropped into the tawdry chair, heart pounding through her chest. When it didn't calm on its own, she crossed to the vanity, poured herself a glass of water, and leaned on the wall to slowly sip it. Then she dropped back onto the bed, but knew she'd never fall back to sleep.

She couldn't keep on like this. Unsure what to do, terrified and paralyzed like a trapped mouse waiting for the cat's paw to swipe down on her, hoping Aunt Lucy would respond to her e-mail. What if she never did?

Marissa shook herself mentally. She could only remember half of her life, true, but what she did remember hadn't been smooth sailing. She'd dealt with obstacles then, she told herself, and she could deal with them now. She'd always had a talent for figuring out how to get what she wanted, and who could help her get it. When school hadn't worked out for her, when the soap and the cupcakes hadn't panned out, she'd taken inventory of her assets and weaknesses, then figured out how to maximize the assets, and compensate for the weaknesses.

The missing twenty-odd years of her memory was her current most obvious weakness. Time and money were also in short supply, so she needed to figure out something quickly and act smartly, rather than just petering out her money on hotel rooms.

As far as strengths, she didn't have many. But she'd remembered her childhood and her early adult years, and there had to be something there she could use to her benefit. And she knew more than she had back at Sunset Gardens—she knew her daughter was having an affair and being blackmailed. And her father always used to say *knowledge is power*.

But what power? What good did knowing that do? She was still here, trapped, trying to figure out how to hide from some homicidal maniac—

Another of her father's expressions flashed through her mind. *Take the fight to the enemy.*

That was it, that was the problem. She was playing defense, allowing herself to be a victim, thinking only about how to run and hide. She'd never come out on top that way, even if she had the time and money to continue.

Fuck running from the killer. One of the things she *knew* was that someone was after her, and the power in *that* was it took away their element of surprise. She needed some way to exploit that, to use his search for her to her advantage.

Her eyes landed on the bear spray she'd brought to bed with her. She couldn't afford to be stupid, or naive, about this. If she was going on the offensive, she'd eventually put herself in danger. She'd need to protect herself, and most likely would have to incapacitate the killer, or kill him herself.

Bear spray wasn't going to cut it. She needed a real gun.

PART THREE

Tuesday, April 16th – Friday, April 19th

CHAPTER THIRTY-NINE

The moment Lopez handed them the information identifying Lucy Huggusi as Zoë's biological aunt, Jo and Arnett raced out to Worcester. As they pulled up to Lucy's worn red-brick house, an odd sense of apprehension, enhanced by the fading sunlight, filled Jo. She peered warily around the property as they strode up the drive. "I can't see how this can go well."

Arnett's nod was slow, and pensive. "You gonna take the lead? This might need finessing."

"Might?" She rapped on the door.

A woman's voice came through. "Who's that?"

"Lucy Huggusi? I'm Detective Josette Fournier and this is Detective Bob Arnett, Oakhurst County State Police Detective Unit. We'd like to talk to you about your niece and her daughter."

"You got ID?"

Jo shot Arnett a look as she held up her badge to the peephole. She thought she heard the word *shit*, then the door opened.

A woman wearing an orange waitress' uniform labeled Tommy's Diner and a wary expression opened the door. "What'd she do?"

Jo slipped her badge back onto her belt, then held up a picture of Zoë on her phone for Lucy to see. "Is this your niece?"

She glanced at the picture. "Yup, that's Marissa. What'd she do?"

"That's a long story, I'm afraid. May we come in?"

She threw up her hand in a resigned gesture and turned around. "Might as well. I *knew* something like this was gonna happen when she showed up at my door. Living room's over there, have a seat. You'll have to excuse me a minute, I just got home from work and I can't stay in this thing a minute longer."

Jo assessed the room as they waited. The decor was shabby and dated. The only new item in the room was a small TV that hung across from the couch, and the only personal items she could find were two pictures of Lucy with a man, most likely her late husband.

Lucy returned a few minutes later in jeans and a faded Worcester Sharks sweatshirt. Jo summarized the situation for her, leaving out mention of the blood. "She left the care facility, and we're trying to find her. We're worried she might be in danger. You said she showed up here?"

Lucy's eyes widened as Jo spoke, and she sat up straighter in her chair. "Two nights ago. Which really freaked me out, because we haven't spoken in ten years, and I wasn't sure whether to believe her or not when she told me she couldn't remember who she was. But I guess she was telling the truth."

That was a lot to unpack in a couple of short sentences. "You haven't spoken in ten years? Why?"

Lucy took a moment before answering. "We weren't close. She's always been difficult, since she was a baby."

"Difficult how?"

Jo watched Lucy choose her words carefully. "If I'm in a compassionate mood, I can admit most of it comes from insecurity. She has a good heart, but she's oversensitive and she's selfish. She's charming as a hypnotist when she wants to be, but when she doesn't, she won't hold back."

"So you just never kept in touch with her as an adult? Or was there a falling-out?"

She laughed bitterly. "There was a falling-out. There was a lot of stupid crap over the years, like items she'd borrow and return broken, then refuse to replace. Money she borrowed and didn't pay back, but claimed she did. But that was easy enough to deal with, I just stopped lending her things. The last straw for me was when my sister Ellen, her mother, died."

"Why's that?"

"Ellen left her house to me. Marissa always assumed she'd get it, since she was an only child. It was a complete shock to me, I didn't know Ellen planned to do that. But I understand why. Marissa was married, and had a nice house with her husband. But my husband and me, we always struggled. Kevin was in a motorcycle accident when he was young, and he damaged his spine in several places and fractured his skull. It was a miracle he survived it, but he was never the same. It was hard for him to work regularly, certainly not a full-time job, and I barely graduated high school so I've never made more than minimum wage. We went through long stretches where we had to live out of our RV. Ellen knew we needed the house more than Marissa did. But Marissa didn't see it that way. All she could see was I'd screwed her out of her inheritance. She put all sorts of pressure on me to sign it over to her, even at the funeral in front of everybody, and threatened to sue me for it. Maybe she tried and the lawyers told her she didn't have a case, I don't know. But she harassed me to the point where I told her I'd get a restraining order on her if she kept it up. She stopped after that, I don't know why. My guess is her husband Miguel told her to cut it out for Sara's sake. Sara's their daughter. He was usually a pushover where Marissa was concerned, but he stood up to her once or twice when it concerned Sara. And I remember the look on his face at the funeral: he was mortified by Marissa's behavior. I wasn't surprised when they got a divorce a few years later."

"She was wearing a wedding ring. Did she remarry?" Arnett asked.

Lucy nodded. "Yep. To Bruce Stasuk."

"What was Miguel's last name?"

"Navarro."

Jo scribbled down the names. "You said Marissa has a daughter. Did she have any other children? I'm guessing you weren't in contact with them, either?"

"Wrong. I'm very close with Sara. And she's an only child."

Jo didn't hide her surprise. "How did that work if you weren't on speaking terms with Marissa?"

"Sara was thirteen when Marissa divorced Miguel. He was a big believer in family, and wanted Sara to have a relationship with me. They split custody, so he made sure she spent time with me when he had her."

"And Marissa was okay with that?"

Lucy laughed bitterly. "What she doesn't know doesn't hurt her."

"That must have put Sara in a difficult situation."

"Sara's always been her own person. She's never been one to let anyone else make up her mind, even when that might have saved her time and trouble." Lucy's eyes narrowed. "But why all the questions about Sara if you're here about Marissa?"

Lucy was sharp—Jo would have to walk a careful line. "When was the last time you heard from Sara?"

Fear replaced suspicion on Lucy's face. "Just over a week ago. Why?"

Jo glanced at Arnett, who nodded. She explained about the blood on Marissa's clothes, and the DNA results.

The color drained from Lucy's face. "I knew Marissa was capable of ugliness, but I never thought she'd kill her own daughter."

CHAPTER FORTY

"What makes you think she killed her daughter?" Jo asked.

Lucy rose and crossed to the window to stare out at her yard.

"Mrs. Huggusi?"

She turned back to them and wiped the tears from her eyes. "I'm sorry, that just bubbled up and out of me. I'm not really sure why. I don't really think she killed Sara. She truly loved her daughter, more than anything in the world." She waved her hand. "Well, except herself. It's just, last I heard, Marissa and Sara were going away on a mother-daughter camping trip."

Jo watched her face closely—something was happening here that she didn't understand. "But a camping trip seems like a good thing. Why would you assume something went wrong between them?"

Lucy sat back down, and her eyes searched the carpet. "I guess part of it is the fear I felt when she came after me about her mother's house. It really shook me that she could turn on me like that. I get that from her perspective, *I* was the one that turned on *her*, but I just can't make the logical link to why a reasonable person would feel that way. I needed a place to live, and she didn't. And the way she came after me, it wasn't just like a family dispute, it was like I was an enemy. I wasn't just throwing out a threat about a restraining order, I really was minutes away from getting one. Which I know sounds dramatic, because she never raised a finger to me or even threatened to."

Jo leaned forward and put her hand over Lucy's. "That doesn't sound dramatic at all. I wish more people listened to their instincts.

It would give us a lot less work to do. Do you think something may have caused her to turn on Sara?"

"No, not that, exactly. It's just—well, it's complicated. One thing is, Sara's fiancé, Hunter, really doesn't like Marissa. Sara's been pulling away from her more because of that. They've never been really close, Marissa's just a hard person to be close to, and Sara has always had to keep an emotional distance, if you know what I mean. She's been spending less time with her the past few months, and I can't imagine Marissa has been happy about that. The more distance you try to put between yourself and Marissa, the more she grasps hold and won't let go. That's why they were going on the camping trip, because Marissa wanted to *reconnect* with her."

So Sara's fiancé was controlling. That surprised Jo—she'd have guessed that's the last thing Sara would be attracted to after a controlling mother. "I get the sense there's something more," Jo said, voice soft.

Lucy's brow furrowed. "Okay, well, Sara's been going through something recently. She didn't want to talk about it, so I don't really know the details. Like I said, she's always known her own mind, and if you push her on something, she'll really dig her heels in. And she's the kind of girl who takes a while to process things, you know? She'll clam up for a few days, and then it'll all come pouring out. So I figured she'd tell me when she was ready." Tears slid down Lucy's face.

"Does Marissa have a history of violence?" Arnett asked. "We didn't find any criminal record for her when we ran her prints and her DNA."

"No. She's more the key-the-side-of-your-car type of person. And she's smart, really smart. She'd check to be sure there are no security cameras first. I watched her do exactly that to Miguel's car when she found out he wanted fifty-fifty custody of Sara. Truth be told, she's too much of a coward for a direct fight."

"And yet something made you want to get a restraining order, and something made you wonder if Marissa had hurt Sara."

Lucy nodded. "I guess it's just that if you're on Marissa's shit list, you're done. You're either friend or foe, there's no in between. And it's very rare to ever come back off of it."

Jo nodded, and shifted gears. "What's Hunter's last name? Where can we reach him?"

"Hunter Malloy. He lives with Sara." She pulled up the address, and both phone numbers. She also gave them the name of Sara's employer.

"And you didn't worry when you didn't hear from her after the trip?"

"No, not at all. We don't talk every day, and she was only supposed to be back a few days ago. I figured she was busy catching up on all the stuff that piles up when you take a vacation."

"Right, that makes sense." Jo flipped a page in her notebook. "You said Marissa was here two nights ago. What did she look like? Was she in a car? Did she say where she was going?"

Lucy recapped Marissa's visit for them, and gave them the address for Marissa's house. "At least, that's the address she found, I'm not sure if it's legitimate or not. Then, yesterday she left me a message saying she still doesn't have a phone number, but she gave me an e-mail address. Sarasmom2019@freemail.com."

"Do you have the number she called you from?"

"I should." She tapped and scrolled, and pulled up the number.

Jo copied it. "And since you weren't close with her, I don't suppose you know where she worked?"

Lucy shook her head. "I'd be surprised if she did work. She never really did. Odd jobs here and there when she needed extra money, but mostly she stayed at home, even before Sara was born."

"How did she support herself after the divorce? Did Sara ever say?"

"I tried not to pry about things like that, partly to avoid putting Sara in an awkward situation, and partly because I frankly didn't care. But I'm certain Miguel had to pay her alimony until she remarried."

Jo nodded. "Just one more issue. Do you know someone named Logan Tremblay?"

Lucy thought for a moment. "I might, but the name doesn't ring a bell."

"So you don't know if Sara knew anyone by that name either?"

Lucy's gaze snapped back and forth between them. "No, why?"

Jo explained. "Does she have any connections to any software companies that you know about? Or anyone in Montreal?"

Her eyes darkened. "Software companies, I don't know—Sara always did enjoy coding. She used to write little games, but she never did anything with it. I do remember Hunter mentioning he had family in Ottawa. Montreal's not far, he might very well have family there, too." She leaned forward. "And isn't Ottawa the Silicon Valley of Canada?"

Jo glanced at Arnett, then stood up. "Thanks so much for all your help, Mrs. Huggusi. If you hear from Marissa again, please let us know."

"Of course. What about Sara?" Her eyes welled up again.

"It'll be much easier to find her now that we know her identity. We'll let you know as soon as we find out anything."

But Jo's gut told her whatever they found wouldn't be news Lucy Huggusi was eager to hear.

CHAPTER FORTY-ONE

The moment he remembered Aunt Lucy, the man had thrown on his clothes and left the hotel.

He drove to a Home Depot and grabbed what he needed. Then he headed to McDonald's, because he'd need food. He ordered a sack of burgers and fries, a cup of coffee, and a large soda to get him through the day. Then he drove to Lucy's house.

He parked kitty-corner one house down, then climbed in the back seat and measured the angles. He pulled out the two extending inspection mirrors he bought and duct-taped them in place to maximize his view. He didn't need to see everything clearly, he just needed to see if and when someone came to or left the house.

Hunched over, he devoured a quarter-pounder and downed his half-cooled coffee. Not falling asleep would be the most difficult part. He lay down on the back seat with the empty cup next to him so he could relieve himself easily when needed, and settled in to watch.

Even with the caffeine and sugar from a large coffee and an extra-large Coke in him, he still almost fell asleep twice. But he'd anticipated that, and set a timer on his phone to go off every fifteen minutes. And he brought along headphones so he could at least listen to pirated versions of stupid sitcoms on YouTube while he kept his eyes glued to the mirrors. And *still* it was boring enough that he couldn't understand how cops kept their sanity on stakeouts. Sure, every once in a while a hot soccer mom would power walk by, but mostly it was long stretches of cramped nada. By the time the sun started to set, his brain was tapioca, and he had no clue how he was going to make it through another however many hours.

That's when the Chevy Cruze pulled up.

The detectives he'd followed to Sunset Gardens approached the house with slow deliberation, him dressed in a cheap suit, her in slacks and a blazer. Even if he'd never seen them before he'd've known they were cops.

Shit. That meant they knew who Marissa was. And *that* meant they'd be talking to everyone she had any relationship with. They'd figure out the rest in a matter of days, maybe hours. Which meant he was pretty much screwed, and he might as well head for Mexico right now.

But no, wait—that wasn't true. If they were here, they still had no idea where she was. He could still get to her before they did, he just had to be smart about it.

He pulled the earbuds out and kept as still as he could, eyes glued to the mirror for the half hour before they came back out, with nothing to do but think. But he still couldn't come up with any place to look for her that they wouldn't figure out, and he had no guarantee she'd show up anywhere, anyway.

No *guarantee* she'd show up.

That's what he needed—a way to guarantee she'd show up.

He didn't have a way, but Aunt Lucy just might.

CHAPTER FORTY-TWO

Marissa spent Tuesday googling and planning. For the first time, the internet failed her. She quickly discovered that, contrary to what you might see on TV, guns weren't easy to get illegally. Or at least not unless you already knew the right type of people. If you didn't, one website said, all you had to do was talk to a banger, or you could approach a drug dealer and ask his boss to sell you one. A third option was to approach a dirty cop and ask to buy a throw-down weapon. But, the site also warned, those methods were far more likely to end with you dead, arrested, or sold into sex trafficking than in possession of a firearm.

She spent quite a while chasing the possibility of the gun-show loophole down a rabbit hole, but eventually had to abandon it. The loophole didn't exist in Massachusetts and most of the surrounding states. And even if she drove to a state where she could capitalize on it, there wasn't a gun show she could find sooner than two weeks away.

But as she spent a good portion of the morning googling, Facebook groups popped up in her search results with strange regularity, and were mentioned in quite a few pro-gun articles. Apparently Facebook had groups that catered to just about every interest, and guns were no exception. Maybe she could finesse what she needed there.

She logged on to her newly discovered proxy network, then into her newly made Facebook profile. She spent another couple of hours filling out information to flesh out her invented identity, and took Facebook's random suggestions for people she might want to add as friends. She was astonished at how many of them accepted her requests almost immediately and without question.

Once she had a convincing profile as a solid foundation, she searched through gun groups. Most weren't tied to a location, but she did find a few that were oriented around people in the northeast. She requested invites to the three she found, and to two more general groups whose descriptions seemed to carry the sort of general vibe she was looking for.

She sighed. All she could do now was wait and hope at least some of her requests would be accepted, and sooner rather than later. She gathered beef jerky, a protein bar, and two oranges, then settled in to watch TV as she waited.

CHAPTER FORTY-THREE

"You want to drive, or make the phone calls?" Jo asked.

"Drive." Arnett got into the car, and plugged Marissa's address into the GPS. He pulled away from the curb as Jo dialed the number Marissa had used to call Lucy.

"Woodland Public Library, how can I help you?"

"Wrong number, sorry." Jo hung up.

"Yeah, that's pretty much what I expected," Arnett said.

Next, Jo tried Marissa's, Bruce's, Sara's and Hunter's cell phone numbers. In each case, the phone went directly to voicemail. She did a basic search for each of the names, then ran through the cell phones again, with the same result. She put a call through to Lopez.

"Jo, what did you find out?" Lopez's enthusiasm crackled over the line. "Please don't tell me Zoë was put up for adoption at birth and Miss Lucy has never heard of her."

"Quite the opposite. We got an earful about Marissa—that's her real name—and the family dynamic." Jo caught her up. "I think we need to get as much information as we can about everyone involved. Including any information about Hunter's family in Canada, and any potential software connections that might exist. See if we can locate any of the phones, and we need to see what we can find out about that e-mail address. We're on our way to what we think was Marissa's house to see if she's there, or if she talked to her ex-husband. We'll update you as soon as we know anything."

"On it."

"Thanks." Jo hung up. "Which reminds me. How do we handle this in terms of press?"

"You mean, releasing the identity?" Arnett asked.

"Exactly. My feeling is, if the murderer thinks we still don't know who the victim is, they'll feel safe. If they realize how much we know, they may flee."

Arnett looked over his shoulder for a lane change. "Agreed. Best to keep it under wraps for now."

The sun had fully set by the time they arrived at Marissa's house. "No lights on," Jo said as they stepped out of the car.

"Got the license plate on that car?" Arnett asked, jutting his chin at the red Chevy Malibu.

"Yep." Jo jotted the number down.

Nobody answered the door despite their loud, repeated attempts, so they circled around to the back.

"Window's been punched in." Arnett knocked loudly on the back door. "Oakhurst County State Police Detective Unit welfare check. Is anyone home?"

Nobody answered. They entered the premises, calling out their identification as they went from room to room.

"No sign of the husband. Plenty of valuables around, so not a robbery. Dollars to doughnuts Marissa broke that window," Arnett said.

Jo pointed toward the living room. "Somebody was searching for something." She walked over and examined the detritus spilling over the coffee table to the floor. "A baby book and photo albums right next to it all. That has to be Marissa trying to remember."

Arnett pursed his lips. "So she wasn't lying to Lucy, she still doesn't remember who she is."

Jo stepped carefully around the piles, searching around and behind the furniture while she spoke. "So, Marissa and Sara were off on a mother-daughter camping trip. But the kid at the campgrounds said a man checked them in, not that he was the most reliable witness. So he was wrong, or it wasn't just a mother-daughter event."

"Could have been Bruce, or Hunter." Arnett slipped on gloves and flipped through a stack of mail.

"That seems most likely as things stand. And I don't like that neither Bruce nor Hunter are answering their phones, and that neither of them have filed missing persons reports."

"Maybe they have. We haven't checked since we got word about Marissa leaving Sunset Gardens on Sunday."

"Excellent point, we need to double-check." Jo sent a quick text to Lopez, then checked the time. "And I really don't like that Bruce isn't home. Maybe he's just not home from work, but based on the dust and the smell, my guess is nobody's been here for at least a week."

Arnett nodded. "I say we interview the neighbors and hope he shows up in the meantime, then go find Hunter."

*

The neighbors weren't much help. Nobody remembered exactly when they'd seen either Marissa or Bruce last, but guessed it hadn't been recently. They also couldn't remember the last time Marissa's vehicle had moved, or Bruce's vehicle was home. The Stasuks weren't the friendliest of neighbors, not the sort to let anyone know when they were leaving, and not the sort that inspired trust from others. In fact, Marissa was the sort of neighbor who, if you did something that annoyed her like burned your lawn trimmings at the wrong time, would pour chemicals on your plants to kill them. The best thing about having the Stasuks as neighbors, one woman said, was that they never entertained because they didn't have any friends. Bruce worked some sort of manual labor job during the day, or so they guessed based on his coveralls and the way he looked in the evenings. And yes, he normally worked typical daylight hours and should probably be home by now. As far as anyone knew, Marissa didn't work at all.

Just as they approached the house on the lot behind the Stasuk home, Lopez called.

"Hey, guys. I have some information for you. First off, I checked Marissa Stasuk, Navarro, and Pesaro. She has no record of any kind, which isn't surprising or we'd have tagged her with the fingerprints. So however bitchy she may or may not be, she's never crossed a line with the law. Her husband, however, is a whole different story. Bruce Stasuk has several arrests, although not under that name, and not in our jurisdiction. One for robbery, one for dealing heroin. He's also been Bruce Caligiri in Las Vegas, and Bruce Rondstat in New Jersey. He managed to avoid jail both times, the robbery because it was a first offense, the drug charge because he turned in an accomplice who was a bigger fish. I'll keep digging, but I can already tell you he seems to be a magnet for the scary boys in the playground."

"I wonder how much of that Marissa knew?"

"It's plausible she didn't know any of it, because it happened before they were together."

"When did they get married?"

"About a year and a half ago. But he moved into her house about five years ago, from what I can tell. He's been at his current job, Sanderson Construction out of Oakhurst, about a year, which is a record for him. I double-checked the DMV records and he owns a white 2014 Chevy Captiva Sport. Marissa drives a red 2012 Chevy Malibu. I've already updated our APBs with the makes, models, and plates."

"We just saw the Malibu in her driveway," Jo said, and confirmed the license plate number.

"So she wasn't stupid enough to start driving that again, unfortunately. I also checked out her divorce settlement, since her employment records are almost non-existent. She and her ex,

Miguel Navarro, split assets fifty-fifty, plus she got alimony from him that continued on until she remarried."

"Lucy suspected as much," Jo said.

"On to Sara. Not much I can tell you about her that you don't already know, except she works at Wynassett Mutual Bank and she drives a silver 2018 Tesla Model S, which is bad ass and tells me she cares about the planet and instantly magnifies how pissed off I am that she's in trouble. To round out our little auto show, Hunter drives a 2014 black Toyota Corolla. And yes, Hunter's address is listed as the same one you have for Sara. He's a graphic designer for Beast Communications. His full title is actually graphic designer and PR coordinator, whatever that means."

"You're e-mailing all of this to us, right?" Arnett asked.

"Already did. On to Marissa's e-mail account. Super easy to track, but ultimately worthless, since I can only track it back to the library, where she used Dolores' name and address. But they have several cameras, so we can get a look at her if you like. I'm not sure what that would tell us, but I guess you never know."

"Okay, thanks. I'm guessing all that means we can't use the e-mail address to our advantage."

"That depends. She'll need to access her e-mail somehow, and depending on how she does it, we can potentially track her IP address. I can list out all the possibilities for you, but what it boils down to is we have to hope she's not too smart about technology."

"That sounds like the doors slammed right back in our face," Arnett grumbled.

"Ah, but there are two possible doors we can cut right into the wall." Lopez paused for effect.

"Have her aunt send her an e-mail and hope she responds?" Jo said.

"Eyes on your own paper. Yes, that's one option. The other is, I can write up a little Trojan that'll snatch up her phone's information when she opens the e-mail."

Jo missed a beat before responding. "That can't be legal."

"I didn't say anything about it being legal," Lopez said. "Of course you'd have to get clearance."

"Lieutenant Martinez will never okay that," Arnett said.

Lopez sighed. "Yeah, you're right. Then we're back to Aunt Lucy sending an e-mail. I'll call her and ask her to do that as soon as I get off the phone with you. But back to our journey up the ladder of bizarre—I can't get a location on any of the phones involved."

Jo paused, stunned. "None of them?"

"Nope. Marissa, Sara, Bruce, Hunter, either they're all some-where that's blocking them from GPS, or their phones are all dead. Which I'm sure I don't have to tell you is really, *really* weird. So I'm going to track down a history of the towers they pinged before they disappeared."

"Speaking of which, I'm sure you would have mentioned it, but there's still no missing persons report filed on Sara or Marissa, by chance?"

"Nope."

A dark pit had formed in Jo's stomach. "I know this sounds odd, but can you start paperwork on a warrant to search Sara's house? Something tells me we're going to need it. And we should probably start the process of accessing everyone's credit cards and financial records, see when they last spent money, and where."

"No problem. Godspeed."

CHAPTER FORTY-FOUR

Marissa looked up from the TV when her e-mail notification chimed, and smiled when she saw Aunt Lucy had finally responded.

Hello Marissa,

Thank you for sending me your e-mail address. I'm worried about you. The police came looking for you, and told me Sara's missing, and I'm worried about Sara, too. Can you please tell me what's going on? Can you find a way to call me, or at least tell me over e-mail? I wasn't able to sleep last night, and I won't be able to until I know Sara's okay.

I was able to find Sara's address. She's still living at 9829 Bulkin Road, in Wortham, where you and Miguel used to live. I drove by, and it looks like nobody's been there for quite a while.

Please let me know what's happening as soon as possible.

Love, Aunt Lucy

Several sets of alarm bells rang in Marissa's head. The police had come looking for her? She sprang up and paced the room. That meant they knew who she was, and weren't far behind her, and wanted to take her in. Dammit, she knew she was right to avoid them.

And something about the content of the e-mail felt off to her. *Love, Aunt Lucy?* That was quite a change in tone from the suspicion and lies just a couple of days before. But maybe she'd tried to reach Sara, and when she couldn't, realized Marissa was telling the truth? Or maybe she was just desperate for news about Sara? That would make sense.

But no. Something was still off about it. She snatched up the phone and read over the e-mail twice more, parsing it carefully. There was a stilted formality sprinkled in with the rest that didn't match. *Thank you for sending me your e-mail address. Can you please tell me.* Those weren't the words of a spontaneous message from a worried relative. They were calculated. Why?

Her heart sank. No matter what the reason, she couldn't trust Aunt Lucy. She'd have to think carefully about her reply.

In the meantime, she checked Facebook, and found that four of her group requests had been accepted. Time to dive in. She made herself a pot of coffee in the tiny hotel percolator to drink while she worked her magic. She scrolled through the posted messages in each, absorbing the group culture and fine-tuning which possible strategy had the best possibility of success.

She ultimately decided to post in a group called *New England Gun Lovers (NO BUY SELL TRADE!)*. The group had a good percentage of women, and they were treated with respect. Of the four groups, it had the most flippancy about gun laws, with more than just an undercurrent of rebellion against the idea of background checks and other gun-ownership limitations. And while there was a strict admonition against any talk of ways to circumvent gun laws in the group's rules and all the posts adhered to this, she noticed the group administrators gave a fair amount of leeway in the comments. The deciding factor was that several conversations ended with comments like 'I know how you can deal with that—DM me." There was at least a contingent of members who weren't averse to bending the rules.

She took time composing her post, then hit send.

Hello everyone, thanks for adding me to the group. I'm in western Massachusetts and I'm wondering if anyone knows

*of a shooting range in the area that rents firearms to practice
with. I don't mind if I have to drive far because it's really
important, so even if it's a couple of hours away, that's fine.
I'm really anxious about my waiting period because I need
my gun like yesterday, so I want to at least brush up on my
shooting skills while I wait. I did my training course and all,
but I haven't gone shooting since my dad took me when I was
a little girl. Thanks in advance for any help you can give.*

She wasn't sure how long she'd have to wait before she got a
response, let alone the sort of response she wanted. But within
half an hour, five people had responded, three with the name of a
range about an hour west of where she was currently staying, and
the other two with a range just over the border in Rhode Island.
Two more expressed general sympathy with her frustration over
the waiting period. Then, a few minutes later, she got her first hit.

*Sounds like you're in a bad situation if it's been that long
since you went shooting. Why do you need it so fast? Family
of deer eating all your tulips, LMAO?*

She knew she had to play this carefully.

*LMAO, I wish. My ex violated the restraining order I have
against him. I know he's gonna do it again and I need
something in the house to protect myself.*

That got the reaction she wanted. Over the next half hour,
several people chimed in with comments like *See, this is the problem,
good people can't get a gun when they need to take care of themselves,
but domestic abusers get as many as they want* and *I bet HE has an
armory full of guns while she's a sitting duck at home.*

But more importantly, three members of the group sent her friend requests, and DMed her when she accepted. Two were women who'd been in similar situations, who wanted to commiserate and give her tips about how to protect herself and deal with the law. The third was a man, James Rafferty, whose sister had been hospitalized by her ex-husband when he violated his restraining order and beat her nearly to death. She'd been in a coma for a week, and the asshole only got sentenced to six months in jail for assault. James made damned sure his sister knew how to shoot and had a gun in her end table in case the bastard came back.

She spent the rest of the evening juggling conversations with James and one of the women, Delilah Sound. She played up the damsel-in-distress for James, and the sister-in-solidarity with Delilah, planting seeds she hoped would take root. As she got to know them, she checked their profiles for any verification they were who they said they were. Family pictures, posts about hobbies, cute cat videos—both profiles looked real, and harmless.

Neither made the sort of overture she was hoping for, but she hadn't really expected they would quite so quickly. But she had complete faith that they would. Most people were decent, or so her mind kept telling her, and most decent people expected that you were decent, too. It was easy to take advantage of that. This would work if she just gave it a little more time. And, she had no other option.

So she crawled into bed early, hoping to catch up on the sleep that had been so elusive. But even if she wasn't able to, she needed time to think anyway—she still had no idea what the next step was after she got her hands on the gun. It was all well and good to decide to take the fight to the enemy, but how did she manage that when she didn't know who the enemy was?

Just as she started to drift off, another flash of memory came back to her.

In it her line of vision was low and awkward—she must have been kneeling or sitting on the floor, and she was staring over her shoulder to the left. At a cot—or rather, under a cot. Halfway beneath was a strange rectangular-triangular-hybrid blade, lying like someone had tossed it there. And just at the corner of her vision, a pair of feet in athletic shoes cuffed by jeans.

She bolted upright and pressed her palms into her eyes, desperate to pull the flash back up, trying to make out any additional detail she could—but it was gone again.

CHAPTER FORTY-FIVE

Instead of trying to guess where Marissa would go, the man needed a way to get her to show up where he wanted her to be. And Aunt Lucy was the perfect way to make that happen.

He waited a fair while after the police left before going in. Partly because he needed to be sure they wouldn't come back, and partly because he was still hoping Marissa would show up. But mostly because he didn't want Lucy to connect his appearance with the police, and guess he'd been waiting for them to leave. He needed her to trust him, as much as possible.

He waited as long as he could before he risked her going to bed for the night. Then he ripped the mirrors down, emptied his bladder again, and jogged up to the door. He pounded on it with the side of his gloved fist and called out, "Lucy, open up, it's me!"

He waited, listening. He was certain he heard footsteps.

He pounded again. "Lucy, I need your help! Sara and Marissa are missing. Please!"

The door opened, and she waved him inside. "Hurry up and get in here, I don't need the neighbors going nuts. Where the hell have you been?"

"I was away on a work trip, and I come back, and all hell's broken loose. You know about all this? What's going on?"

She led him into the living room, an odd look on her face. "When was the last time you saw them?"

"When they left for the camping trip. When was the last time *you* saw them?"

She looked at him for a long minute, then sat down and rubbed her eyes. "Same. Well, that's the last time I saw Sara."

He picked up the strange wording. "What do you mean? Have you seen Marissa?"

"Marissa was here on Sunday."

He furrowed his brow. "She came here? Why would she come here?"

She stopped rubbing her eyes but left her face in her hand, like she was thinking. "She said she was in an accident, but she didn't remember what happened. Or where she lived, or even that she had a daughter."

"Shit. Was she okay? Did she go to the police?"

Lucy shook her head. "She seemed fine except for her memory. And—no. No, she didn't go to the police. I mean, I don't think so—maybe."

He noted her strange pauses—she was lying. "She's not home, I checked, neither of them are. Why wouldn't they go home?"

Lucy shook her head again. "I don't know."

"What did she say to you? She must have said something."

She took a deep breath. "Let me try to remember."

His eyes stayed on her face as she stood and crossed the room. She was agitated, yes, but he was sure she was stalling for time. He couldn't let her think too long, she might start putting pieces together. "Please, anything will help. If she didn't remember anything, how did she find you? Did she say anything at all about where she was going?"

She turned on him, her frustration boiling over. "Stop! She saw an RV that made her remember me. And I showed her some pictures of her childhood and she remembered that, but she still didn't remember Sara. That was it, I just wanted her out of my house!"

She was feeling guilty—he could use that. He put on an angry expression. "So wait, let me get this straight. Your niece, your own flesh and blood, comes to you after she's been in an accident, and she can't remember anything, and you just wanted her out of the house? What the hell?"

Her eyes shifted around the room. "I just—no, it wasn't the smartest thing to do, but I didn't even know she was telling the truth until—"

He didn't miss a beat. "Until what?"

Panic flashed across her face, and he could practically see her searching for a way to cover up her mistake. He couldn't let her. "Until what? Come the fuck on, this is serious!"

"Until I got the voicemail from her with the e-mail address," she said.

Yeah, right. She'd been about to mention the police, he'd have bet money on it. But it didn't matter. In her hurry to lie about what she thought *did* matter, she'd given him exactly what he needed. "What e-mail address?"

She looked relieved, but still guarded. "She called and gave me an e-mail address where I could reach her. I just sent her an e-mail about half an hour ago."

He purposefully deflated. "Oh, thank God. What's the address?"

"Hold on, I have it next to the computer."

He followed her down the hall. Her posture tensed—she must have expected him to stay back in the living room, but she was too off-kilter to object. She turned into a spare bedroom half repurposed into an office, and bent over the desk to pick up a Post-it note.

"Here it is. I'll write it down for you."

"Thanks so much." He leaned on the other side of the desk as if to reach for the pen there, and brushed against the mouse pad of the open laptop. The screen came to life, displaying Lucy's e-mail account—and he almost let his excitement show. He didn't *need* access to her e-mail, but it would make things so, so much easier.

He stepped back so she wouldn't think he was trying to get at the computer. "Oh, I'm sorry—but—is that the e-mail you sent her?"

She glared at the screen, clearly annoyed, then took the pen and scribbled the address on the next Post-It. "Yes, I was just checking before you got here to see if she'd responded yet, but she hasn't." She pushed past him toward the living room.

As soon as her back was to him, he pulled a length of cord from his jacket pocket. With one end in each hand, he lunged to loop it over her head and around her neck. He wrenched the garrote deep into her throat, pulling her head into his chest with one arm, and restraining her arms with the other.

She struggled harder than he'd expected, raining blows onto his legs wherever her flailing fists could make contact. He braced against the attack, wincing, but held strong, reminding himself she was doing him a favor. The more bruises she gave him to join his others, the better; they'd just lend credence to his cover story.

After an eternity of willing his strength not to fail, he felt her go slack. He kept the cord tight for another minute, then released her to the ground and made sure she had no pulse.

He pulled his gloves off, hurried back into the bedroom, and sat in front of the computer. He read over the e-mail she'd sent to Marissa, and checked the time on it. She'd only sent it a few hours before, but the situation was urgent enough that another e-mail coming so quickly after the first would make sense. He typed a second e-mail, and sent it. Then he changed the password on Lucy's account and jotted down both her e-mail address and the new password. Then he slipped his gloves back on, grabbed a towel from the linen closet to wipe down the keyboard and the chair he'd touched, and slipped out of the house.

CHAPTER FORTY-SIX

Jo scanned Marissa's block. "It doesn't look like Bruce is coming home anytime soon. I say we get over to Sara's house as soon as possible."

"Can't wait to hear why Hunter hasn't filed a missing persons report for his beloved fiancée." Arnett opened the passenger door and climbed into the car.

Twenty minutes later, they pulled up to Sara Navarro's house, and Jo was flooded with a feeling of déjà vu. No lights were on, and there was a single car—Sara's Tesla—in the driveway. "I'm not feeling good about this. Do we have enough probable cause to force our way in?"

Arnett grimaced. "That'd be a hard argument to make. It's been days since she bled on Marissa, and if she made it home, she's probably okay. And since there's another resident…"

"Right." Jo scanned the house and the yard. "We can't check the perimeter with that fence in the way, and both their places of business are closed for the day."

"Neighbors?" Arnett asked.

Jo nodded her agreement, and took off toward the house directly across the street. As she did, a tall, golden-haired, middle-aged woman who identified herself as Missy Arguello stepped out onto her porch to talk with them.

Jo went through the introductions. "We'd like to talk to you about your neighbors, Sara Navarro and Hunter Malloy. When was the last time you saw them?"

Missy's blue eyes widened. "I'm not sure, exactly, but at least a week for both her and Hunter. Why, are they okay?"

"You can't be any more specific about that timing?" Arnett asked.

"Like I say, I know it was at least a week, because we put out our garbage cans on Wednesdays, and they didn't put theirs out this week. I assumed that meant they went away somewhere. After that I've been checking, and the house has been dark."

"So nobody has come or gone, nothing suspicious?"

Missy pulled her jacket closer around her. "No, nothing like that. Why?"

Jo resisted the urge to explain. "How well did you know them?"

"Sara I know well. I watched her grow up. Quiet and a bit moody, but a sweet girl. Hunter I don't know as well. He moved in about six months ago, but he's always been pleasant."

Jo was surprised. "You watched Sara grow up?"

"Sure. The house belonged to her father before he passed away. And both their parents before they got divorced. Sara inherited everything when Miguel died."

"Marissa Navarro used to live here?"

A shadow crossed Missy's face. "She did."

"You don't look like you were sorry to see her go," Arnett said.

She raised her eyebrows. "I guess I wasn't, really."

"She wasn't a good neighbor?"

She paused, considering her answer. "I wouldn't say that. She never did anything obnoxious, or caused any problems. I guess it's just that, well, we didn't ever click."

"She was difficult?"

Missy wagged her head. "Not exactly. She could be very sweet, in fact. But I guess after I knew her a while, I got the sense that everything she did was calculated. And she was very sensitive. I remember at a neighborhood watch meeting once, Gladys, our neighbor over there, said her peach preserves were too sweet. I don't think Marissa ever talked to her unless she had to again after that."

Jo nodded. "You said Sara's father lived in the house before he died? When was that?"

Missy's expression darkened, and her head dropped. "About eighteen months ago. It hit Sara hard, losing her father that young."

Jo thought of her own reaction to her father's cancer. "You miss him, too?"

"I do. Miguel was a good man. The kind where if he saw my husband trying to fix something on the house or the car, he'd come over and help."

Jo made a mental note to find out more about Miguel Navarro. "And you don't know Hunter well?"

"Not yet. But so far, he seems like a good guy. He dotes on Sara, and the way he looks at her—like she's his whole world. It reminds me of when my husband and I were newlyweds." She smiled at the memory.

"So no problems then? No fights, nothing like that?"

Missy's eyes flicked to Gladys' house, and she leaned forward ever so slightly. "Everyone fights, I guess, but nothing like Marissa and Miguel. I wouldn't know, of course, but Gladys' bedroom faces theirs, and they used to have some rip-roarers before they divorced."

"Sounds like that was the right choice, then. But you said everyone fights? Does that mean Hunter and Sara did?"

Missy's gossipy posture straightened. "No, not really. Only once that I know of. And I'm not sure it was a fight, Sara might just have been mad about something. I was out here trimming the roses when she slammed out of the door and stormed down the porch steps. She didn't even wave to me, just jumped in her car and tore off down the street."

"And Hunter was home when that happened?"

She nodded. "His car was in the driveway and when a pizza guy arrived an hour later, he opened the door."

Jo reached into her blazer for a card. "We need to talk with Hunter as soon as possible. If you see him, can you call us?"

Missy took the card without breaking eye contact. "I can. But, please, Detective, what's going on?"

"I'm sorry, I can't tell you anything more at the moment. Only that we need his help with an ongoing situation."

"Is he dangerous?"

Jo was surprised. "What would make you think that, Mrs. Arguello?"

She flushed. "Absolutely nothing. But I know what *help with an ongoing situation* means."

Jo chose her words carefully. "We have no reason to believe he's dangerous. In fact, he might be in danger. So we'd appreciate any help you can give. If you remember anything, please let us know."

CHAPTER FORTY-SEVEN

The other neighbors didn't add anything to Missy's information. They called Lopez to update her with what they'd learned, then returned to the Cruze to confer in privacy.

Jo slipped the key in the ignition. "First Bruce doesn't show up after work. Now Hunter's been gone for a week? And we can't find anybody's phones?"

"So what, they all go camping, some mass-murderer stumbles on them and starts slashing, and only Marissa gets away?"

"Maybe Logan was the murderer, and Marissa returned from a hike to find him slashing up her family." Jo's fingers flitted to her neck. "But if that's the case, where are the other bodies?"

"Maybe one of the family killed the others?"

"Better, but we're still missing at least one corpse if so, and we have no idea how Logan fits in." She shook her head. "But we're getting ahead of ourselves. Bruce might be hanging out with buddies, and Hunter may be on some sort of business trip."

Arnett checked the time on the dash. "Nobody else we can talk to today."

Jo nodded. "No. The only other thing I can think of is to try to find some next of kin for Bruce or Hunter, and see if they know anything. But Lopez is already looking into Hunter, and I can search Bruce's family myself. Go home and spend an hour or two with Laura."

They went over the facts of the case again as they drove back to HQ, but didn't make any further progress. As Jo considered contacting kin, she remembered her own—she needed to check on her father.

She detoured over to her Chevy Volt, turned on the seat warmers, then reached for her phone.

"Josette." Her father's voice rang out over the speakerphone, vibrant and happy.

It took her a minute to recover—she hadn't expected him to pick up. "Dad. How are you?"

"I'm doing fine. Nick's here with his girls, we just got back from the aquarium. Jacqueline must have said fifty times how she wished you were here."

Jo's eyes filled with tears at the memory of the little cousin who'd greeted her with a nosegay the previous fall, during her visit out to Brenneville. She wiped them away. What the hell was wrong with her? Was even the mention of a child going to send her over the deep end on the drop of a dime?

"I wish I were there, too. Hopefully I can come out soon."

"I'd like that. Hey, I haven't put it on the tree yet, but I found Terese Langlois' parents. I'll try to update it this weekend."

Jo and her father had been working on their family tree for several months, slowly wading through records and chipping away at brick walls, trying to trace as much of the family as possible back to the grand deportation from Acadia in 1755.

"Sorry, Dad, I haven't had much time so far this month. But I have a list of records we need to search." She heard a little voice in the background calling out.

Her father's voice muffled; he must have put his hand over the phone. "Hold your horses there, *cherie*. Make the popcorn and we'll start the movie in a minute." His voice cleared again. "Sorry about that. Now, why'd you call? Your sister got you all riled up?"

She bit her tongue. "I just wanted to check in. But she told me you rescheduled an appointment?"

He paused for a beat, probably trying to gauge how much she knew. "I did. I'm going tomorrow, and that'll be just fine."

"Yes, it will. Anyway. I don't want to keep you from your movie, so I'll call back later in the week." She tried to add the words *I love you*, but the words stuck to her tongue. Despite the progress they'd recently made, he still wasn't that sort of father, which made it hard for her to be that sort of daughter.

He paused again. "Your voice is strange. There's something you're not telling me. You okay?"

Tears filled her eyes again, and she coughed to cover the rasp she knew she'd have in her voice. "I'm fine, Dad. I gotta go grab a glass of water. I'll talk to you soon."

She hung up the phone and stared down at it like it was a block of Chernobyl concrete. Mood swings or not, she couldn't function if she kept bursting into tears. She needed to find a way to pull herself together.

She strode inside to her desk, hoping a few hours of good old-fashioned detective work would distract her again. But her work ended up largely fruitless. She'd found Hunter Malloy's parents, and a sister, who all lived in Wyoming. As it turned out, he was born and raised there, and had come to Massachusetts to go to college at OakhurstU. They hadn't heard from him for about two weeks, but said that wasn't unusual. They hadn't expected to talk to him until Easter. No, he didn't have any family in Ottawa, but they were fairly sure he had a friend from college who lived there. They couldn't remember his name.

She had less luck with Bruce Stasuk's family. She searched each of the aliases she had for him, but couldn't come up with a living relative. Maybe they hadn't stumbled on his real name yet? Whatever the reason, not having their phones slowed everything to a crawl. Hopefully Lopez could work some of her magic once she had access to their phone records.

At the end of it all, she was just as emotional as she'd been earlier, but now she was frustrated, too.

She picked up the phone again. Her finger hovered over Eva's contact information for a long minute while she tried to figure out what exactly she could possibly say.

She needed to not deal with this right now. She needed something positive, something warm and happy, something that would allow her to stop the endless circular thinking and just *be*.

She scrolled through her contacts and sent a text to Matt.

CHAPTER FORTY-EIGHT

Marissa woke Wednesday morning to another e-mail from Aunt Lucy, sent the night before:

Marissa,
  I can't find Sara, and the people at her job say she hasn't shown up for days. I don't understand what's happening, please contact me as soon as possible. I think you should come stay here with me where you'll be safe. Or if you're worried about coming here, I'll come to you. I know you don't have a phone, just let me know where to meet you and I'll be there as soon as I can. We have to figure out where Sara is, and we have to keep you safe.
  Love, Aunt Lucy

Marissa poured a cup of coffee from the teeny pot as she considered the e-mail. If the previous e-mail was strange, this one was downright bizarre. In the course of an evening, her aunt had gone from deep-freeze to *love* to *come-stay-with-me*. Marissa's recovered memory of her aunt, combined with what she saw Sunday night, was enough to give her a basic sense of who Aunt Lucy was, and this just didn't fit.

As far as she could see, there were two possibilities. One, that the police had figured out Marissa's identity and were using Aunt Lucy to bring her in. Two, that Aunt Lucy was the attacker, or was working with her attacker. No matter which, she couldn't risk going to the house again, or even calling her. That was exactly what whoever was behind the e-mail wanted.

She tapped her fingernail on the side of the cup. This was the opportunity she'd been looking for, the way to turn the situation around. She knew the e-mail was bullshit, which gave her the advantage. She could name the time and place, and could set up everything carefully. If it turned out to be the police, she'd run. And if it turned out to be the killer, she could force them to tell her where Sara was. Maybe even call the police to come get them. Or, if all else failed, she'd kill them herself.

But she couldn't do any of that without getting a damned gun.

For the rest of the day, she checked her notifications obsessively, almost as stir crazy as she'd been in Sunset Gardens. She searched through additional Facebook groups and considered posting to another of them, but couldn't risk someone noticing and pegging her as a scammer.

So she distracted herself as best as possible, praying someone would take the bait.

CHAPTER FORTY-NINE

Jo woke early the next morning with an uneasy sense of something pulling at her mind. At first, she assumed it was a new side effect of waking in Matt's bed, and she pushed it aside. When he pulled her into him, the feeling fled, replaced with something far, far more pleasant.

But as she drove back to her house, the unease returned. Something about the conversations she and Arnett had the day before was niggling at her brain, and she couldn't remember what. She replayed the day from start to finish, and finally hit on it—in her hurry to find anyone related to Bruce or Hunter, Miguel Navarro had been pushed to the back of her mind. But until they got access to everyone's phone records, Miguel was the only other person involved in Marissa and Sara's life, and that meant she needed to know about him.

She ignored a wave of morning sickness as she showered quickly and threw on her clothes. She made a stop for coffee, then drove early to HQ, settled into her desk, and began her search. Almost immediately, she hit pay dirt.

When Arnett arrived, she called him to her desk before he could take off his coat. "Hey, I put your coffee on your desk. But come check this out."

"You're up bright and early—or have you just been here all night?"

She half-smiled. "Get this. When Missy told us Miguel Navarro *passed away*, I assumed it was from some sort of medical issue. But he was murdered."

"Say what now?" He grabbed his coffee, pulled his chair over next to hers, and stared at the screen in front of her.

"Eighteen months ago he left work at the end of the day, went into the parking garage next to his office building, and rode the elevator up to the third floor. When he got to his car, someone shot him in the head."

Arnett's eyes scanned the screen. "Did they catch the killer?"

"Nope, the case is still unsolved. Their theory is he interrupted a drug deal, since there had been an increase in drug-related drive-by shootings in that area for the few months before."

"No surveillance cameras in the garage?"

"There were, but the locations didn't cover that particular area. They did catch a car leaving shortly after that, but of course when they traced the car, it turned out to be stolen."

"So you're thinking it might be related to our case. How?" Arnett sipped his coffee.

"I don't know. Maybe I'm barking up the wrong tree, Lord knows I've seen families with far worse cases of bad luck than that, and the gap in timing is strange if it's related. But since we're tapping out on every lead we get, I figured it might not be a bad idea to dig deeper."

Arnett nodded. "So then the question is, was there someone in his life that wanted him dead, and if so, how does that relate to Sara and Marissa?"

"Exactly. The file mentions a woman he was dating at the time, Alana Lyon. I'm thinking we might want to fit her into our schedule today after we go check out all the workplaces."

CHAPTER FIFTY

The first interviews went quickly. Bruce Stasuk's boss at Sanderson Construction told them he hadn't seen Bruce since April fifth, but he'd never been a reliable employee, so they didn't lose any sleep when he didn't show back up. Hunter Malloy's supervisor said he'd asked for several days off, but had been expected back on Monday. They'd tried to reach him but when they failed, they'd assumed he got a better job offer somewhere—employees 'ghosting' their employers was a growing trend, they said.

Tyler Franks, Sara's branch manager, met them inside the beige-and-russet interior of Wynassett Mutual Bank, and brought them inside a glass-fronted office. He pointed to two beige chairs with a shaking finger, and while Jo explained their purpose, she could hear his chair squeak as his leg bounced under the table.

He glanced out to the bank floor before he answered. "Sara took last week off, but I expected her back on Monday. I've been worried about her, in fact."

Jo's eyebrows rose. Both other employers had expressed annoyance with their employee's absence, and had become defensive when asked why they didn't file missing persons reports. "Just earlier today we were told that it's not uncommon for employees to just stop coming to work. I guess that's not true for the bank industry?"

"I'm not sure I'd call it common, but it happens," he answered distractedly. "Is Sara okay?"

"We're not sure. She's missing, and we're looking for any information that might help us find her." Jo watched the blood drain from Tyler's face. "Are you okay, Mr. Franks?"

His eyes dropped and scanned the carpet. "Like I said, I'm worried. This isn't like Sara. She's one of our best workers."

"And yet you didn't file a missing persons report," Arnett said.

His face went paler still. "I didn't think it was my place."

Jo fought back her impatience—didn't he understand what was at stake here? She reminded herself not to let her emotions get the best of her, and softened her voice. "Mr. Franks, if there's anything else we need to know about Sara, now's the time to tell us. She may be in danger somewhere, and in need of help. Time is of the essence."

His eyes flipped up to hers, then resumed jumping along the carpet's herringbone pattern. Then he stood up abruptly, pulled the blinds over the glass walls, and sat back down.

His eyes jumped between the two of them. "Anything I tell you, it won't be made public, will it? It could cost me my job."

"We can't promise that. But we'll do everything in our power to keep it quiet if possible," Jo answered.

"The thing is… Well, we were having an affair," he said. "And of course that's not allowed. But I'm worried because I think her fiancé may have found out about us."

"Okay, back up. You were having an affair with her. For how long?"

"About four months now."

"How did it start?" Arnett asked.

"It's hard to say. We'd always been attracted to each other, and we flirted. I'd been on the verge of asking her out when she started dating her fiancé two years ago. I wasn't her boss then, but I got promoted shortly after. Then, a few months ago she made a few comments to me about problems in her relationship. Ever since they moved in together, all he did was play Xbox in his spare time.

And he didn't like her mother. She had to admit he wasn't fully wrong, but it put her in a difficult position. I took the comments as a signal. We were at the company holiday party and we'd both had a little too much to drink, and she was upset because Hunter had refused to come, and…"

"It just happened?" Jo asked.

"Yes, exactly." He searched her face, a plea for understanding in his eyes.

"If I had a dollar for every affair I've heard of that started at an office holiday party." She shook her head sympathetically. "What makes you think Hunter found out about the two of you?"

"Nothing specifically. It's just, a couple of weeks ago when we were leaving my house after, um, a stopover, I could have sworn a car followed us."

"Are you sure?"

"Not positive. But the timing was odd, and the car stayed on my tail as I drove us back to work. A few blocks before we arrived, the car turned another way, so I told myself I was being ridiculous. But it stayed with me."

"Anything else?"

"No. I know I'm probably overreacting, but when she didn't show up for work and didn't return any of my calls, I didn't know what to do."

A thought popped into Jo's head. "When did you last hear from her?"

"The day before she left for her camping trip."

"You didn't hear from her at all while she was gone?"

"No, but I didn't expect to. I assumed she wasn't getting signal out in the woods, and that Hunter was around once she got back. We tried to keep our communication to a minimum, anyway, because those things get you caught. We had little codes that sounded work-related, but of course I couldn't send anything like that when she was on vacation."

"And that didn't bother you, that she was with another man?" Arnett asked, unable to hide the judgment in his tone or on his face. "Not being able to have her for yourself? Having to play those sorts of games to spend time with her?"

He straightened in his chair. "She was deciding whether or not to leave him. I believe they'd have been broken up within the next few weeks. And yes, I know that sounds ridiculously naive. But she was feeling pressured."

"Pressured about what?"

"The main issue was her mother. He wanted Sara to make a clean break from her. Sara was resistant. Her relationship with her mother was complex, sure, and sometimes her mother could be overbearing and insensitive. But you only get one mother, and most mother-daughter relationships are tricky. He kept insisting it was a toxic relationship, and that she needed to be done with her mother for her own sake, and the sake of their relationship."

"Sounds controlling," Arnett said.

Tyler was quick to jump on this. "That's what I said. And the thing is, she was really only with Hunter because of timing. She'd just started dating him when her father died, and he was there for her when she was vulnerable."

"So she wasn't sure if she'd have stayed with him had she not been in such an emotional place?" Jo asked.

"Exactly." Tyler jabbed a finger onto the desk.

"Do you know if Sara and her mother went alone on the camping trip?" Jo asked.

His brow creased. "I assumed so, but I don't know for sure."

Jo caught Arnett's signal from the corner of her eye, and stood up. "Thank you, Mr. Franks. You did the right thing telling us this. We'll do our best to make sure nobody else hears about it." She handed him a card. "If anything else comes back to you, please let us know immediately."

He took the card, and met her eyes, his gaze imploring. "Will you let me know when you find anything out? I know I'm not officially anything to her—"

Jo nodded, and softened her voice again. "We'll let you know what we find as soon as we can." Affair or not, Jo had no doubt Tyler Franks had deep, genuine feelings for Sara. Judging by how nervous he'd been, possibly *too* deep.

CHAPTER FIFTY-ONE

As soon as they exited the bank, Arnett turned to Jo. "Sara's missing. Bruce is missing. Hunter is missing. This many people don't go missing for this long without someone being dead."

She nodded. "Agreed. Here's what I'm thinking. Did we stop too soon when we were searching for Sara out at the campgrounds? I assumed we found the dumping site, and that if there was another corpse nearby, Marzillo's team would find it, and I know they did a thorough job. But maybe there was a second dumping site farther out in the area?"

Arnett rubbed his chin. "Maybe our killer could only carry one body at a time, and lost track of where he dumped the first one."

"But wouldn't the dog have alerted us if there was another corpse somewhere nearby?" Jo asked.

"No idea. You saw how Garrison went into reward time with Bones, played with him and gave him treats for finding what he was looking for. Maybe the dog would have to be instructed to look again."

"True. And we only thought we were looking for one person at that point, but there was certainly enough blood in that cabin for more than one victim." Jo pulled out her phone and called Garrison Hutter. She explained the situation to him.

"No, he wouldn't automatically search again, I'd have to give the command. I didn't realize there was a possibility of a second body," Garrison said.

"I don't suppose there's any way you can meet us back up there, and try again?"

"We're supposed to go talk to some grammar school kids today, but I think they'll understand if I cancel."

An hour and a half later, they met Garrison at the cabin, Marzillo in tow.

Arnett peered at the dog. "How do we keep him from just going to the same site again?"

Garrison shook his head. "Not a problem. Since the corpse has been removed, the scent trail won't be there, at least nowhere near as strong as it was. If there's a second body around here somewhere, that'll drown it out no problem. So just say when you're ready."

Jo nodded, and Garrison gave the command, and they started off.

Sure enough, Bones took a different route from his first trip through the woods. He raced down the left branch of the path, then veered off into the left, western portion of the forest.

After a few minutes, Jo checked her watch. "It feels like we're going farther this time, or is that just because it's daylight?"

"Nope," Garrison answered. "The last one wasn't much more than a third of a mile in. We've gone nearly half a mile in."

As he spoke, the smell of decomposition, much fainter this time, reached her, and Bones stopped.

Two feet away, behind a large rock, a figure lay wrapped in a blanket. Long, dark hair fanned out over the dirt, away from a skull with only a patchwork of remaining skin.

CHAPTER FIFTY-TWO

Once burned, Jo and Arnett had Garrison check for any additional victims. They worked their way back to the cabin, but Bones didn't pick up another trail.

When they returned to the scene, Marzillo called them over. "The team's searching the area, and obviously our vic will have to be transported and everything will have to be confirmed by the ME. But with so much decomposition, I'm able to get a fairly good look at her injuries right here. What I see is similar to what we saw on Logan, although not as severe, so unless we find something very strange, cause of death here was also blunt force trauma to the head. I can also confirm that we're looking at the same weapon or type of weapon that was used on Logan. And the stage of decomposition and insect activity puts her right on time to be your missing daughter, killed at approximately the same time Logan was."

"So nothing on her that identifies her? The hair color matches Sara's, but other than that…" Jo asked.

"Nope. Unlike Logan, there's no ID, no phone, no nothing. The blanket also has a Target label, and her clothes are generic retail, from what I can see so far." Marzillo rubbed her nose with her forearm. "We won't know for sure until we get DNA back."

"Can we get a picture of the clothes with the head cropped out? Maybe her Aunt Lucy will recognize them," Jo said.

"I'll have Pepper send some over to you. In the meantime, there's a little more that I can tell you." She knelt down and pointed toward the woman's skull. "Her head injury has two locations, somewhat more differentiated than Logan's were. One is here, at the temple. The other is under here, at the back of the head. The hit to the side of the head is shallower, and the fracture isn't as long."

"Head wounds bleed like crazy, so that potentially matches Marissa's bloody shirt," Arnett said.

"Correct," Marzillo said. "The injury to the side of the head is horizontal front-to-back and long, while the injury to the back of the head is short and roughly diagonal, with the most damage at the top of the fracture. I can't be sure, but my guess is she was standing, possibly running, when our killer hit her the first time, and he caught her with a swing parallel to the floor. Then she dropped to the ground, and standing over her, he hit her again."

"Which could also match the blood high on the wall in the cabin, then lower on the wall."

"Just like I said with Logan, I can't be sure without pattern or directional information, but it's not inconsistent. There are other scenarios that could account for what we saw, this is just the theory my brain pops out when I put this information into it. The only thing I can say for certain is she was hit at least twice with a long hard object of some sort. And based on the fracture, I'd guess the object had a cornered edge to it, not smoothly round like the billy club we discussed before."

"Did she die immediately?" Jo asked.

Marzillo stood back up. "I can't determine that."

"I know you don't have a reference with you here, but does this match up with Marissa's head injury?"

Marzillo shook her head. "No, the shape of her contusion was completely different. Bigger and less centralized, with no laceration to the skin, and according to the X-ray, no skull fracture."

Jo stared at the woman's head. "So while someone attacked this woman directly, Marissa seems to have run from the same crime scene, and, based on her flash of memory, hit her head when she fell."

Marzillo shrugged. "I can't say for sure, but that's possible. And that's about all I can tell you for now."

"Thanks, Janet. We'll get out of your hair," Jo said.

She and Arnett trudged through the forest back in the direction of the cabin. "So what are we looking at here?" Arnett asked. "Logan's a secret serial killer? He kills Sara, and Marissa shows up in the middle of it? She kills Logan, and then panics about going to jail for it? So she cleans up, then drags both bodies out into the forest, then slips and falls on the way back and knocks the memories out of her head?"

Jo inhaled a deep breath. "That works better than anything I can put together, except it doesn't account for Hunter and Bruce's whereabouts."

"Dammit."

"It's possible one of them killed the other, along with Logan and Sara. We know Sara was having an affair, maybe Hunter came up here because he thought the mother-daughter camping trip was a cover for a rendezvous. And maybe when he got here, Logan, who they'd happened to meet earlier in the campgrounds, had come over for some innocuous reason or other, and Hunter thought he was the guy Sara was cheating with."

"And Marissa got caught in the crossfire. It's possible, but then where's Bruce?"

"Okay, here's another possibility. Tyler seemed a little too scared when we talked to him, and I couldn't figure out if he's really just head over heels for Sara, or if he was scared of us."

"Because he killed her?"

"Maybe. We only have his word for most of what he said. Maybe she told him their affair was a mistake, and he didn't take it well. Maybe he followed the family up in the woods and killed them all."

"Like a fatal attraction. Except where does Logan fit into it all, then?"

They both fell silent a moment, then Arnett spoke. "Maybe she was having an affair with Logan. Maybe this trip *was* a cover to meet with someone, and maybe she *had* broken things off with Tyler. Lucy said Sara had interests in coding, and maybe she met him through Hunter's friend."

Jo nodded. "Or maybe she wasn't meeting up with him to have sex. Maybe Tyler was right, and she was looking to break things off with Hunter. Maybe she was looking to start a whole new life. Maybe she wanted to be more than a bank teller, maybe she wanted to be a game designer."

"Interesting. But we're still left with a dramatic mass slaughter and two missing corpses."

"We keep coming back to that." She shook her head. "I have to go to my mother's house for Easter dinner tonight—don't ask—so maybe something will come to us as we sleep on it."

"Or maybe when we have Lucy ID the clothes tomorrow, she'll remember something relevant," Arnett said.

CHAPTER FIFTY-THREE

That evening, as Marissa chased down two bags of Cheetos with another protein bar, James pinged her again. She lay back on the bed to chat with him.

Hey, how's it going? You sleep better last night?

A little, but not much. Every sound I heard outside woke me up and scared me half to death.

That much was true, at least.

Yeah, I didn't figure you would. I'm so sorry. But, I have an idea.

She sat bolt upright on the bed, and leaned forward over the phone. *I'll take any bright ideas I can get, haha :)*

Okay, so, I totally get it if you don't want to do this. But I was talking to my sister about you when I got home from work, and she let me have it. Yelled at me and told me if I didn't offer to sell you one of my guns, she'd find you and give you one of hers.

Marissa jumped off the bed and did a little victory dance on the motel's disgusting carpet. When she picked up the phone again, he'd already sent another message.

*But I get it if you don't want to. I know I'm a stranger, and
I don't blame you if you're not super trusting right now. But
my sister said she'll come with me to meet you, and you can
bring whoever you want to so you feel safe. We can meet at,
like, an IHOP or something. Well-lit and in public.*

Oh, this was beyond perfect. Not only was he not worried that
she was some sort of psychopath, but he wanted to assure her that *he*
wasn't. Which, of course, he still might be, but if she took precautions,
she could minimize the risk. She'd find a way to meet up with them
where she could bolt if anything felt even the slightest bit off. But
nothing about him made her suspicious, he felt like a genuine person
with no motive to harm her. And what other choice did she have?

She sent her reply. *No, sorry. I was just thinking. Are you
sure you'd be okay with that? You have something you don't
mind letting go?*

*Sure, it's no problem, I can always get a replacement. I'll just
download a record of transfer form and then we just have to
report it and it's all good. I'd never forgive myself if something
happened to you and I could have helped it.*

*Then I'd be extremely grateful! The only thing is, I already
paid for my gun at the gun store, so I can only afford to give
you about $300. Do you have something that would be
worth less than that?*

*Sure, I have a semiautomatic .22 Beretta I can replace for
that. I can even give you a box of ammo with it for that.*

*Omg, you would be absolutely saving my life. I don't know
how to thank you!*

Just keep yourself safe, that's all I care about.

She made arrangements to meet him and his sister at an IHOP in Springfield the following day, then turned in early again, finally falling into a deep sleep.

CHAPTER FIFTY-FOUR

Jo arrived at her mother's house cradling the apple pie she'd forgotten to order and nearly forgot to pick up on the way. Thankfully, DeMarco's, her favorite bakery, wouldn't feel the full brunt of the Easter crunch until Friday, so she was able to sweet talk them into letting her have one.

"Josie, I was starting to worry about you." Her mother stepped back from the door and took the pie from her.

Jo leaned in for a hug. "You said dinner was at seven, right? It's just after six."

"I told you we were doing an egg hunt first." Her mother released Jo and gave her the evil eye.

Dammit, she had said that. "You're right, you did, I'm sorry." Jo shrugged out of one arm of her coat, set down the bag she was carrying, then shrugged out of the other.

"It's okay, we haven't started yet." As her mother hung up the coat, Jo noticed a bounce to her movements and a twinkle in her eye. Her mother lived for get-togethers like this, and the apex for her were the rare occasions where both her daughters were together with her at the same time. Guilt ran through Jo. It had been petty of her to be so pissy about changing the date, and she was glad she'd found time amid the press of the case.

"Aunty Josette! Aunty Josette!" Her two nieces bolted toward her as soon as she stepped into the gray-and white beach-styled living room, nearly bowling her over.

"Careful, now, you're getting too big to tackle me! Let me look at your dresses."

The girls took a step back and did little ballerina twirls. Emily, who was a few months away from turning seven, wore a pale pink dress with a fluffy tulle skirt that whirled out when she spun. Isabelle's dress was a dusty lavender A-line more suited to her mature, eight-year-old sensibilities. Both girls had on white patent leather Mary Janes with kitten heels, ringers for the ones Jo and Sophie'd worn with their Easter outfits as children.

"Look how elegant you two are! You're practically grown up. In fact…" Jo made a show of looking down at the bag in her hands. "I think I made a mistake with the Easter gifts I bought you. I think maybe I better take them back."

The girls shrieked and threw themselves at her again with such a loud chorus of no-no-nos and gimme-gimme-gimmes that even Sophie had to laugh. "Girls, is that how you act when someone has a present for you?"

They stopped straining to reach the bag that Jo had lofted above her head, dropped their arms to their sides, and took a step back. "Please may we have our presents, Aunty?"

Jo pretended to think about it, then pulled out two presents wrapped in rainbow pastel paper. The girls took the packages, careful not to grab, and dropped to the floor to rip them open. They both squealed as they pulled out matching unicorn hoodies, decorated with rainbow manes and silver horns.

"Mama, can we wear them to do the Easter egg hunt?" Emily asked, legs and arms swinging in separate directions in her excitement.

Sophie shook her head. "You know we're going to take pictures when you do, don't you want your pretty dresses to show?"

The girls' faces dropped. "Please, Mama? Please?"

Sophie flashed her mother an I-told-you-so-look before she started to speak. Jo cut her off. "Hey, I know. Why don't you wait and wear them after dinner? I've always wanted to play Monopoly with a unicorn." She crossed her eyes and stuck her tongue out the corner of her mouth.

They both giggled. "You're crazy, Aunty Josette," Isabelle said.

"You, my darling, are not the first person to tell me that. But I think Mémé is waiting for you to go find all the stuff the Easter Bunny hid for you. You better hurry, before a pack of raccoons comes and steals it all!" She pointed toward the backyard.

They ran, tiny heels clicking on the hardwood floor, as Jo's mother led them into the kitchen. Sophie got up to follow.

"Sorry, Soph," Jo said. "I just figured the hoodies were better than more chocolate."

"The hoodies aren't the problem, Jo, it's the timing. You just don't get it." Sophie walked through to the kitchen.

You don't get it. That was Sophie's favorite refrain, constantly telling Jo she didn't understand what it was like to have a normal life. What it was like to have a husband. But most of all, to be a mother.

Jo had forgotten about Greg, her stepfather, and startled as he got up from his lounger. "Don't let her get to you, kiddo. You're great with those girls, and she knows it. I promise you she fully intended to put those girls in coats before she saw your hoodies." He patted her upper back, and made a 'come on' gesture toward the kitchen with his head.

Jo's jaw dropped. It wasn't like Greg to take sides in any argument, in fact he made a concerted effort not to. He'd married her mother when Jo was a teenager, which thrust him as a male outsider into a family of three strong-willed women. His strategy had always been to do the best impersonation of the invisible man as possible—he spoke little, offered opinions on almost nothing, and only interfered when Jo's mother demanded it. As a result, Jo was never quite sure where he stood on any issue involving family dynamics, and had always assumed he didn't care.

She closed her mouth and followed him out to the backyard, where her mother and Sophie were readying cameras. David,

Sophie's husband, was handing out baskets and flashlights. The sun hadn't fully set, but the light was low enough to hamper a good hunt.

"Okay. On your marks… get set… go!"

The girls tore off into the yard with the adults trailing behind, making quick work of the first ten candy-stuffed plastic eggs. But once the easy, same-spot-each-year eggs were exhausted, they were forced to slow down and strategize. At first Emily decided the smartest thing to do was follow Isabelle, but she quickly realized she was always going to be one step behind that way. So she did a one-eighty, and ran over to the opposite side of the yard to search. Jo smiled wryly to herself, trying not to put too much stock in the parallels that jumped to mind between her and Sophie's relationship.

"Thirty more to find," Jo's mother said.

As Emily stretched to the tips of her toes to reach an egg stuck in the crook of a tree branch, a fusillade of questions slammed into Jo out of nowhere. The baby she was carrying—would it be the grandson her mother always wanted? Did it look like Eric? Or if it was a girl, would it look like Emily and Isabelle, whose chestnut hair and green eyes mirrored hers and Sophie's? Would she be a little spitfire like Emily, fearless and no-nonsense, or would she be serious and pensive like Isabelle? Or something else entirely her own?

She stared at Emily's Easter dress. A year from now she might be picking out an Easter outfit for her own daughter, a tiny, frilly concoction topped with one of those headbands with a bow or a flower, and little white shoes the baby would outgrow long before she learned to walk.

"Ten more to find, girls."

This signaled that the time had come to help the girls. Jo was nearest to Emily, so she swept her up and held her high, where she couldn't fail to see the egg Greg had perched on the porch of the birdhouse. She waited until David had hinted Isabelle over to an egg, then scooted Emily to one devilishly hidden in plain sight on top of her mother's blue garden gloves. Emily grabbed the egg, and Jo turned to find another of the last six, the adults now as enthralled with the hunt as the girls were.

Once the last egg was secured, everyone suddenly realized how cold it was in the dying light and hurried inside, laughing and chattering as the girls counted their bounty, eager to see who had found more. Jo and Sophie peeled off toward the food, and helped their mother put the dishes on the table. Greg carved the lamb as Jo ladled pea soup with dumplings into bowls, and Sophie set out au gratin potatoes and roasted Brussels sprouts.

Once the meal was finished and the traditional post-feast game of Monopoly had been played, Sophie called the girls to her. "Time to change into pajamas and pick your story."

Sophie eased the girls into the end of every holiday dinner with this ritual. Usually they fell asleep by the time the story was done, and David carried them out to the car. But even if they didn't, the story calmed them, counteracting any residual sugar or adrenaline in their systems. It was a brilliant strategy—no tears, no fuss, and everyone left happy. One of the hundred different tricks that, Sophie would be fast to point out, Jo had no experience with.

Emilie grabbed *Madeline* from Grandma's magical toy stash. "I want Aunty Jo to read it!"

Jo ignored the annoyed look on Sophie's face, well aware Sophie would have gladly welcomed the reprieve had the girls chosen anyone else. But as Jo's mother had pointed out, part of the evening was about Jo spending time with the girls, and if Sophie didn't like it, she could suck it.

Jo smiled. "Of course, honey. Did you know *Madeline* was my favorite book when I was your age?"

Emily nodded. "That's why I chose it."

Jo laughed and grabbed the book. "You tricked me!" She patted the spot on the couch next to her. "Isabelle, do you want to come listen?"

But Isabelle had another book in her hands, a Nancy Drew mystery. "That's a baby book. I'll read this one while you read that one."

"Good choice. I loved those when I was young, too," Jo said, and shifted to make room on either side for the girls.

But Emily climbed directly into her lap, and rested her head back against Jo's chest. She was asleep before Jo had finished the second page, but Jo kept reading. Something about the weight in her lap and the rise and fall of Emily's head against her bosom filled her with the most relaxed, cozy peace she'd felt in as long as she could remember.

Was this why people did it? This feeling of warmth and purpose, the sense of *home* residing within a person rather than a place?

As Jo reluctantly finished the last page and closed the book, Isabelle rubbed her eyes, and Sophie stood up.

"Isabelle, put on your coat while your dad carries Emily out to the car," she said.

Isabelle's face screwed up like she'd just bitten into a lemon. "But I didn't even get to read a whole chapter!"

Sophie put her hands on her hips. "Isabelle, you know the rules. Once the story's done, it's time to go."

"That's not fair! Emily got to hear a whole story! And I want to know what happens!"

Jo glanced over at David, who stared up at the ceiling like he'd rather be anywhere else.

"Isabelle, don't argue with me. You have to get up early tomorrow, and it's time to go."

Isabelle's voice rose. "No! You never let me do what I want to do!"

"Be quiet before you wake your sister, and don't back-talk me. Get your coat now, or you get no Easter chocolate tomorrow."

But it was too late. Emily was awake, and rubbing her eyes. She saw the look on her sister's face and heard the threat about chocolate, and burst into tears.

Sophie snatched her up out of Jo's arms. "David, can you deal with your daughter, please?"

Half an hour later, both girls were bundled into the car, dishes of leftovers had been handed out, and Jo found herself in an oddly pensive mood as she drove back to her house. Yes, the angelic sleeping child on her lap had been beautiful, but what was that, five minutes out of a whirlwind-hectic day? The majority of which was the temper tantrums and constant moral lessons to be instilled? During the good moments, the egg hunt and the hugs and story time, she'd almost convinced herself she could do it. But the rest? By the end of the night Sophie had looked like she was on the edge of madness.

But Jo's spirit rebelled at being told she wasn't capable of something, and it fought back. *Of course* a baby would change her life. But there were babysitters and childcare, and she could make it work, if she became a different sort of detective. Still an excellent one, but one who turned off her cases in the evenings and on weekends. Plenty of successful detectives did it, and plenty of single women balanced career and children just fine.

But did she want to be that sort of detective?

As the signal light in front of her changed, she growled in frustration at the thoughts ping-ponging around her head. Why was this plaguing her? It was simple, she wanted a child or she didn't. And she'd spent all of her life *not* wanting a child, so there was no way that could have suddenly changed out of nowhere. This wave of sentimentality was born of the fear her mother had invoked, and the natural stubbornness of wanting something because her body might soon take away her ability to have it. This was all just her mother's voice in her head, and her own raging against the inevitable aging process. She was being ridiculous.

But when she got home, she walked past the kitchen to the bedroom, again forgoing her evening snifter of calvados.

CHAPTER FIFTY-FIVE

Jo slept restlessly, and woke early to another round of nausea. She showered, threw on her clothes, and pulled up to HQ. Arnett was already waiting for her, so they grabbed the Cruze and headed out to talk with Aunt Lucy.

Arnett hugged the latte she'd brought him. "Ran into Lopez this morning. Aunt Lucy sent a second e-mail to Marissa, this one saying she wanted to meet up."

Jo's eyebrows shot up. "Gutsy move, but a really bad idea. Then again, maybe we can use this to our advantage, and intercept their meeting."

"If Marissa responds."

"Right. What exactly did the e-mail say?"

"Lopez sent it to us, hang on." Arnett pulled up the e-mail and read it to her.

Jo signaled a turn and waited for the light to change. "I admire her initiative, but I wish she'd talked to us first. That sounds fake as the day is long."

He reread the e-mail again, then closed out the window on his phone. "Heartening to know not everyone's a natural-born liar."

A call came through Jo's phone, showing a name and number she didn't recognize. She hit the number on the dash to answer through the car's speakerphone. "Detective Josette Fournier."

"Detective. I'm Officer Dailey, Worcester PD. We received a call this morning requesting we do a welfare check on a Lucy Huggusi. We entered the house when we got no response, and found her on the floor, deceased. We also found your card out on her coffee table, and since it's a clear homicide, we figured we might as well call you directly. Is this related to something you're working on?"

"Shit. Yes. In fact, we're almost to the house now."

Five minutes later they pulled up to Lucy's curb. They identified Officer Dailey, a tall, young woman, protecting the perimeter while her partner, an older man, filled out paperwork in the squad car. Jo introduced herself and Arnett. "What exactly happened?"

Dailey pushed a hank of hair off her dark skin and jutted her chin toward a gray-haired woman standing on the sidewalk, arms tightly crossed over her housecoat. "Her neighbor called us this morning, concerned. She hadn't seen any activity at the house for a couple of days, no lights on, nothing. She came over this morning, supposedly to give her a piece of mail that was delivered to her by accident, and nobody answered the door. When she lifted the mail slot to put the letter through, she said the smell almost knocked her over. We entered the residence and found Mrs. Huggusi dead on the floor, apparently strangled."

"Got it. We're going to suit up and take a look while we wait for our medicolegals to get here."

"We'll keep the perimeter secure," Dailey said.

Once outfitted, they climbed the stairs to the porch, but still smelled nothing. "Yeah, she didn't just lift the mail slot. She bent down and stuck her face into it. Whatever would we do without nosy neighbors," Arnett said, and reached for the doorknob. It twisted in his hand, and the door swung open; the stench of decaying flesh crashed over them like a wave.

They swept through the living room, and turned into the hall.

Lucy lay face down on the carpet, a length of white cord around her neck stuck in an angry red-purple slash across her throat, her face tinged with blue.

CHAPTER FIFTY-SIX

James couldn't meet the following day until after he got off of work. Marissa passed the day watching TV and wanting to be anywhere but inside the hotel room. But when the time came, James and his sister turned out to be good, well-meaning people, and by late evening, she was the owner of her very own cuddly black Beretta.

The upside of spending a day locked inside the hotel was she had plenty of time to come up with a plan for meeting whoever was behind the e-mails from Aunt Lucy. She needed to see them before they saw her, so she needed a place where she could watch from a safe distance, preferably under the cover of darkness. If the police showed up, she'd need to slip away—so she had to be familiar enough with the location to escape quickly. But her hope was that her attacker would be the one to show up, and trigger her memory of whatever the hell happened. But she couldn't count on that happening—she hadn't recognized her own house—so she had to be prepared to face a dangerous stranger.

What would she do then? Sneak up behind them and put a gun to their back? Probably fine if it turned out to be a woman, but just about any man would be able to overpower her and take the gun. So maybe walk up and show him or her the gun, and threaten to shoot if they didn't answer her questions? What if they came at her? She'd have to be prepared to shoot—but somehow she didn't foresee having a problem shooting the bastard that attacked her and her daughter. Refraining from emptying the entire clip into them would be the problem. But all that meant she needed someplace secluded, with no witnesses, and no fast response if there was gunfire of some sort. That severely restricted her options.

But despite her limited memory, she did remember one place that might work. When she attended Columbus Community College, she went out to Lake Victoria, on the western edge of campus, to study. Large for a suburban lake, the perimeter was about five miles, dotted with fishing coves and a couple of docks. She'd discovered a small clearing bounded by rocks a few hundred feet off the perimeter trail near the southern dock, and loved to study there while listening to the sounds of wildlife and the water lapping against the shore. You could approach via the trail from two directions, both of which were visible from the clearing, but the clearing wasn't visible from the trail if you sat down behind the rocks—more than once she'd scared someone when she suddenly appeared out of the trees after an afternoon of studying. And while people fished there during the day, it was more or less deserted later in the afternoon, especially at this time of year.

But, that had been at least twenty-five years ago. She needed to check it out, in the dark, to be sure it was still there. But even if the spot was overgrown, she'd be able to plan out another location in the area that would work.

So after meeting James at the IHOP, she made a detour before returning to the hotel. She loaded a clip into her new Beretta, drove out to the lake, grabbed her flashlight, and went for a stroll. The dock was where she remembered it, about a five-minute walk down the trail between the two closest parking lots. She examined the surrounding forested area, weaving in between the trees to where she thought she remembered the clearing. She didn't find it at first, but as she expanded her search, she noticed a familiar rock a few yards away. The clearing was behind that, smaller than she remembered, and more bumpy than flat now because of expanded tree roots.

She stepped into it, hunched down, and gazed back out over the trail. Three light poles kept the path bright enough that she could watch whoever approached, with dark areas just behind them in either direction. If she spotted the police, she could slip through the trees in the other direction until she passed the lit area, then continue down the dark trail to the parking lot beyond. If that turned out not to be the lot where she'd parked, she could double back down the main road until she reached her car.

Satisfied with her plan, she returned to the Suburban. She stopped to pick up a Big Mac meal on the way back to the hotel, then settled in to savor the hot food as she composed her response to Aunt Lucy.

> *Dear Aunty,*
>
> *I'm so glad you contacted me. I can't find Sara either, and when I left her house the other night, someone followed me. I managed to get away, but I'm terrified. What could have happened that someone would hurt Sara, then come after me? I feel like I'm caught in a nightmare and I can't get out. I'm worried that they may be watching your house, waiting for me to show up. I've been living out in the woods, so I'm thinking a good place to meet might be at Lake Victoria? That way it would be easy for us both to be sure nobody is following us. There's a dock on the south end that's well lit and has benches, so we can sit while we talk. I don't feel comfortable in the broad daylight with other people around, so maybe eight tomorrow night? Please e-mail me back and let me know.*
>
> *Love, Marissa*

She read and re-read the message, weighing the emotion to be sure it sounded genuine. It read to her as scared and paranoid, which she was, so that should work. The reasons for wanting to meet somewhere remote were legitimate, so they shouldn't raise any suspicions. If Aunt Lucy really had sent the e-mail, she might prefer somewhere well lit and populated, and if so, she could say so. But if the killer was behind it, they almost certainly would prefer a clandestine spot as well.

She made herself a warm mini-pot of coffee, climbed under the hotel blanket, and settled in to watch TV while she waited for a reply.

*

The man was just beginning to fear Marissa had been too smart to take the bait when the alert chimed on his burner phone.

He read the e-mail, and his initial reaction was excited relief— not only had she bought the e-mail hook, line, and sinker, she'd even suggested the perfect location. All he'd have to do was pull out the gun and tell her to walk calmly back to the car. Then he'd drive her out to the woods to kill her, and leave her body in the same general location as the others. Perfect.

Too perfect.

He read through the e-mail again. Why wouldn't she suggest someplace safer? Was she suspicious about the e-mail, or just legitimately paranoid after the car chase? He couldn't be sure, and that meant he had to be smart about this. He had to assume she was taking precautions, that she'd plan on getting there early and would watch for him.

Something else about the e-mail tugged at his memory.

He pulled up a map of the lake and zoomed in, then went into the satellite view. He found the dock she was referring to on the southern end, and studied the location.

Yes, just what he thought. He chuckled—she thought she was being clever.

He fired off a confirmation to her, then spent the rest of the evening cleaning his gun.

CHAPTER FIFTY-SEVEN

"I'm pissed I didn't see this coming," Arnett said to Jo as they drove out to meet with Alana Lyon while Marzillo's team processed the scene.

"It didn't occur to me either," Jo replied. "Why would it? She and Marissa weren't close. We had no reason to believe Marissa or anyone else involved in this would come after her. I *still* can't wrap my head around why, but at least I think we can say this rules out a random attack of some sort."

"Agreed. Maybe Lucy was lying to us and knew about the affair? If the affair is the root of the attack, maybe Tyler or Hunter or Logan knew she knew, and decided they had to shut her up."

"But why lie to us? She'd want us to find Sara as soon as possible."

"Unless she was lying about more than that. Maybe she wasn't as close to Sara as she wants us to believe. Tyler said someone was following them, maybe that was her. Sara just inherited a large sum of money, and Lucy *is* struggling. Nobody works an on-your-feet waitressing job at a cheap diner at her age unless they don't have a choice, and you saw the house. Her income is limited at best."

Jo tapped her fist on her leg. "Blackmail. Interesting."

Arnett slid into a parking lot outside Le Poulet Blue, the upscale café where Alana Lyon, the woman Miguel Navarro had been dating when he died, worked. The restaurant's contemporary black-metal-and-glass outside seating hadn't yet emerged from the cold of spring, but the inside, filled with white and tan faux-exposed brick and wrought-iron accents, was warm and welcoming.

They found her near the bar, folding silverware into napkins. She smoothed down her long black ponytail as she rose to greet them, then squirted sanitizer from a bottle after she shook their hands. "No offense, I just don't like touching people's utensils unless my hands are germ-free," she said.

Jo laughed. "I can't tell you how much I appreciate that. I'd make that a law if it were up to me."

Alana returned her laugh. "That's a relief. I hope you don't mind if I continue while we talk? I have to wrap up all of these and then polish all the wine glasses before we open for dinner."

"No, not at all. We just appreciate you taking the time to talk to us. We'll try to make it quick. I mentioned we'd like to talk to you about Miguel Navarro. How long had you been dating him when he was killed?"

Tears sprung into her wide brown eyes. "About a year. I was supposed to move in with him when my lease was up at the end of that year."

"How well did you know his ex-wife and his daughter?"

"I knew Sara well. She was the apple of his eye, and it was important to him that any woman he dated got along with her. She and I weren't getting pedicures together, but we enjoyed each other's company fine."

"Are you still in touch?"

"No. I talked to her once or twice after the funeral to be sure she was okay, but that's it. She's the type that keeps to herself mostly."

"And how well did you know Marissa?"

She shrugged. "Not well. I met her a few times, and tried to be cordial. Miguel had a lot to say about her, but that's always true with exes. No happy marriage ever ends in divorce."

Jo half-smiled at the witticism. "What was your impression of her?"

She met Jo's gaze. "Honestly? I got the impression she was watching me carefully, even when she wasn't paying direct attention to me. Not that I blame her. I'd be very wary about anyone stepping into my ex's life that way, what with a child involved. But the result felt cold."

"You said child. Just to make sure I have the timing right, Sara would have been twenty-two when you started dating her dad?"

"That's right. I just mean I can understand her wanting to be sure anyone dating Miguel was relating well to her daughter. I've known women who actively pushed their stepdaughter out of their husband's lives. And I don't know what she was like when I wasn't around, but I'd say she definitely hovered over Sara when I was."

"I see," Jo said.

A waiter who'd been changing tablecloths stepped over to them. "Can I grab you something to drink? Water, coffee?" He winked. "Chardonnay?"

Jo and Arnett smiled, and both asked for coffee.

Jo took a deep breath. "I realize the detectives involved asked you at the time, but was there anyone in Miguel's life who had reason to want him dead? Any bad blood or grudges, even if small?"

She shook her head. "Miguel didn't make enemies. He'd give you the shirt off his back. If anything, he was *too* giving. He's the guy that if he saw you broken down by the side of the road in the rain, he'd stop to help. That's how we met. At my previous job, I dropped a tray of food, and he jumped up to help me clean it up. My manager was a huge jerk, and he fired me right in front of the customers because it was the second tray I'd dropped that week. Miguel looked right into his eyes and said that it was his fault, that he'd bumped into me when I'd walked by, and that he'd pay for the food and the plates. He was nowhere near me, and my manager knew it, but he didn't have much choice but to say I wasn't fired after all. Then, before Miguel left, he told me about this place, how they were about to open and they were looking for waitstaff. He knew the owner's brother, and I guess he put in a good word for me, because they hired me without an interview." She paused and waved a spoon at each of them in turn, with a teary smile. "And no, it wasn't because he wanted to date me. I had to ask about him several times before I found out his full name, and then I asked *him* out. That's just who Miguel was. Always wanting to help people."

Jo nodded gently. "Sounds like he was quite a guy."

"He was." She sniffed.

The waiter appeared with their coffees, and a miniature pitcher of cream. Jo added some to her cup. "Did that extend to Marissa and her new boyfriend?"

Her eyebrows rose. "Miguel wasn't fond of him, and there was some tension, sure. But nothing out of the ordinary for an ex-husband."

"Do you know, did Miguel have any life insurance, anything like that?"

"Of course, there was a hundred-fifty-thousand-dollar policy, essentially one year of his salary. But Marissa wasn't the beneficiary, Sara was. Sara inherited the house, and used a big chunk of the money to buy a car. She offered to share it with me, because Miguel would want me to have something. But I refused. I've never been comfortable with that sort of thing, profiting from someone's death. It feels ghoulish to me."

Jo nodded. When her father was battling his cancer, Sophie had broached the topic of a will with him. He'd assured her he had all his ducks in a row, but she hadn't believed him. She'd tried to get Jo to join forces with her and demand to see the paperwork, but Jo had refused. She didn't want to think about any of it, and she didn't care where his house or money went. The whole discussion felt presumptuous and distasteful to her.

Alana continued. "And, like I said, Miguel would give you the shirt off his back. If she wanted anything from him, all she had to do was ask. He gave her the money for the down payment on her new house right before we met. She didn't like her old neighborhood, and couldn't afford to move. He didn't have to do that."

"So your feeling is the detectives were right, he was just in the wrong place at the wrong time?" Arnett asked.

A tear slid down Alana's cheek, and she wiped it away with her forearm, a move that reminded Jo of Marzillo. "I can't imagine it was anything else."

Jo took a long sip of her coffee, then set it back down carefully. "If I have my timing right, Sara was dating Hunter when Miguel died. Did you know him at all?"

She shook her head. "No. She'd mentioned him once or twice, but they'd just started dating. They weren't to the meeting-parents stage yet. I did meet him at the funeral, though, and I think briefly one other time after that."

"Did you form any impression of him?" Jo asked.

"Not really. I wasn't in a very good headspace. I do remember he was taking good care of Sara, and I was glad she had someone to lean on."

Jo noticed a man in a suit peek his head out from the kitchen entryway for the second time. After a surreptitious confirmation glance at Arnett, she took another deep breath. "Just one more question and we'll let you get back to work. When was the last time you saw Sara?"

"I think it was, what, a month after Miguel's funeral? She had some things for me that I'd left at his house. We had coffee and we cried a lot, and we said we'd be in touch, but we both knew that most likely wouldn't happen. At that point we'd become reminders of Miguel to one another." Something seemed to occur to her. "Why do you ask?"

"Unfortunately, both Sara and Marissa are missing."

"Missing? From where? For how long?"

Jo gave her a sanitized version without mentioning that Sara most likely had been found dead.

Her face paled and her brows creased. "And you think this may have something to do with Miguel's death?"

"We don't know. We're just following up every lead we can. So if you can think of anything at all that you think might help us, we'd really appreciate knowing about it." She pulled a card out of her blazer, and handed it to Alana.

She stared down at the card. "Have you talked to her aunt Lucy? She was always close to her aunt Lucy. Maybe she'll know something?"

"We have, thank you. But if you think of anyone else who might know something, please call me."

Alana nodded, still staring at the card.

CHAPTER FIFTY-EIGHT

Arnett took the driver's seat and pulled out into the road.

"I need more coffee after that, the sweet little cupful wasn't near enough caffeine to pull together all of these threads," Jo said.

"Pretty sure there was a Starbucks on the left just up ahead," Arnett replied, switching lanes.

"So what do you think, is Miguel's death just a coincidence?"

"Sure seems like it. I can't see why she wouldn't finger someone who had a beef with him. So my next instinct is always follow the money, but that's a dead end, too. The person who should have inherited did inherit, and that new Tesla in her driveway would have drained most of the insurance money. And I can't see her committing patricide for a house and car when Miguel sounds like he would have helped her buy them, anyway."

"Marissa was angry at Lucy when she inherited her mother's house. Maybe she was angry at Sara for inheriting Miguel's?"

"Except she had a reason to think she'd inherit from her mother, but she had to know Sara would have inherited as Miguel's next of kin. She got a solid divorce settlement and alimony, so she had no reason to think that house was hers. And from what Alana said, he gave her money for the down payment on her new house, too."

"Excellent point. Lopez is pulling their credit card and financial records, let me check on that." She pulled out her phone.

"Jo, what's up?"

"Just wondering if you know when we'll have credit card and bank records for Marissa and Bruce."

"Actually, I have them, for Sara, Hunter, and Lucy, too. But I didn't mention it because there's nothing to mention. They're all disgustingly responsible—other than their mortgages, they're all clear of debt. No student loans, they all own their cars outright, and none of them even runs a balance on their credit cards. Marissa and Bruce got a second mortgage about a year ago, they must have done some repairs or something, but apart from a late fee or two, they've kept up on both sets of payments. Not that anyone's rolling in it, either, because none of them have much money in the bank. Except Sara, sorta. She had that large influx a few months ago from her father's insurance settlement, but spent most of it on her car. She put the rest, except for about twenty grand, into her 401K. That's far more than the average American has in the bank, but I still wouldn't call it stacks on stacks."

"Got it. Thanks."

"My pleasure." Lopez hung up.

Arnett shook his head. "So much for that. I'm out of ideas for where to go next. So, recap?"

Jo nodded as Arnett pulled into the Starbucks drive-thru. Once they had their drinks and were safely back on the road to HQ, she started. "Marissa and Sara went away to bond over a camping trip because their relationship had hit a rough patch, likely complicated by Hunter. We've heard this described as a mother-daughter trip, but it might have included Bruce, Hunter, or both. Something happens that ends up with Sara and Logan, an apparent stranger, each dead and buried separately about half a mile away out in the woods, and Marissa wandering around the Berkshires covered in blood. Marissa then bolts from her care facility, and a few days later, her Aunt Lucy turns up dead."

"Correct."

"Random violence is out because no random murderer would have a reason to kill Aunt Lucy, and it was unlikely anyway because of the false name in the campground registry. And, no matter what scenario we manage to come up with, we can't find Bruce and Hunter. If they were there, too, we'd expect one or both of them to be buried out in those woods with Sara."

Arnett held up a finger. "Follow that through, because that has to be at the crux of this, no matter who the killer is. We're also missing a car in that case. Carrying dead weight through the forest in the dark isn't easy—maybe he got tired and drove the remaining body away somewhere."

"Very possible. Okay, so, either they're all up there and somebody killed the others, or one of them wasn't up there, but came there, probably with the express purpose of killing one of the others. And, we've been assuming all this time that Sara was the primary intended victim, but do we have any reason for thinking that?"

Arnett signaled a lane change. "Not that I can think of. So what motive would someone have for wanting to kill the others?"

"Marissa doesn't seem to be very well liked. We've heard from several people now that she was cold at best, selfish and calculating at worst. We know Hunter wanted Sara to distance herself from Marissa, and supposedly this trip was meant for them to reconnect. Maybe Hunter didn't want them to reconnect, and went up there to make sure that didn't happen."

"By killing her?"

"We've both seen people kill for less. But my guess is it's more likely he and Marissa ended up fighting, or he and Sara did, and it escalated."

"Or maybe Marissa just plain decided to get rid of his influence. Maybe she made the reservation under the fake name—I don't believe for a second that guy knew for sure a man made the reservation, I still have a contact high from talking to him. Maybe she planned to make it look like an accident, took Hunter out into the woods and shot him when his back was turned. Comes back and pretends she has no idea what happened to him, but Sara's not buying it, and Sara attacks. Comes at Marissa, and Bruce jumps in to defend her." Jo twirled her finger in a circle. "Convoluted, I know, but whatever happened here isn't straightforward, I think we can be sure about that."

Arnett took a gulp of his coffee. "And Tyler's also a possibility, if he went up there to get Hunter out of the picture. And Bruce. He's been in trouble with the law. Big jump from his penny-ante charges to murder, but it's worth checking into."

Jo nodded. "That's a pretty big leap to murder, but you're right. Past behavior is the best predictor of future behavior."

Arnett tapped the steering wheel with his palms. "But we can sit here all day coming up with a hundred crazy scenarios and get nowhere. We need evidence."

"What we need is the search warrant to get us inside Sara and Hunter's house."

Arnett glanced at his watch. "Any idea when—"

Jo's phone rang. "Fournier."

"I have some preliminary findings if you want to head over." Marzillo's voice sounded surprisingly energetic.

"On our way," Jo said.

*

Fifteen minutes later, Jo and Arnett hurried into the lab. Marzillo had a picture of Lucy waiting up on a large central monitor, and she launched right in. "Unless something strange comes back from the ME, cause of death is asphyxiation due to strangulation, which won't surprise you. I didn't find any other wounds or anything else suspicious. From the position of the injury, the killer must have been behind her. Best I can calculate, time of death is sometime Tuesday. The stomach contents may be able to help pin it down more than that."

"We interviewed her Tuesday evening, so it must have happened after that," Arnett said. "You said the killer was behind her? She was facing the living room, so someone must have been hiding in the back of the house?"

Marzillo pursed her lips. "I'd say that's most likely. She might have struggled and gotten turned around, but I didn't see a lot of evidence of that. Some bruises across her arms, probably where the attacker restrained her, but not the sort where someone is trying to grab her after she made a break away, or from a struggle. Also, we didn't find any evidence of a break-in, or a robbery."

"The door was unlocked when we got there, but we heard her unlock the door for us when we visited. I'm guessing she let her attacker in," Jo said.

"As far as the cord, I did a few quick searches, and it's about as common as you can get. They sell it at just about any home-improvement store in the country. So, basically, not a lot of help that I can give you. Lopez is going through her phone and her computer."

They turned, and Lopez waved from her workstation. "I, on the other hand, have some interesting news for you. Nothing out of the ordinary on Lucy's computer, or phone. She texted and talked about once a week with Sara before she went missing, and there were a few assorted texts. Two friends she texted to now and then, all benign shooting-the-shit type messages about *America's Got Talent* and some books they all read." She pulled over several printouts, and handed one each to Jo and Arnett. "I got back the data on all the missing phones. No surprises with Marissa's, Sara's, and Bruce's; they last pinged in Wortham on Friday April fifth, during the day. Then, starting that evening, they ping towers close to the campground. Then the pings stop at around eleven-thirty that night, again for all."

"So that must be about the time Sara was killed and Marissa ran off."

"That's what I'm thinking. And here's where it gets interesting. Hunter's phone doesn't ping at the campground that night. But then on Saturday it takes the same ride up to the campground the others did, then stops, just like the others did."

Jo and Arnett stared to where Lopez was pointing on the sheets, processing the information. "Like he went up there looking for Marissa and Sara, and then disappeared himself."

Lopez gave a wide-eyed nod. "Stuff like this is why people believe in the chupacabra."

"You're obsessed with the chupacabra," Pepper called out from a far corner of the lab.

"Tcha, of course," Lopez yelled back. "The chupacabra is bad-ass. But that doesn't mean I believe she's real."

"She?" Arnett asked.

Lopez pointed at him. "Make no mistake. Women are far more dangerous than men. We're just less obvious about it."

"Usually," he mumbled.

An *aah-oo-ga* sound blared from Lopez's computer, making both Jo and Arnett jump. Lopez turned to check one of the three monitors in front of her. Her smile widened. "Yes! Bingo, ladies and gentlemen!"

"What?" Jo asked.

"I had Lucy set up her e-mail to forward me anything that came from Marissa's address. Marissa just responded to Lucy's e-mail."

They both bent in to read the text. "No way we can tell where it's sent from, right?" Jo asked.

Lopez ran a hand over her head, following the line of the slicked back hair to the ponytail. "I can try, but no guarantees."

"It may not matter anyway—she just gave us a way to find her." Jo gestured to the screen as she finished reading.

"Do you think it's legit? That she's really trying to meet up with her aunt, or do you think it's bullshit?" Lopez asked.

Arnett laughed. "Doesn't matter. Either way she'll be there, and we got her."

"Can you pull up the lake she mentions?" Jo asked.

Lopez pulled up the satellite view, and navigated to the dock at the southern end. "Smart choice. Open location surrounded by lots of cover."

Jo and Arnett studied the location. "Two ways to come in and out, but we can cover those easily." Jo straightened back up. "Should we scout it beforehand, or just cover the two trail entrances and lots?"

Lopez grabbed her Rockstar. "I say no. If I were up to something, I'd get there really early, or I'd already have a camera somewhere to watch for anything strange. If you show yourself too much, you risk scaring her away."

Jo pointed at her. "Nice catch. So we need to make this look like we're just there to enjoy the lake. An undercover car, a romantic couple having an intense conversation, something of that nature that won't arouse suspicion. We can stake out each lot that way and grab her when she arrives. I'll also check for any cameras in the lots. It must be a part of the Mass state park system, which means—"

Lopez's computer *aah-oo-gaed* again. Everyone turned to stare.

"Well, now, that's certainly odd," Lopez deadpanned. "Aunt Lucy just responded to Marissa."

Jo and Arnett exchanged glances. "Quite a trick for someone strangled two days ago," Jo said.

Lopez nodded her head to the left as her fingers flew over her keyboard. "Not to mention I have both her phone and her computer sitting right there."

"Somebody hacked into her account," Arnett said.

"Yup. Changed the password and everything," Lopez said.

"How do you know?" Jo asked.

Lopez shot her a look. "Let's just say I had access to her account, and now I've been bounced out."

"For my sanity and for the sake of all our jobs, I'm going to assume Lucy gave you the old password." Her face froze as a thought occurred to her. "Oh, wait a minute. Can you pull up the e-mails Lucy sent to Marissa on Tuesday?"

Lopez clicked each of them open, and Jo examined them. "She sent this one right after you called her and asked her to. Then, this one went out, what, four hours later? But according to Marzillo, she must have been killed sometime that evening. So did *she* send this, or did our hacker friend send it? At the time I wondered about her going out on a limb like that without talking to us first. Can you tell when the account was hacked?"

"I'll need a few minutes to get back into the account, but I should be able to tell you once I do."

"Great. But considering how excited our hacker seems to be about the meeting, I think we can assume they sent it. Which gets us one step closer to a motive for killing Lucy."

"And means not only will Marissa be at the lake, so will our killer," Arnett said.

"Lopez, you said you have Lucy's phone and computer?" Jo asked.

"Right over there."

"Is it too late to check them for prints or DNA?"

She wagged her head back and forth. "Yes and no. I've been all over them, but before that they were collected with gloves and evidence bags. Any prints on the phone and keyboard are probably gone, but you might get lucky with DNA."

"Let's see what we can find." Jo turned to Arnett. "But in the meantime, I think we need to arrange for some backup."

"My thoughts exactly. Let's go catch this bastard."

CHAPTER FIFTY-NINE

Marissa woke early the next day and checked out of the hotel.

Her quarry wasn't stupid. They'd get to the lake early, so she'd need to get there still earlier. And since they knew what she looked like and what sort of car she drove, she'd have to change both.

She drove to a Denny's two towns away from Wortham. Far enough away that likely nobody would recognize her, but mostly because it was part of a standard-mall-plus-strip-mall combination that sprawled over more than a mile, with a surrounding parking lot that circled the stores. She parked on the opposite end of the complex and made her way through the mall, shopping as she went. First for an exercise outfit, running shoes, hip-pack and earbuds that would make her look like just another middle-aged woman power-walking around the lake, then for a bobbed blonde wig. Finally, for a large messenger bag, a legal pad, and several folders.

When she reached the Denny's, she asked the jaded hostess for a table rather than a booth, indicating one in the back of the section by the restrooms.

The hostess shrugged, led the way, and plopped a menu down. "Your server will be right with you."

Marissa pulled out a legal pad and a sheaf of papers, all paperwork from the motel, and began making notes on them, while she waited, pretending she was consumed with important work.

"What can I get for you today?" Olivia, an older woman whose uniform's seams were stressed to the brink stood waiting with pen poised over her pad.

"I'd like a chef's salad and a Diet Coke."

"What kind of dressing?"

"Honey mustard, please. Oh, also, can I pay now? I'm waiting for a call, and when it comes, I'll need to leave quickly."

She picked up the menu and pointed to the register. "You can pay whenever you want, up front."

Marissa smiled. "Perfect."

Marissa resumed scribbling. Now and then she'd pause, pen tapping her chin, to glance around the room, pretending to think while she evaluated her fellow customers.

A scattering of older couples, which she wanted to avoid if possible. Several business people who'd come on their lunch hour, who were too unpredictable. Several teens who were either cutting class, or had an open campus.

She'd finished her chef's salad before what she needed walked in. Two young mothers, both with a toddler and a preschooler, took a table across the room from her. She smiled—she might not remember much, but she remembered plenty of restaurant meals plagued by other people's out-of-control children. Sure enough, these women paid more attention to each other than the children—this was probably their only time to get out of the house and catch up. It was only a matter of time before one or more of the children lost it, but she didn't have forever to wait.

Marissa strolled over to the machines that lined the far wall of the room, stared into the toy claw machine long enough to draw the children's attention, then put money into it. She tried twice to get a toy, then returned to her table. Sure enough, when she walked back by the children, they were clamoring for a turn at the machine.

Their food came. The mothers plunked the children down in front of their plates, and turned to gossip in earnest with each other. As soon as their attention shifted, the oldest child slipped down from his chair and made a break for the machine. Not wanting to be left out, the child across from him followed. The toddlers, who were belted into plastic high chairs and couldn't follow, screamed bloody murder. Both mothers turned to see what was wrong, noticed the missing children, and bolted after them. The entire restaurant turned to watch, some in amusement, some disapproval, and some downright annoyance.

While everyone was distracted by the spectacle, Marissa shoved her pad and phone into her messenger bag, held it at her side, and strode smoothly toward the table. Without pausing, she swiped the purse one of the mothers had hooked over the back of her chair, and slipped it over her shoulder along with her messenger bag in a single fluid motion. She continued on past the women who were now wrangling the boys, without breaking stride until she made it outside.

She rounded the corner and pulled the woman's keys out of her purse, then hit the remote control. The lights of a blue Ford Focus flashed. She slipped into the driver's seat, threw the purse and messenger bag onto the seat next to her, and started the car. Keeping her pace casual, she turned out of the parking lot toward the highway.

After she finished at the lake, she'd drive the stolen car over to where she'd parked earlier, slip back into the Suburban, and be on her way.

CHAPTER SIXTY

Jo and Arnett decided a half-day stakeout would be the safest bet to catch Marissa and their mystery hacker. Lieutenant Martinez assigned Detective Eli Goran, a young, newly promoted addition to the unit, and Detective Charles Coyne, a middle-aged veteran, to cover the second parking lot at the lake. He also agreed to enlist Wortham PD to circle the lake's perimeter in an undercover car; they sent over two uniformed officers, Dan Turcotte and Sheila Meyers.

Jo and Arnett briefed everyone in a conference room at HQ. Jo distributed folders, then brought them up to speed. "Marissa may have changed her appearance, so we're not sure how accurate these pictures are. We also want to be on the lookout for a silver 2018 Suburban, although it's likely she dumped it and grabbed another car since we haven't had any alerts to those plates." Jo pointed to pictures of Hunter, Bruce, and Tyler. "We believe the person she's meeting is most likely one of these three men, driving the cars noted in the folder. But we may be wrong, and our killer may be someone we haven't accounted for."

"Got it." Goran learned forward, intense brown eyes scouring the pictures.

Arnett took over. "Goran, Coyne. If you see her head in, let us know immediately. We want to bring her in, but what we really want is to catch this killer, and since we don't know for sure who he or she is, we may not be able to positively identify them until they make contact with Marissa. So we'll follow her in, but need to make sure we're not seen. Stay a minute or so behind, no more. Then find cover where you can watch her and anybody else who approaches without being seen. Turcotte, Meyers, as soon as we move in, we'll let you know, and you'll patrol back and forth between the two lots until we need you. As soon as we see someone approach her, we grab 'em."

"What if he gets there before she does?" Coyne asked.

"Hopefully we'll recognize him in the lot, and nail him before we even get started. But if he gets by us, we don't want to be too far behind her, we want to hear if she calls out or takes off through the forest."

"Makes sense," Coyne said.

"Any other questions?" Arnett asked.

Everyone shook their heads.

Jo grabbed her blazer. "Then let's do this."

CHAPTER SIXTY-ONE

Marissa slipped into the lot farthest from the highway. She'd agonized over which lot was less likely to be chosen by the person she was meeting, but finally flipped a coin to save her sanity.

With the messenger bag safely stowed in the trunk, she put her newly purchased earbuds into her ears, strapped her hip-pack around her waist, grabbed a bottle of water, and climbed out of the car. She glanced around the parking lot under the cover of her mirrored sunglasses, but couldn't see anything suspicious. There were a fair few cars in the lot, and while she would've liked to examine them more closely, she couldn't risk drawing attention. She started down the path to the main trail without a look back.

She maintained a brisk pace on her way to the clearing. The day was cool and beautiful—the sun sparkled off the lake, and the green of the pine trees stood out against the blue of the sky—and she used the scenery as an excuse to gaze around and check that she wasn't being followed. A woman came at her down the trail, perspiring and panting from the pace of her run, but didn't even smile at her.

When she arrived at the dock, she scanned the area. Two fishermen stood in the middle of the pier, and a large bass boat tied up at the end bobbed on the water. When she passed by a small copse of trees along the shore that blocked her view of the fishermen, she slipped into the trees on the other side of the path and made her way to the clearing. She sat strategically, with her back to one of the rocks, and her eyeline just above the rock in front of her. Then she pulled out water, a protein bar, and a squashed half roll of toilet paper from her hip pack.

She settled in to wait.

CHAPTER SIXTY-TWO

As the time crept past seven, the sun floated toward the lake with a brilliant display of purple and periwinkle.

Jo, dressed in an Ariana Grande graphic tee and jeans, glanced at her ponytail in the rearview and winced.

"Not a fan of your new look?" Arnett sipped from the thermos of coffee.

"Not used to *your* new look." She made a face at his OakhurstU sweatshirt, then texted Goran and Coyne to be sure they hadn't had a sighting. Their negative came almost immediately.

She shifted in her seat. "But seriously. She should be here by now. The very latest I'd have expected her is seven-thirty, and it's almost that now. Something's wrong."

"Agreed. Either she's not coming, which I don't believe, or we must have missed her somehow."

Jo pointed across the lot. "That Focus, it's been here the whole time we have. I think she got here before us."

"Shit." He pulled up a picture he'd taken when they arrived. "You're right."

She tapped a nail on her leg. "So what's our next move?"

Arnett scanned the entrance to the trail. "Tricky to wait here and hope we spot whoever's coming to meet her, because if it's our killer, they're not going to just saunter up. The other option is to go in and monitor the spot. But then if something happens in the parking lot, we'll miss it."

Jo cast a last look around the parking lot, but couldn't come up with another option. "Yeah, that could work. We can pull Turcotte and Meyers in and have them monitor the lot. Let's get in there."

She texted the details of the strategy change, and asked the officers to check into the Focus. Then they threw on their holsters and their jackets and headed down the path holding hands, pretending to be a couple out for a romantic stroll.

"Think Goran and Coyne are doing the same?" Arnett asked.

Jo smiled. "I'd like to think so."

They lapsed into soft, intermittent comments about the scenery: how pretty the trees were, how the lights from the lampposts danced on the surface of the dark lake. Arnett made a joke about the lake containing Wortham's version of Nessie, and Jo made a show of chastising him for scaring her. When they rounded the final bend and the dock came into sight, they slipped off the trail and melded back into the trees. Jo sent a quick text confirming they were in place, and that there were no people around the dock. She waited for a confirmation that Goran and Coyne were ready as well, then shoved the phone back into the pocket of her jeans.

They settled in to wait.

CHAPTER SIXTY-THREE

As Marissa listened for the smallest sounds and watched for the smallest movements, she entered into something close to a trance. She followed the joggers and mothers with strollers as they passed, wondering who they were and what their lives were like with envy. *They* could remember their lives. *They* knew what happened to their children. *They* weren't plagued with vague memories of arguments and running through the woods and oddly shaped blades. And when the fishermen packed up their tackle and walked down the dock toward her, she envied the happy ease in their faces—they'd caught no fish, but that wasn't the point. They'd had a relaxing day with a friend, and now were ready for a good meal and a beer. She couldn't imagine ever being at ease again.

As the sun set, the people on the trail dried up, and a growing anxiety replaced her trance. She checked the time on her phone: seven-forty-five. She'd been sure whoever was coming to meet her would arrive at least half an hour early to head her off, and it unsettled her that so close to the time, nobody had appeared. Her pulse picked up, and she took several deep breaths trying to steady it.

She gasped as something landed with a thud and a rustle to her left. She whirled around, fighting the temptation to turn on her flashlight, praying that a raccoon had jumped from a tree limb.

An arm snaked around her neck, and pulled her up onto her feet. Then something hard poked into her ribs.

"Yep, that's a gun. Stay quiet, and you'll get out of this alive. We just need to go somewhere we can talk this out."

She couldn't see her attacker, but she didn't need to. His voice alone brought her memory of him flooding back.

Her husband. Bruce.

CHAPTER SIXTY-FOUR

She couldn't let him know she'd remembered him—that was the only advantage she had left, and maybe if she could divert his attention, she could get her hip pack unzipped, and reach her gun. "Who are you? What do you want with me?"

He nudged her in the direction of the trail. "I just told you. Walk. We're going to go have a little talk. Say one word and I'll kill you. I'm already at the end of my rope."

"How did you know I was there?" she asked, voice shaking.

He laughed dryly. "You really *don't* remember, do you? You told me about your little study grotto years ago. We've had picnics here for fuck's sake. *Now move.*" He dug the gun into her ribs.

She did what she was told, mind racing to find a way out. But all the reasons she'd chosen this spot were now working against her. As they reached the trail, he wrapped one arm around her shoulders while using the other to bury the gun into her side. A black gun, held by a black-gloved hand, indistinguishable from one another even in the pools of lamplight. To anyone who walked by, he'd look like a boyfriend reaching for her breast, and her horrified expression would read as embarrassment at his public behavior. And if she called for help or tried to break away, she had zero doubt he'd kill her—he'd already killed Sara.

The only possibility was her gun. She reached one hand slowly up her side.

"Uh-uh. Cut that shit right out. Hand back down, princess."

Shit. She forced herself to think. The walk back to the parking lot would take time. Could she use the terrain to her advantage somehow? Maybe pretend to trip on a tree root and grab his hand in the process? No, he could shoot her accidentally. If she could catch him off guard, she could kick him, in the shins or preferably the genitals, and dash into the woods. He'd be shooting among the trees then, and that would make it difficult to aim for her, especially in the dark—

But he didn't continue on the path. He turned up the dock. What was he going to do, throw her in the lake?

He stopped at the bass boat—the boat she'd assumed belonged to the fishermen. *Damn it*—how had she not noticed that they left on foot and the boat was still anchored to the pier?

He grabbed her arm with one hand and put the gun to her head with the other. "Get in. Don't *accidentally* fall in the water or I will shoot you. Don't try to pull me down or into the water, or I will shoot you. Basically, don't give me any reason to get your whiny, passive-aggressive, lazy, user ass out of my life for good. Get the point?"

She nodded. He kept a firm grip on her arm as she stepped into the boat, and as he stepped in after her.

He pointed at a tarp on the bottom. "Sit there on the floor behind that seat, facing the bow, with your legs stretched out along either side of it."

She did what he said, shifting and struggling to fit into the narrow space and slide her legs into place. She could barely move, so there was no way she could try to jump over, or even rock the boat, before he had plenty of time to react. But while he was steering the boat, maybe she could reach her gun—

"Very slowly remove that fanny pack and throw it into the water."

Dammit! Tears of frustration pricked at her eyes as she clicked the plastic connector, pulled it off, and tossed it over the side. Her last chance, now resting at the bottom of the lake.

He sat sideways on the chair in front of the steering wheel so he could keep the gun trained on her while he watched the water in front of them. He turned on the motor, and took off across the lake.

CHAPTER SIXTY-FIVE

"What the hell?" Jo said, as a boat engine roared to life.

She and Arnett jumped from where they'd been watching the path, and sprinted toward the dock. They reached it a minute later, in time to see a bass boat slip away, carrying a man holding a gun pointed at a woman's head.

"Fuck!" Arnett kicked the edge of the pier.

Goran and Coyne emerged, running, out of the darkness.

"That our guy?" Goran called.

"Pretty sure. There's only one other dock on this lake, and we need to get to it before he does. You stay here in case he decides to get cute and doubles back." Jo turned and sprinted down the path toward the parking lot, calculating as she ran. The main dock was directly on the other side of the lake. A boat could cut almost a straight path across the half-moon-shaped lake without interference, but their car would have to go the full half perimeter. Even using their sirens, if his boat was anything like her father's back home, it could do fifty mph, easy. No way were they gonna make it to the other dock before he did.

She stopped and pulled out her phone. She hit Lopez's number, then resumed running. "Come on, Chris, come on," she chanted as her feet pounded the path.

Lopez picked up.

"Lopez, just listen. Our target is on a boat, crossing the lake. I need you to call Turcotte and Meyers and tell them to haul ass over to the main dock. Then call Wortham PD and have them send whatever squad car is closest. Got it?"

"Got it." She hung up.

CHAPTER SIXTY-SIX

Marissa's memory kicked in, not with the instant clarity she'd had when she remembered her childhood and her early marriage to Miguel, but also not like the vague, dream-like flashes. Instead, a sequence of disconnected scenes flowed through her mind as she sped through the darkness.

Three men had come to the house looking for Bruce. They were big and slimy, with polyester suits and slicked-back hair, and when she opened the door, they pushed their way in. They searched the house for him, and when they couldn't find him, they broke the big-screen TV and shattered her breakfront and everything in it. He had a week, they told her. A week to pay back the money he owed them. If they didn't get it by then, they'd be back to break more than the TV, and they really didn't care if that meant him, her, or somebody else.

Fifteen minutes after they left, Bruce snuck in the back door. She pushed out a disgusted puff of air at the memory—he'd known she was in there with them, but had left her to deal with them by herself. He'd seen them come in, and had hidden in the neighbor's yard until they left. Her knight in fucking shining armor.

"Who the hell were those men?" she'd asked as soon as the door closed behind him.

"I don't know them. They were sent by the casino."

"Whoa. Wait a minute. When did you go to the casino? After you promised me? After what happened in Vegas?"

His face flushed. "Yeah, I guess I lied. Is that what we're gonna focus on right now?"

She'd been so angry she had to struggle for words—but why was she surprised he'd lied to her again? Their entire relationship was one long lie, and everyone had known it except for her. When they started dating, Sara had warned her he was no good, and so had her friend Debbie. She'd never even met him because she'd moved to Wisconsin just before they started dating, but even from across the country she'd sensed the truth about him. But Marissa hadn't listened. What did Sara know—she was young and naive. And what did Debbie know—she'd never even met him! Bruce wined her and dined her, and made her feel like the most beautiful, cherished woman in the world. She hadn't had that since Miguel, had been terrified trying to make it on her own, and she missed the security of a partner to take care of her. By the time they took the trip to Vegas, she was already way too far in. Pot committed, Bruce would have said.

Vegas.

Her sinuses were still dried out from the recycled plane air when she found out the truth. They'd dumped their bags at the hotel and gone for a stroll through the old-school casinos on Fremont Street, reveling in the flashing light show strung across the sky. As they left Lucky Stars, two men in black suits stepped straight out of a bad gangster movie and flanked them. The man next to Marissa put his hand on the small of her back like he was guiding a date into a fancy restaurant.

"Bruce Caligiri. I gotta hand it to you, I didn't think you had balls nearly big enough to ever show your face here again."

Bruce stopped in his tracks, but the man next to him propelled him around, back into the hotel. "Keep moving. Although now I got a whiff of your breath, I get it. You're not ballsy, you're shit-faced. But your pretty little lady here looks sober, so she'll translate for you later. Sam told you never to set foot in his casino again, and best I can tell—" he looked down "—you just set two feet in there."

The man with his hand on Marissa's back laughed. "So now you've lost *all* Vegas privileges. You're gonna leave town right now, or we'll take you and the missus out to the desert and feed you alive to the vultures. And if you're ever stupid enough to come back, the vultures will sound like a good option next to what we do to you."

They rode down an employee elevator, and walked through a series of underground corridors to a back entrance. A limousine was waiting for them. "Ah, look, here's your ride. Don't say we didn't send you off in style."

The limo took them straight to the airport. When they pulled up curbside, Marissa said to the driver, "But we need to go check out of our hotel first, get our luggage—"

The driver eyed her like she was crazy. Bruce waved him off as he pulled her away from the car. "Forget about the luggage, Marissa, I'll buy you some new clothes."

"But my jewelry—"

His hand clenched her bicep, and he pulled her into the airport. "We'll call the hotel and have them send it to us."

She'd glanced back through the sliding doors. The driver was watching them, while talking to someone on his cell.

Bruce came clean while they waited for the next flight back to Massachusetts, and swore up and down it was a problem he'd left firmly in the past. He hadn't gambled since, he said, and he'd never gamble again.

Less than a month later, one of her credit card statements showed up with a five-thousand-dollar cash advance on it. He lied about it, but she picked away at him until he admitted the truth. He'd gone up to the Indian casino and lost what he came with, then lost what the card would allow him to withdraw. But it was no big deal. They had the money in the bank to cover it. He'd learned his lesson. He'd never do it again.

Sara told her to leave him, but she justified it all to herself. He worked hard at his job, and it was just one slip. He'd pay her back. Not the end of the world. And she'd been so lonely after she and Miguel divorced, and so scared. So scared. The alimony only went so far, and she just couldn't face nine-to-five work. Plus, she wasn't a spring chicken anymore, she was dipping into her forties, and she wasn't going to win any beauty contests. How likely was it that she'd find somebody else, especially someone who was okay with her not working? Bruce treated her like a queen. Had a job. Well, he'd been let go from the job he had when he first met her, but that wasn't his fault. He found another one after a couple of months. Now he could take care of her. And nobody was perfect.

But it happened again. And then again. And the jobs never seemed to last for long. She remembered the pain of it all with a horrible rush—secret after secret, discovering that everything she thought she knew about him was complete bullshit. He was like that old joke: *How do you know Bruce is lying? His lips are moving.*

If she had any sort of a brain, she would have gotten out then. But she made more excuses, and the next thing she knew, the goons showed up.

The first memory returned, and she was standing again in her smashed-up living room, terrified that the men would come back and kill her. "How much money do you owe them?"

"You don't want to know," he answered.

She pointed to the crushed remains of the TV. "You're motherfucking right I want to know."

He stretched both sides of his neck, avoiding her gaze. "Fifty large."

She gaped at him. "Fifty *thousand* dollars?"

"Last time I checked that's what fifty large meant."

She dropped onto the couch, stunned. This wasn't a single trip to the casino. This wasn't even a few trips to the casino. "How—?"

He paced up and down the living room. "Does it matter? We just have to find a way to pay it back."

"We? I don't have to find a way to pay back anything. This isn't my mess, it's yours. We're not married."

He turned on her then and laughed, a cruel, snarling sound. "Like they care. They'll kill you just the same. Except since you're so useless, they'll probably just put you in a wheelchair to teach me a lesson, so *I'll* still be able to get them their money back."

Panic froze her in place.

He took in her expression, sighed, then came over to her to hold her hand. "I'm sorry. I shouldn't have been so blunt. Look, it's going to be okay. I have a plan."

As she remembered his plan, nausea ripped through her. She clutched her stomach and retched.

Bruce waved the gun and yelled at her. She struggled to hear what he was saying over the motor.

"I swear to God, if you puke in this boat, I will shoot you *just because*."

CHAPTER SIXTY-SEVEN

The sound of Arnett's footsteps behind Jo faded. She stopped again to turn back toward him.

"Go!" he yelled. "I'll hitch a ride with the backup."

"I just sent them over to the dock parking lot," she said as he caught up to her. "You can do this, we're almost there. And I'm buying you a treadmill for your birthday."

She raced ahead to the car. She dove in and drove it back to the mouth of the trail, cutting off a few hundred yards from the distance for him. She leaned across the car and flung open his door.

Still panting, Arnett slid in, then pulled out the siren and stuck it on the roof while Jo screeched out of the parking lot.

CHAPTER SIXTY-EIGHT

Marissa had no doubt now—there was no way Bruce was going to let her out of this alive, even if he was pretending there was a chance of that. If she let him get her away from the lake, nobody would ever hear from her again. She needed to come up with a way to escape, fast.

Even if she managed to jump overboard, she wasn't a strong enough swimmer to make it to shore alive. And once they got to the dock, he'd strong-arm her out of the boat the same way he'd strong-armed her into it. Her memory of the main dock was vague, and most likely it had changed, regardless, so she couldn't count on an opportunity there.

What would he do after that? He'd have to get her to his car. Was there anything in the parking lot that she could use to her advantage? There'd be a few cars at least, and probably the same slatted wooden fencing as the other lots. If she could break away from him, maybe she could duck behind a car long enough to scream for help? Maybe he'd give up on her and just go?

It was primitive, but it was all she could think of. He'd probably just shoot her, but at least she had a chance of getting away. Because if he got her in the car, she was done.

CHAPTER SIXTY-NINE

Jo leaned forward, gripping the steering wheel with both hands as she blew through lights and around corners. She glanced at the clock. Ten minutes gone.

Eleven.

Twelve.

She slammed her palms onto the dash. "Shit! Unless his boat's a complete dinosaur, he'll be at the dock in a couple of minutes at most, and we're still at least ten minutes away."

"Turcotte and Meyers should be a couple of minutes ahead—" Arnett's head turned as Jo flew past them. "Or maybe Wortham PD had a squad car close." He stabbed at his phone, then shook his head. "Lopez says their closest car is ten minutes out."

"Shit, shit, shit."

"He still has to get her out of the boat and into a car. We can make it."

Jo glared out the windshield, unable to take her eyes off the road, and shook her head. They were too far behind, and they both knew it.

CHAPTER SEVENTY

As soon as Marissa stopped plotting, the aborted memories flooded back, faster and faster, details making her head throb.

The first part of Bruce's plan was to call in a few favors. He knew some guys in mortgage lending who helped him set up a little shell game. A line of credit based on the equity in her home—seventy thousand dollars, which would allow them to pay off his gambling debts, with enough left over to keep up on the new mortgage payments until they put the second part of the plan into action. But they had to get married, he told her, because his name would need to be on the papers. Another lie, but she didn't find that out until well after their ceremony at city hall. And what did it matter? She was in the shit anyway, married or single. They might as well get the tax deduction.

He wouldn't tell her in advance how he planned to pay off the second mortgage. And she hadn't pushed too hard because she figured he was still working the details out, and she didn't have much choice, anyway. Even if it meant losing her house, that was far better than having those men come back and put a bullet between her eyes, or her spine, while she slept.

Or at least, that's what she told herself. But was that really why she hadn't pushed? Or had she suspected all along what he'd planned, but just wanted to keep her hands clean?

If only Sara—Sara! She remembered Sara now, could picture her as plain as day!—if only she'd been willing to give them the money to pay back the mortgage. Had it really been that much to ask of her? After she'd inherited her father's house and insurance policy?

But Marissa's already-rocky relationship with Sara had deterio-rated further after she married Bruce—Sara was wary of Bruce, and then became wary of Marissa by association. Then Hunter came into the picture, his disapproval of Marissa and Bruce clear in his every breath and movement. Marissa tried to counter his impact: she bought little presents for the both of them, baked Sara's favorite brownies, always took an interest in their beyond-boring lives. And she'd been making progress.

Until the day she made the overtures about her money problems.

They'd been at Sara's house—well, Miguel's and Marissa's house, really—sharing a pan of Toll House cookies and coffee on a Friday night. Hunter was off on some business trip, so Marissa suggested they eat junk food and give themselves facials while watching reality TV. They'd found some stupid makeover show and were making fun of the contestants, laughing until their sides hurt, which hadn't happened for years. Then the show ended, and a *flip-your-house* type show came on. Marissa decided the segue was too good an opportunity to miss, and under the guise of continuing the joking, made a few comments about how she and Bruce might have to flip theirs, because they were having money problems.

Sara stood up and left the room.

Marissa followed her into the kitchen. Sara shoved a bag of popcorn into the microwave, then stabbed the popcorn button. She said nothing, just stared at the microwave while the seconds ticked down.

Marissa put her hand on Sara's shoulder. "We were having such a good time, what did I do wrong?"

Sara practically growled her answer. "Hunter called it. He said you'd do exactly this. He even predicted you'd try tonight, when he was out of town."

Marissa's veins froze. "What do you mean?"

"Look, I hoped he was wrong, and I'd like to hold on to some sort of relationship with you, so I'm going to put down a really clear boundary, okay? I'm not giving you any money. Not a penny. Dad gave you more than a fifty-fifty settlement when you divorced. Then he supported you for years, and even gave you the down payment on your house. I warned you about Bruce, and I know Debbie did, too, because she told me. But you wouldn't listen. It's not my fault that Bruce has a gambling problem, and I'm not going to support you like Dad did, or waste what he worked his whole life for to pay off someone else's debts. When I became an adult, I became responsible for my own choices. You need to do the same."

Marissa's mouth dropped open, her shock only half-faked. "I didn't ask you for a dime, Sara. I think you owe me an apology."

"Maybe I do, and if so, I'm sorry. You can prove it to me by never asking me for money. Because don't you see? The very fact that I have to wonder about your motives? That means this relationship is toxic."

"That's Hunter speaking, not you."

"He's right. You refuse to respect my boundaries and you make me feel like shit about myself. You stopped after Dad died, right when you knew I was going to inherit, and suddenly became Wonder Mom. Now you're dropping hints and when I call you on it, you try to turn it around like I'm the one that did something wrong."

"You are! Did I ask you for a penny? No. You just assumed that's what was happening because Hunter said so. And then when I'm hurt by your accusation, you say I'm turning it on you? I've worked for months to improve our relationship, and now you're even turning that into some ulterior motive."

Sara watched her for a moment in silence. Then she turned back to the popcorn. "I think you should go now."

"Come on, Sara, this is ridiculous—"

"Please, Ma, just go. We've said all we need to say."

The memory of Sara's stony, betrayed face made Marissa retch again. Bruce had put her in a situation she couldn't win. She wanted a good relationship with her daughter, but she needed the money. *Desperately* needed it. What else was she supposed to do?

Besides, Sara had plenty. And, dammit, she shouldn't have to *beg* her daughter to do the right thing. Any *good* daughter who loved their mother should *want* to help her out of a horrible situation if they were able. Marissa had never wanted a daughter, but she hadn't aborted her—she had the baby anyway, and wasted her entire life raising her. God knew the pregnancy had ruined her body. She'd done all that, given her life to Sara, given Sara *life*—and Sara couldn't give her a few thousand dollars to keep her from being homeless? What kind of ungrateful bullshit was that?

The nausea intensified as the small doubt in her head got louder. *Is that what happened in the cabin? Did you kill her because she refused to give you the money?*

She pressed her palms into her eyes again, and they slipped in the tears streaming down her face. Dammit, why couldn't she remember that night? Everything *but* the few weeks before that damned trip had come back. She couldn't remember who had suggested it, or why, or what her plan for it had been. Had she decided Bruce was right, that Sara owed her the money? Had she tricked her own daughter into going away with her so she could kill her for it?

That would make her a monster. What sort of mother would do something like that? What sort of mother would kill her child?

Was that why she couldn't remember, because she'd done something so horrible her own mind couldn't deal with it?

"Heads up," Bruce yelled.

She wasn't sure she'd heard him right, but when she looked up, a gray slab loomed out of the inky blackness a few hundred yards in front of them, lightly kissed by the boat's lights. The dock.

"You hear me? Same rules as when we got in, or I kill you."

She heard him clear as a bell—because the motor died as he said it.

CHAPTER SEVENTY-ONE

"Motherfuck!" Bruce kicked the engine, then tried to start it. He tried a second time, and a third.

"You're out of gas," Marissa said.

"You think I don't know that, you stupid bitch?"

Rage flooded Marissa, temporarily blotting out her fear. "I'm the stupid bitch? I didn't kidnap someone without checking to be sure I had a full tank of gas!"

His fist hit her face so hard she saw bursts of light, and it took a moment for her vision to clear. When it did, she looked back over her shoulder to find him dipping an emergency oar into the water.

He rowed from the tip of the bow, alternating sides, trying to keep the boat's slowing momentum strong enough to carry them to the dock.

"Don't get any ideas. If you move, I'll smash this oar right into your head."

Right into your head.

The rest of her memory exploded into her consciousness like a supernova.

CHAPTER SEVENTY-TWO

As the boat glided toward the dock, she sat, still frozen, trying to process what she'd just remembered. He grabbed her arm, jolting her out of her fugue, and forced the gun back into her side. He hopped onto the deck, yanking and heaving her along as he went.

The high whine of sirens in the distance broke the still air.

"Fuck! Move!" He shoved her along the dock.

She tried to run, but tripped, and fell onto her knees. He fired the gun. She screamed as she felt the bullet whiz by her face, but the bullet plowed into the wooden plank next to her.

He pressed the gun to her head. "Simple choice. I shoot you in the head right now and give myself time to escape, or you run your ass off and come with me. If they catch us, we both spend the rest of our lives rotting in prison."

She struggled to get back to her feet, and then ran as fast as she could. Knees on fire, lungs bursting, trying to think.

As they turned into the parking lot, an unmarked car with a siren on its top pulled into the far end—nearly half a mile away. He might make it to the car, but he'd never get past them now. If she knew it, he must know it. He yanked her back out of the parking lot and to the left, toward a building with a *boat rental* sign.

As he pulled her around its corner, a car screeched to a halt, and two doors slammed.

CHAPTER SEVENTY-THREE

Jo bolted from the car as the man tugged Marissa around the boat rental building. She unholstered her weapon and gestured to Arnett to indicate she'd take the long end of the building. He nodded and pointed toward the short end. She took off running.

She scanned the darkened landscape as she closed the distance to the building. A few hundred feet beyond it, several trees thickened into a dense copse that lined the trail and curved out of sight. If Marissa's kidnapper reached the trees, they'd disappear immediately. He could hide for hours in the miles of forest, then backtrack out to the main highway when and where he pleased—she had to get there first.

She summoned a burst of speed, still monitoring the lit pavement between the building and the trees. They hadn't yet appeared as she neared the far corner of the building, so she slowed her pace to a jog. She raised her weapon and peered around the back corner. Scanned the line of locked-up boats in their pen. Nothing.

She turned and jogged toward the front corner of the building. She heard footsteps, and panting. She raised her weapon again and peered around the second corner—and spotted them immediately. Only a few hundred yards away, but their pace was slowing. They were tired, and Marissa was limping. Leading with her gun, she stepped around the building to face them.

At the sight of her, the man pulled Marissa in front of him, and pointed his gun directly at her temple. "Don't move!"

For the first time, Jo was able to get a good look at him. She stepped forward. "Bruce, it's over. Let her go."

"No way I'm going to take the rap for what she did! Drop the gun and let me go or I'll kill her!" He stepped to his left, edging toward the woods.

Jo kept her gun trained on him. "I don't want you to take the rap for anything you didn't do. But you have to talk to us. Let her go so we can straighten this out."

"I said drop the gun!"

Something moved in the corner of her eye. Arnett, sneaking silently up the path. If she kept Bruce angled toward her, he wouldn't see Arnett until it was too late.

She froze. "I can't do that, Bruce. Talk to me here if you want, but you know I can't drop my gun."

Bruce stepped again, turning sideways as he moved past Jo, keeping Marissa between them. "Drop it! I *will* shoot her!"

Arnett was almost there.

She shook her head. "If you shoot her, there's no way out. It's over. Explain what's happening, because this doesn't look good. Innocent people don't take hostages."

Bruce took another step toward the woods—as he did, he spotted Arnett. "Freeze, fucker!" he yelled.

Arnett froze, weapon up. "She's right, Stasuk. Let her go and let us help you."

Bruce kept shifting toward the woods, backwards now so Marissa faced them both. Jo and Arnett slid forward, matching his steps. His head flicked back to check his location, but never for long enough that they could get a jump on him. Then he turned and fled, dragging Marissa behind him into the trees.

Jo leapt forward into a sprint, only seconds behind him. The strip of woods was still narrow enough to allow in light from the lamppost, but in a few hundred feet he'd be gone in the darkness.

She couldn't stop, but she couldn't risk a shot with both of them in motion.

Then, Marissa tripped—or did he push her?—and fell.

Bruce turned the gun back toward Jo, and fired.

The force of the bullet threw her back. Her head smashed into something and she bounced back forward, landing face down on the ground.

The last thing she heard before she lost consciousness was a barrage of bullets whizzing past her.

CHAPTER SEVENTY-FOUR

Jo woke in a hospital bed.

Her mother, sitting in the chair closest to the bed, was the first to notice. "She's coming out of the anesthesia." She jumped up and grabbed Jo's hand. "Eva, can you get the doctor?"

Eva and Arnett both rose from their chairs. Eva hurried out of the room, and Arnett crossed over to the bed.

Jo tried to sit up, but her head and arm exploded with pain, and nausea crushed her back down.

"Don't move, honey. I'll adjust your bed." Her mother clicked on a remote hanging next to Jo's head, and the back of the bed rose slightly. "There. How are you feeling?"

Jo blinked and tried to take inventory, head still swimming from the anesthesia. "My head feels like someone's smashing it with a hammer and my arm's on fire." She met Arnett's eyes, and tensed. "Did you catch him?"

Arnett nodded. "Shot him twice in the leg. That slowed his pace."

She half-smiled. "And Marissa?"

"Also in custody."

She relaxed back against the bed. "What time is it?"

Her mother squeezed her hand. "Just after midnight. Luckily, they didn't have to operate, they just had to sew you up."

A doctor pushed through the door, chart in hand, with Eva following behind. He paused at the foot of the bed, face somber. "How are you feeling…" he glanced down at the chart "… Josette?"

"Jo. My head's throbbing and my arm hurts like hell." She closed her eyes for a moment to focus. "My stomach, too. Was I shot twice?"

The doctor's brow knit. "No, just once. The good news is, the bullet missed the bone, so while you lost quite a bit of blood and have a fair amount of damage to the bicep, it should heal quickly and well. A few inches difference and you'd have had shoulder problems for the rest of your life."

"Oh, thank God," Eva said. Jo's mother crossed herself.

The doctor cleared his throat, expression still dour. "As for the abdomen. We noticed bleeding when we had you in the operating room. At first we thought—well, it doesn't matter. The point is, I'm so sorry. The trauma to your system triggered a miscarriage. You'll likely have residual pain and bleeding for a few more hours, maybe days."

Stunned silence filled the room. Her mother and Eva gaped at her, then at each other, lost for words.

Arnett met Jo's eyes. Then he turned to her mother and Eva. "Ladies, I have a few police details I need to deal with. I'll let you know when we're done." He took them by the elbows and shuffled them out of the room. He left them in the hall, too shocked to object, and closed the door behind them.

He turned to the doctor, jaw tight. "When can she be released?"

"Now, if she has someone to drive her home."

"And Bruce Stasuk? What's his status?"

"He's still in surgery, but he's stable. One of the bullets shattered his femur. Don't worry, your lieutenant already made it clear he's to be kept under guard until you can take him into custody."

"Thank you. I'll drive Detective Fournier home. Can you prep the paperwork?"

"Of course." The doctor turned to leave, but seemed to remember something, and glanced awkwardly back over his shoulder. "I'm sorry again for your loss."

Jo turned to stare out the window, and counted his footsteps as he continued out the door.

Arnett made no move to touch her, and she was grateful for that. If he so much as held her hand, she'd fall apart.

"Tell me what you want me to do, Jo, and it's done."

His voice alarmed her, and she turned to read his face. Concern for her, primarily. But there was also a glowing, barely controlled anger.

"It's nothing, Bob, really. I just found out about it a week ago. Not even a week ago. I haven't had time to process it yet, so you don't have to worry about me. It's probably for the best, actually." Her voice broke as she spoke the final words, and she paused before continuing. "No need to put it in the report, either. I don't need the whole department tiptoeing around me. It's bad enough I have to figure out what to tell my mother and Eva now."

He held her eyes. "Whatever you need."

*

As Arnett pulled up to Jo's curb, Elisabeth and Eva parked behind them. They insisted on seeing her into the house and settling her into bed with a cup of chamomile tea.

"Here," her mother said, opening the pain pills she'd picked up from the hospital pharmacy while Jo was still sleeping. "The doctor said you could take one of these when you got home."

"What is it?"

"Percocet."

Jo pushed her hand away. "No, thanks. Can you just bring me the Advil from the medicine cabinet?"

"Advil? Josie, you were shot. And you—" She stopped short.

"I know what happened, Ma, I was there. I'll take the antibiotics in the morning, but Percocet makes me feel too out of it." Jo positioned the pillow beneath her and leaned against the backboard.

"You need to sleep. It doesn't matter if you feel out of it when you're asleep." Her mother shoved her hand toward Jo again.

Eva, who had slipped out of the room, appeared again with the Advil. She wrestled off the childproof cap and poured out five tablets. "If you're only gonna take Advil, take a lot. Don't worry, when I had my dysmenorrhea, the doctor gave me one-thousand-milligram Ibuprofen tablets and told me I could take up to one and a half if I needed to. Those are only two hundred each."

Jo tossed the pills into her mouth and chased them down with a swig of the chamomile tea. Then she looked up at the two women. "You guys really don't have to stay. I'm fine, I just need to sleep."

Her mother stepped forward and grabbed her hand. "Josie, you're not fine, you—"

Eva met her eyes. "Jo, maybe your mom's right, maybe—"

Suddenly it was all too much. Without warning their voices became drills in her head, and their hovering suffocated her, making her roomy bedroom feel like a claustrophobic closet. "Stop it!" she screamed, throwing her good hand over one ear and squeezing her eyes shut. "Both of you! Stop it!"

Both women took a step back and stared at her. An awkward silence filled the room.

She instantly felt guilty. This wasn't who she was, and it wasn't who she wanted to be. They were just doing the best they could during a situation they didn't understand. They were worried and frightened, and also probably more than a little hurt she hadn't trusted them with her secret. And she was sorry for every bit of that, but there wasn't anything she could do about it, at least not now. She needed to be alone.

She calmed her voice. "I just can't do this right now. I know you mean well and I love you for that, but I need you to just go. Please."

Eva and Elisabeth looked at each other, then back at her.

"Okay, Josie, whatever you need. Call me tomorrow, okay?" Eva said.

Jo nodded.

"I'll check on you in the morning," her mother said.

"That's fine, Ma. And I'm sorry I yelled. I just—" But she couldn't find the words.

"We get it, Jo. Get some rest," Eva said.

Jo could tell from their faces that they didn't get it.

But then, neither did she.

PART FOUR

Saturday, April 20th – Sunday, April 21st

CHAPTER SEVENTY-FIVE

When Jo walked through the doors of HQ the next morning, shoulder bandaged and in a sling, Arnett smiled and shook his head. "How did I know? First thing on a Saturday, after almost being killed the night before?"

She rolled her eyes. "Don't be a drama queen. It's a flesh wound. No way I'd let you off the hook for all the paperwork if the situation were reversed."

He watched her face closely, expression turned somber. "And you talk about how stubborn your father is."

"Be nice to me, I brought you this." She looked down at the coffee in her hand.

He leaned back in his chair. "Liar. You can only carry one and you're hoping I'll tell you to keep it."

She set the cup in front of him and eased into her chair, careful not to jostle her abdomen or her arm. "Not true. I got myself a latte, I just made sure to finish it on the way over."

"Since when is one enough for you?" He stood and set the cup in front of her. "No way I'm taking coffee out of the mouth of my injured partner, I have a reputation to uphold. And I know why you're really here. You don't want to miss the interrogations."

She tapped her temple. "Who's up first?"

He paused, then seemed to think better of whatever it was he was about to say. "Marissa's on her way over now. The doctor says Bruce should be coherent enough for us to visit him at the hospital in an hour or so."

Jo turned toward her computer. "Then we have a plan."

The two lapsed into a companionable silence while they finished up the paperwork generated by the previous night's incident. Once Marissa was delivered, they grabbed a refill on the coffee from the break room; Jo downed another six Advil tablets, then continued on to the interrogation room.

The woman waiting for them looked the same as the one they'd last seen at Sunset Gardens, but her facial expressions, the way she held herself, even the way her eyes took in the room engendered a completely different person. Jo's mind brought up a Saturday-morning movie she'd seen as a young girl, about pod-people aliens who took over people's bodies.

Jo and Arnett settled into chairs across from Marissa, and nodded at the cup of water on the table. "Before we start, can we get you anything else? Coffee, or something to eat?"

"No, thank you." Marissa's eyes were glued to Jo's arm. "I'm so sorry you were hurt. I'm not even fully sure what happened last night."

"Let's start with that." Jo took a sip of her coffee before continuing. "What was it you thought was happening?"

"I thought my aunt was coming. I'd e-mailed her asking her to meet me. Then Bruce showed up and pulled a gun on me."

Jo kept her face blank. "Okay, let's take a step back. You've recovered your memory."

She nodded. "It came back in fits and spurts. That image at Sunset Gardens, then my childhood and early adulthood. But the parts around Sara's murder only came back to me when I saw Bruce."

That fit with what Matt had told them about memory loss—so she was most likely telling the truth. "Speaking of Sunset Gardens. Why did you leave the way you did?"

Marissa glared at them defiantly. "You told me my daughter was missing and injured, and then you wouldn't listen to me. I had to find a way to help her. I'm sorry about the money I took, I'll pay back every penny. And I already told the officer that booked me where to find the Suburban."

Jo's hands gripped into fists in her lap as she forced herself to put aside Marissa's attacking tone and focus on what she'd gone through. Jo would have done the same thing in the situation if a loved one was in danger.

"Why not just let us handle it?" Arnett asked.

She leaned forward. "You couldn't even figure out who I was, let alone protect me. A man turns up trying to get at me and all you could say was the system worked. But I guarantee he would have come back, and more prepared the second time around. And I was right. He found me within a day."

Jo forced her fists to relax, and took another sip of her coffee. "What did you do then?"

Marissa took them through everything, ending with the pictures of Sara and the memory they'd stirred.

"But you didn't remember who had blackmailed her?"

"No. And when I went to Sara's house, Bruce found me." She took them through the car chase, and her next steps. "It's terrifying to know somebody's after you, who knows more about you than you know about yourself."

"Tell us about Sara's murder," Arnett said.

Tears sprung instantly into Marissa's eyes. "Bruce killed her, up at the cabin." She explained about the gambling problems, and the mortgage. "Bruce figured Sara could lend us the money while he got back on his feet. But she never liked him, so she said no. Then he came up with the idea that if we all went together for a camping trip, maybe we could talk to her about it in another way, make her see how much it meant to me, how I'd lose my house if she didn't." She paused, eyes flicking between their faces.

"What then?" Arnett asked.

"We went, and that's what I thought was going to happen. I was looking forward to s'mores around the fire pit and long walks in the woods with my daughter. I'd seen less and less of her since she got engaged. Which is normal, I guess, but it still hurts, you know?" Her eyes pleaded with Jo for understanding.

Jo nodded. "It must be hard to give your whole life to a child, then have to let them go."

Marissa's head bobbed. "And everything started out fun, we were having a good time. But then Bruce brought up the money again, earlier than he was supposed to. He was supposed to give us time to connect. But he jumped the gun, and dropped it like a bomb: *Sara, we need that money for the house if you don't want your mother out on the street.* And of course she didn't respond well to that. She said she was going to call Hunter right then to come get her. That's when he pulled out the photos, of her with this guy who wasn't Hunter. He'd been following her, and he said he'd tell Hunter if she didn't give us the money."

"You didn't know he planned to blackmail her?" Jo asked.

Marissa's head whipped back and forth. "No way. No way in hell I'd be a part of something like that, blackmailing my own daughter. I was shocked and disgusted. But I *should* have known, because I knew what he was capable of, that and much worse. And that's when she said she'd tell Hunter herself before she gave us a dime. And she went to move past Bruce, and all of a sudden he had a—" She broke into sobs.

Jo waited a moment, then pushed the cup of water toward her and told her to drink. Marissa's hand shook so fiercely water spilled over the side as she raised her cup. Arnett pulled over a box of tissues, took a handful to wipe up the water, and placed the rest of the box in front of her.

Jo placed her hand over Marissa's. "Do you need a break?"

She pulled a tissue from the box and wiped her eyes, then her nose. "No, it's not going to get any easier. I just need to get it out." She took another sip of the water, then continued. "He had a hatchet. One I'd had for years, so it was old. He swung it at her head as she passed, but the blade flew off. So he swung again with just the handle, and smashed it across her face. She fell forward and he hit her again, on the back of the head, and I heard a horrible crunch—" She broke down again.

Jo squeezed her hand. "And then what happened?"

She shook her head. "Everything gets so confusing at that point. I must have run to her, because next thing I know I was on the floor, holding her, calling her name, trying to get her to answer me, but she was unconscious. And I remember yelling at him, 'What have you done, what have you done?' and he told me it was the only way to get the money from her, because now I'd inherit everything since I was the next of kin. And I should have just shut up, but I didn't. I jumped up and I told him there was no way I'd let him get away with murdering my daughter, no amount of money was worth that. And he gave me this chilling smile and shrugged his shoulders and said he had a feeling that's what I was going to say. Then he lunged for me."

"How did you get away?" Jo asked.

Tears poured down her cheeks. "I was facing him, so I saw him coming. I threw up my arm out of reflex, and it knocked the handle out of his hands. That must be where I got the bruise up here." She pulled up her sleeve and showed a rectangular, yellow-brown bruise on her upper arm. "Then I took off out the door. He came right after me and grabbed me from behind, by the shoulders, and I fell over by the fire pit. But he fell, too, and slipped over the steps that led up to the cabin. That gave me a chance to get up and run. I could hear him running behind me and I knew I wouldn't be able to run for long. And then this guy appeared on the trail in front of us. He took one look and started running toward us, then ran past me. I didn't look back, I just kept running, into the woods so I could lose him. But I couldn't see where I was going very well and I hit a slope, and I just remember this feeling like I was suddenly moving faster than I should be, and then I was falling. The next thing I remember is waking up in the space between those rocks."

Jo patted her hand. "You must have hit your head in the fall. And from the sound of it, the man on that trail saved your life. His name was Logan Tremblay, by the way."

CHAPTER SEVENTY-SIX

Jo and Arnett asked Marissa a few more clarifying questions, then had her taken to a holding cell to rest while they talked to Bruce.

Half an hour later, they arrived at the hospital. As they neared Bruce's room Jo became oddly hyper-aware, like the world was lit too brightly, and her palms went cold and clammy. Arnett noticed the shift in her, and threw up an arm to stop her. "Are you sure you want to do this? I know you're superwoman and all, but you're as pale as a ghost. I'm not sure it's a good idea so soon."

Jo took a long, deep breath and stared down the corridor to the officers seated outside Bruce's door. She had a high tolerance for pain, at least the throbbing throughout her body, but they both knew that wasn't what Arnett was talking about. "No, I'm not sure. But if I don't walk through that door and look him in the eye, I think something inside of me won't ever be right again."

"You need to show him it didn't mess with you?"

She examined the white tile for a long moment, then met his eyes again. "No. I need to show *myself* it didn't mess with me."

Arnett searched her face for another moment, then continued down the hall. The uniformed officers guarding Bruce Stasuk's room let them through.

Bruce's eyes grew wide when they entered, and he pushed himself up as though trying to crawl away.

"Relax, Stasuk. As much as I might *want* to be in this moment, I'm not that kind of cop. We're just here to talk." Arnett grabbed a chair for himself and another for Jo, and pushed them near the bed.

Bruce's eyes flicked between their faces, but he didn't relax. He turned to Jo. "I'm glad you're okay. I didn't mean to shoot you, you know? You have to understand. You were coming for me, and you were never going to believe me that I was innocent. The only chance I had was to run. I was scared for my life."

Rage and panic wove together and enfolded Jo. Her chest tightened, and the room suddenly seemed too bright again. She forced herself to speak in an even tone. "I told you at the lake I'd hear you out. I always keep my word. So tell us your side of the story."

"What did she tell you? Did she say I killed Sara?"

When Jo didn't reply, Arnett took over. "Did you?"

"Hell. No. That crazy bitch killed her own daughter, then tried to kill me."

Bullshit, Jo thought. But the point now was to allow him enough rope to hang himself, and the more he talked, the tighter the noose would pull.

Arnett kept his face passive. "Start at the beginning."

"The beginning is my fault, I have no problem admitting that. I have a gambling problem. I should have called the eight hundred number years ago, I know that, but I never did. I've been in trouble more than a few times because of it. But this time was really bad."

Jo clenched her jaw to keep quiet as he told them about the debt and the men who'd come to collect it—like it was the most ordinary thing in the world to start the day with a yawn and a stretch and end it owing mobsters fifty thousand dollars.

"Anyway, the point is, all along we knew we'd have to borrow at least some of the money from Sara to pay the mortgage back, because with the interest rates and all, we couldn't afford the payment for long."

Jo leaned forward almost imperceptibly at the subtle difference in his story. Was it an important one?

Arnett made a note of something. "With you."

"But Hunter saw the whole thing coming a mile away. When Sara turned her down, I told her that was that. I'd have to get a second job and she'd have to get a job, too. But she doesn't like working, so she came up with another idea. She'd caught Sara in some lie a couple of months before and when she pressed Sara about it, Sara half admitted she'd been out with another guy. Tried to play it down like it was an accidental thing, but Marissa was sure it was still going on—I swear, it's like that woman has some sort of radar, she can smell bullshit a mile away. So she followed Sara, and lo and behold, Sara's banging some guy that's not Hunter. She took a bunch of pictures, and had a couple of sets printed out so we could hand Sara some physical copies. Then she tricked Sara into going away on a camping trip like they used to do when Sara was a little girl, figuring when Sara gets all gushy and sentimental, she'd ask for the money again. But this time if she refused, she'd hand Sara the pictures and tell Sara that families take care of each other, and that if she wanted Marissa to take care of her secret, Sara needed to help take care of the mortgage."

"Blackmail," Arnett said.

He shrugged. "Technically. Except you're missing the point. She was never going to tell Hunter, that's far too messy and what would be the point? If Sara didn't give her the money, she'd just kill Sara and inherit."

"So you knew there was a possibility she was going to kill Sara when you went on the camping trip?" Arnett asked.

He threw up his hands, face all wide-eyed innocence. "Of course not. I never would have been involved in something like that. I thought she'd show her the pictures, and Sara would either pay up, or the whole thing would die right there. But she refused, and Marissa lost her mind. Started calling Sara an ungrateful bitch, yelling about how Marissa had given her everything over the years and the first time she needed help, Sara was turning her back. Said Sara had never loved her, how she always preferred Miguel, blah blah blah. Said how even the Bible condemned children who didn't honor their parents. Then she grabbed the hatchet and attacked her."

"Just, a hatchet right to the head?" Arnett asked.

Bruce shuddered. "No, that was the weird thing. The actual blade flew off, clear across the room. So she beat her to death with the handle."

"Then what happened? Did you try to stop her?" Arnett asked.

He dropped his head. "I did. I pulled her off Sara, hoping to save her. But then Marissa turned on me. And my mother taught me never to mess with crazy. So I turned and I ran out of the cabin. I figured I'd run a ways down the trail and tire her out, but she was right behind me. So I ran into the woods, hoping to lose her, and I saw this guy running down the trail, directly at her. He must have stopped her but I just kept running. By the time I realized I was safe, I couldn't figure out how to get back."

Jo and Arnett exchanged a glance. "So you were lost in the woods. Then what?"

"I was out there for four days. I found a creek, so I was able to drink, and luckily I know how to make fires and traps, I was an eagle scout when I was a kid. And I had cargo pants on, so my keys were in one of the pockets and I have a Swiss army knife on it, which isn't like having anything real, but it works in a pinch. So I was able to stay alive until I found my way back to civilization. Then I hitchhiked back to Wortham, but I couldn't go home, because who knew if she was still looking to kill me? So I went to Sara's, because I figured the first thing I needed to do was tell Hunter. My spare key to their place was on my keys, so I let myself in, and from what I could tell, he hadn't been there for days. She must have realized he would tell the police about how she was asking for money, and killed him. So I grabbed his keys and his car and went to a hotel and tried to figure out what to do."

"Why didn't you go to the police?" Arnett asked.

He looked back and forth between them. "I don't have the best record with the police. What was I going to do, walk in and admit I was in on a blackmail scheme gone wrong? And I knew Marissa would claim I was behind it all."

"Why would you think that? Maybe when she calmed down and realized what she'd done she would have turned herself in?"

Bruce twisted his face in a you've-gotta-be-kidding-me smirk. "Marissa's never taken any responsibility for anything she's done, ever."

"So you went to a hotel room to figure out what to do. Do you have any credit card receipts, anything like that?" Arnett asked.

"No, my wallet was in the cabin. I usually keep it in my back pocket, but I took it out because it's uncomfortable to sit on. I learned my lesson there. But I looked around for Sara's fire safe. Marissa always keeps some cash in the fire safe in case some emergency happens, I figured Sara might have learned to do the same. Luckily for me, she did."

"So how'd you end up at the lake with Marissa and a gun?"

"I knew I couldn't go empty-handed. I saw a report on the news that the police were trying to figure out who Marissa was. I figured either she had some sort of breakdown, which was gonna look even worse for me, or it was some sort of trick. So I went to Sunset Gardens to try to see which—she wasn't going to kill me there in front of everybody. But pretty much as soon as I walked in, I knew it was a mistake, so I took off. And then I didn't know what to do. The only way I knew to get in touch with her was her aunt Lucy, so I went to talk to her—"

"When was this?" Arnett interrupted.

Bruce looked up to the ceiling and calculated. "That would have been Tuesday night, I think. She gave me Marissa's e-mail address. I told her I wasn't sure what Marissa was telling the police and that I needed to reach her, but I figured if we met up, she'd try to kill me again. So she offered to send an e-mail to her asking to meet, and said she and I could go meet her together. But then when I went back to her house the next day to see if Marissa had answered, she wasn't home. Which was weird, and I figured Marissa must have told her some lies, and turned her on me. I was desperate, so I hacked into her e-mail account."

"You know how to do that?"

"It wasn't hard. She's only ever had one thing that mattered to her in her life. Her password was her late husband's name."

"Someone killed Lucy Tuesday night," Arnett said.

Bruce's eyes widened. "She was alive when I left. Marissa must have done it after I left."

"Why would she do that?" Jo asked.

Bruce shrugged. "Who knows? My guess is Lucy started asking questions she didn't like, probably wondering where Sara was, and Marissa decided she had to shut her up."

Arnett shot Jo a look, then continued, "Okay, so you agree to meet up with Marissa. How does that become you kidnapping her into a motorboat with a gun to her head?"

"I'm not stupid and neither is Marissa. I knew I might be walking into a trap. I waved a wad of cash at some loser at the marina and he sold me his boat. I knew I had to get her to some-place where I was calling the shots, then I could talk to her and convince her to go to the cops. So I snuck up on her and grabbed her gun. And then I saw you guys, and I knew it was a trap. So I had to get away, 'cause I knew you were going to lock me up for something I didn't do."

Arnett nodded his head. "So what happened to Hunter?"

Bruce turned both palms up. "I have no idea. I didn't get a chance to ask her."

Arnett sent Jo a questioning look. Instead of signaling him, she spoke. "There are a few things that I'm confused about. Why did you book the cabin under a false name?"

"That's a private joke between me and Marissa. A long time ago we were talking about how celebrities always register for rooms under a regular name, and joked about how funny it would be to register under a celebrity name. We've done it wherever we can ever since."

Bullshit, Jo thought again. But he had an answer for everything, and they came without hesitation. And from everything they'd learned, Marissa was certainly no angel. Was Jo allowing the fact that Bruce had shot her to cloud her judgment? Maybe Marissa had played a bigger role in everything than they thought? For now, she needed to press him. "Also, you were an eagle scout, but you didn't know to follow the creek to safety?"

"I couldn't. It went down into a ravine and I would have broken my neck going with it. I tried to follow parallel, but I lost sight of it and couldn't find it again, so I had to backtrack."

"I also find it hard to believe that Marissa was able to carry her daughter's body more than half a mile out into the woods."

"She's stronger than she looks, but that doesn't matter. We always bring one of those folding utility wagons when we go camping, so we don't have to make a thousand trips from the car carrying everything."

Shit. Was that the fabric they'd found burned in the fire pit?

"And how did you find out Marissa was at Sunset Gardens?" Arnett asked.

He shrugged, but shifted and looked down. "I called all the care facilities I could find until I found her."

Jo leaned forward, ready to pounce—they'd made sure the staff knew not to reveal her presence there. But then, she realized, one careless attendant was all it took—and they'd certainly had that. The tension drained from her muscles.

"I guess what really surprises me is that Marissa would kill her only daughter to pay off *your* debt," Jo said.

He shifted, and rearranged the pillow behind him. "I don't think there was any rational thought involved. She just lost it. She'd been feeling like Sara was slipping away from her and there was nothing she could do about it, and I think this was just the last straw. But even so, it was out of a horror movie, like she was possessed or something. I can't believe the woman I married would have done something like that."

A nurse pushed into the room with a lunch tray. Jo gestured toward the door to let Arnett know she was done, and they both stood to leave.

"Enjoy your lunch." Arnett's tone suggested he'd prefer that Bruce choked on it.

"Wait, what does this all mean? Am I still under arrest?"

Jo fought a wave of silver-hot fury—how could he have the nerve to sound put out?

Arnett answered before she could. "Yes, you're still under arrest. When you're well enough to be discharged you'll be booked and taken into custody. No matter what else you may or may not have done, you held a woman hostage and shot a police officer. You *will* be serving time." Arnett turned without waiting for a response and exited the room.

Jo followed without a word.

CHAPTER SEVENTY-SEVEN

They nodded to the officers as they passed, and remained silent until they were back in the car.

"How you holding up?" he asked.

She waved the question away. "Of course they're trying to point the finger at each other. I have no doubt he's guilty—there's no reason why Marissa would go back and kill Lucy. "

"Maybe they both planned and executed it, and this whole drama is just to create reasonable doubt?"

Jo rubbed the bridge of her nose. "That doesn't sit right with me. If that was the goal, they could have come up with a far simpler plan. You wouldn't draw all this attention by pretending you didn't remember and wrap it all up by shooting a cop. And, if that was so, why bother to kill Hunter or Lucy? But I admit, I get the sense that Marissa isn't being fully honest with us, either."

"Agreed on all counts. He's a slimeball and Sara was nothing to him—no matter how this went down, he's behind it. And he had no reason not to come directly to the police if his story was true, no matter how much of a record he has. That whole scene by the lake, that was about shutting Marissa up." He banged his palm on the steering wheel. "But none of it matters unless we can find some sort of evidence."

"Then we need to buckle down with Marzillo and Lopez and go over the evidence. And also, we need to find Hunter. I just don't believe he's still alive, and he may be the key to it all. He's up in those woods somewhere. And, where's all the camping gear, and everyone's phones? All the cars are accounted for now except Bruce's, which wasn't in the parking lot at the lake—so where did that go?" she asked.

"My guess is Bruce's car is wherever Hunter is. Either Marissa or Bruce drove him somewhere and killed him."

"From what I can tell, Hunter wasn't too fond of either of them, so I doubt he'd just jump in a car with one of them for no reason. I think the killer lured him out to the campsite on the premise something was wrong. Then killed him, then drove him away."

"We need to convince Martinez to send helicopters to do a fly-over looking for an abandoned vehicle in the area," Arnett said.

"What about drones? They can get closer, and they cost less."

"Let's go."

*

Fifteen minutes later, they'd caught Marzillo up on both interviews.

"So we need to know if there's anything in the evidence that can tell us who's lying, or if they're both lying," Jo said.

"What's the theory, that Marissa was lying about her memory loss the whole time? That she faked that whole scenario?"

Jo fingered her necklace. "No, if she's the killer, I think it's more likely that she cleaned up the scene, then disappeared into the woods, and planned to emerge the next morning and go to the police, but fell down a slope the way she said, and hit her head."

Marzillo pulled up the case files and clicked through them. "Got it. The trouble is, whoever's lying stuck closely to the truth. Both stories are largely the same, so it's hard to pull them apart. Both stories match those strange finger-like bruises—they both claim Bruce grabbed her from behind. And a hatchet handle could have caused the bruise on her arm, but I'm not convinced about the contusions on Logan's and Sara's heads. Hatchets have a smooth handle, generally."

"We wondered about that. We asked her to pick out the right model from Google images. She picked this one." Jo held up her phone, which displayed a handle that was rounded front and back, but flat on the sides.

"Yep, that'd do it," Marzillo said, and pointed first to the hatchet, then the diagram of the contusions. "The edges created here where the flat meets the round could easily create this part of the fracture. And it could cause the injuries to Sara's face."

"How about the falls? Do they make sense?"

"Sure, she had some scrapes and a few other small bruises. Those could easily have come from when she fell down outside the cabin, and down the slope. She was fully clothed, which explains why we don't see more, and why there was some tearing on her jeans and top."

"And what about the blood on her clothes?"

Marzillo shook her head. "There is some spattering, but that could have come from either being in proximity when someone else hit Sara, or if she hit Sara herself. And if she knew she was going to have to cover up the murder, she could easily have cradled Sara after the fact to make the blood look like she was trying to help Sara."

"Bruce's clothes," Arnett said. "We didn't find any bloody clothes. Is that possible?"

She wagged her head. "It's not *im*possible. But we found burned bits of cloth in the fire pit. He may have burned what he was wearing."

"Right, of course." Jo tapped her fist on her thigh. "So nothing jumps out at you that disconfirms either story?"

Marzillo clicked through the pictures of Marissa from the hospital, and Sara's autopsy report. "No, nothing that I can see. And, even if you do find the camping gear, I'd expect to find prints and DNA from both of them all over it."

Jo turned to Arnett. "Then we've gotta hope the drones find Hunter."

CHAPTER SEVENTY-EIGHT

The drones had no problem picking out the white Chevy from amid the green and brown of the forest, located about two miles in the opposite direction from where they'd found Sara's body. The trunk and the inside were packed to the brim with rolling suitcases and camping supplies.

While Arnett waited for Marzillo's team to arrive and set up a tent, Jo accompanied Garrison as Bones searched from that location. But, this time the dog wasn't able to detect a scent.

Garrison shook his head. "I'd say it's pretty certain there's not another body within a mile and a half of here. What we can do is try farther out, see if he picks something up. We do searches like that all the time."

For the next two hours, they did just that, to no avail.

Jo and Arnett returned to the lab tent. "Catch us up," Jo said.

Marzillo grinned a vicious smile. "Not much to tell—at first. Two roller suitcases and a duffel bag. Phones, wallets, and camping gear. But then we found this." She picked up an evidence bag with a hatchet head inside of it.

Arnett took the bag from her, and turned it all around to inspect it, then pointed to the edge. "Holy shit, is this what I think it is?"

"Do you think it's a bloody partial?" She smiled.

"I'm hoping like hell it is," Arnett responded.

"Then today's your lucky day. See how the top's smudged there? Someone wiped it down for prints but missed that part. That's what happens when you clean up in the dark, in the middle of a forest."

"How soon can we have that matched up to Bruce and Marissa?"

Marzillo's eyes gleamed. "As soon as I get back to the lab."

CHAPTER SEVENTY-NINE

By the time Jo got home that night, she was so tired she dropped into bed fully clothed and fell instantly asleep.

She woke the next morning to a deluge of notifications on her phone. She groaned—most of them were texts and missed calls from her mother and Eva, progressively more worried about her. She sent both brief texts letting them know she was okay, hurried to get out of the door and over to HQ.

She rushed into the lab to find everyone waiting for her. "Sorry, guys. I underestimated how long it would take me to shower with one hand and an arm that feels like it's continually on fire."

"This is why I admire you, Jo." Lopez lifted her Rockstar in a *cheers* motion. "You're almost as insane as I am. One arm hanging on by a thread and you still make it in, even on the weekend. That's my kind of bad-ass."

Jo smiled, pleased. Not by the compliment, but by the assurance that Arnett hadn't told them about the baby. If he had, they'd be avoiding eye contact or rushing to ask how she was. "How can you drink that stuff this early in the morning?" Jo asked.

"This one is citrus flavor. Just like the orange juice Mama used to serve." She lifted the can and gulped.

"Alrighty then." Jo shuddered. "Do you guys have anything for us?"

"Yep. First off, that print on the hatchet head belongs to Bruce. I sent the blood off so we can be sure it matches Sara's, but I think it's fairly safe to assume for the moment."

A rush of excitement hit Jo. "That takes care of that, then. His story didn't involve stopping to pick up the hatchet blade before he ran out of the cabin. Did you find the handle?"

"No, it wasn't in with the other camping gear. Odds are he burned it with his bloody clothes."

"Got it. Anything else?" Jo asked.

Marzillo waved her hand dismissively. "Lots of prints on lots of things in the campsite cache that match both Bruce and Marissa. And the handles of the suitcases were all wiped down, which tells me somebody was smart enough to know they didn't want their prints to be the most recent, since those would have belonged to whoever brought the cache to be dumped."

But Lopez's face didn't look happy. "I hate to ruin your easy ending, but… First, I checked the phones. The batteries were removed to prevent any GPS tracking, by the way. The thing is, the pictures we picked up in the Suburban of Sara and Tyler? The originals are on *Marissa's* phone. I double-checked the metadata, and they were definitely taken with her phone, not Bruce's. Of course, it's possible Bruce used her phone to do it, but I'm not sure how likely that is."

"How about texts and e-mails, anything like that?"

"Marissa texted a bit with both Sara and Bruce about the trip, but there's nothing anywhere that points to the direction of guilt."

Jo sprung up out of her seat and paced across the room. "So we're back where we started, with no conclusive answers."

"Not true. We're a one-eighty from where we were. Before, we couldn't prove either one of them did it. Now we have evidence that will put them both away," Arnett said.

She scanned his face as an idea hit her. "You know, you're right. Grab your coffee. I think I know how to get Bruce to talk, but I need to check on something with Marissa first."

CHAPTER EIGHTY

"Stasuk. Wake up, the detectives want to talk to you again." The guard banged on the solid metal portion of the door.

But Marissa wasn't asleep. She hadn't been able to sleep since her memory had returned, and she wasn't sure she'd ever be able to sleep again.

The male detective, Arnett, pushed a cup of coffee across to her when the two of them came into the interrogation room. She sipped cautiously, and when she confirmed it wasn't too hot, she drank half of it in one gulp.

"I'm going to cut to the chase," Detective Fournier said. "We found your suitcases and camping equipment dumped in the forest. Including your phone. We took a look at it. Do you want to guess what we found?"

Tears filled Marissa's eyes, then slid down her cheeks. "I knew I should have told you the whole truth. But I didn't think you'd ever believe I didn't kill Sara if you knew I'd blackmailed her."

"Try me," Jo said.

Marissa closed her eyes, and sunk back into the memory as she spoke.

*

The night Sara kicked Marissa out of her apartment, Marissa ran back to Bruce and told him it was all over.

"I had a feeling this would happen," he'd said. "So here's what you're gonna do. You know she's having an affair with that guy, what's his name? Follow her and get proof. Then you'll explain that families either take care of each other, or they don't."

Marissa had been appalled. "I'm not going to blackmail my own daughter," she said. "We tried, Bruce. It didn't work. We'll find another way. If I lose the house, oh well, but I'm not going to lose my daughter."

He laughed an ugly laugh. "Are you that stupid? You've already lost her. She doesn't want anything to do with you! She just kicked you out of her house! How much more do you think you can lose her?"

His words sliced through her like a rapier, and she started to cry. She stood up to leave the room, but he pulled her back down onto the couch, and softened his voice. "I don't mean to make you cry, but it's the truth. And the thing is, this isn't just about the mortgage anymore."

Marissa's world began to spin around her—the room became impossibly bright, and she gripped the couch to keep from falling forward. No, no, no—not again. He couldn't possibly be stupid enough—and how could she have been stupid enough to believe—

"I figured if I borrowed a couple thousand and took it down to the casino in Connecticut, I could win enough that we wouldn't have to push her for it. But I lost. So I borrowed more, and, well. You get the picture."

She could barely manage to get out words. "Who would be stupid enough to lend you money?"

He shrugged. "Everybody, 'cause they know I'll find a way to get it back to them. But look, here's the thing. I'm not saying we'll actually go through with the blackmail, I'd never want you to do that. In fact, I can be the one to talk to her. We'll take her somewhere for the weekend, and when the moment's right, I'll show her the pictures. You can say you didn't even know anything about it. And if she still won't help us, well, then I'll agree you're right, and there's nothing more we can do. But, baby, we don't really have a choice."

Marissa nodded and pretended to consider. But he was right—they had no choice. "You promise we won't follow through?"

"Of course not. That's your daughter, I'd never want to hurt you or her. But I gotta say, I think we'd be doing her a favor anyway. That Hunter guy, he gives new meaning to the word hipster douche."

That's two words, some part of her brain whispered. But she agreed to the plan.

He didn't honor it, of course.

As soon as Sara said she'd tell Hunter herself rather than fold to blackmail, Bruce killed her—that part of what she'd told them was completely true. And as she sat there cradling her only daughter's head against her chest, she screamed up at him. "You promised—you told me—"

He'd mocked her. "*You promised, you told me*—do you know how ridiculous you sound? Don't pretend for a single second that you didn't know exactly what was going to happen here. You knew she wasn't going to agree, but you wanted me to do the dirty work. *Again*."

"I didn't—I didn't—"

"*I didn't—I didn't—*" he mocked again, then smiled a hideous, nasty smile that twisted his whole face into someone she didn't recognize. "I'll tell you what you didn't know." He paused, and leaned in closer to her face. "Why do you think I insisted we get married right before we started this whole thing?"

"To sign the mortgage—"

"You really do give new meaning to stupid bitch, don't you?" He laughed, then changed his tone as though speaking to a child. "When Sara dies, *you* inherit as her next of kin. But, who inherits when *you* die, Marissa?"

Her mouth gaped open as the implication hit her.

"A *boyfriend* inherits nothing. A *husband* inherits everything."

"You're going to kill me."

He nodded. "I am. But I have to do it slowly. Because when I call the police after I return from gathering firewood to discover that some psychopath came and slaughtered you both, they need to be sure you died after Sara did, or your aunt Lucy will inherit everything." Bruce took a step back. "So, I'm going to back up slowly so I can watch you, and—"

But when he took his second step back, he slipped in the blood that had seeped across the floor, and crashed onto his back.

As soon as he hit the ground, she dropped Sara and fled. But he recovered quickly, and came after her with the hatchet handle, just as she'd told the police. He grabbed her and they fell, but she scrambled up and managed to flee into the night.

CHAPTER EIGHTY-ONE

Jo and Arnett left with instructions to have Marissa taken back to holding. As they made their way back to the hospital, Arnett scratched the day's growth of beard he hadn't found time to shave. "Do you believe her?"

Jo liberated a hank of hair that had lodged under the strap of her sling. "I do. When Lopez mentioned the phones earlier, I remembered something. Hunter's phone pinged until Sunday evening. But we had Marissa in custody then, at the hospital. She didn't touch him."

"Fair enough. But was she really in denial about Bruce's intent to kill?"

Jo fingered the necklace. "I'm not sure we'll ever know for certain."

Bruce sat, alert, watching *NCIS* on TV when they pushed through the door to his hospital room. Jo barely had time to register the irony before she hit the button on his remote with her good hand.

"Time to cut through the bullshit, Bruce. We have hard evidence that you were the one that killed Sara, not Marissa, and we're going to be taking it to the assistant district attorney as soon as we leave here."

His gaze ping-ponged between them. "What evidence?"

"Let's start and end with a bloody fingerprint. Your print, Sara's blood. We found all the goodies you dumped from the camping trip out in the woods."

She caught a micro expression of fear beneath his mask of confusion. "You can't know whether it's her blood so fast."

She leaned over him, bracing her good arm on the bed's guardrail. "I said it's time to cut the shit. We both know whose blood it is, but let me share a few more facts with you. You've been arrested in other states, but maybe you don't understand how things work in Massachusetts. Detectives work out of the District Attorney's office, which means the DAs listen closely to what we have to say." She paused to let the words sink in. "Your little plan to divert the blame to Marissa isn't going to work. We have the evidence to get a jury to convict you, no problem, and I really don't give a shit how long you rot in jail for. But, I don't like loose ends, and I don't like it when families don't get closure. We want to find Hunter Malloy. If you cooperate, we'll talk to the ADA about working out a plea for you. If you don't, well, you're in deeper shit than you realized. You kidnapped your wife, and that's a felony. Which is one of the few things that make you eligible for the death penalty in our great commonwealth. And when it comes time for sentencing, our judges have a thing about assholes who don't allow their victims' families to give their loved ones a proper burial. So, you've got sixty seconds to make up your mind to tell us where we can find Hunter."

Jo took immense satisfaction from watching the blood drain from his face at the words *death penalty*. She raised her eyebrows and cocked her head, staring directly into his eyes.

He opened his mouth twice before successfully speaking. "I'll draw you a map."

CHAPTER EIGHTY-TWO

Bruce admitted his original plan had been to make Sara and Marissa's deaths look like the work of a random serial killer, but once Marissa escaped, he had to come up with a new plan, fast. He decided the smartest thing to do was frame Hunter, say he found out about the affair and came out to the woods to confront Sara. Bruce planned to tell the police he, Marissa, and Sara had decided to leave early, and that while he was packing up the car, the women had gone for one last hike on the trail. When they didn't show back up, he went looking for them, and ran into Hunter on the trail—who then tried to kill *him*. He'd say he escaped but got lost in the woods, and it took him several days to find his way back to safety, and that Hunter must have driven the car with all their belongings out to some hiding place so the police wouldn't be able to figure out what happened.

So he cleaned up the cabin and lured Hunter to the campgrounds. He told Hunter he'd gone to sleep early the night before and left the girls outside by the fire pit, drinking wine and talking. When he woke up the next morning, they were gone, but he didn't worry at first—he figured they'd just gone for a walk on the trail. When several hours passed with no sign of them, he realized something was wrong, and he wasn't sure what to do, and the police wouldn't respond until they were missing for twenty-four hours. Could Hunter come help him look?

Hunter met him in the main parking lot, and Bruce took him to a trail on the opposite side of the campground, miles from where Sara's body was. He killed him, then ditched his own car in a different part of the forest, hiked back, and drove Hunter's car home. Once he found Marissa and killed her, he planned to take Hunter's car to a wrecking lot and have it crushed down into a tin can, make his way back to the forest, and pretend to emerge with his story for the police.

Bruce described the general location where he'd killed Hunter, and Bones took it from there. They found the corpse in an advanced state of decomposition, but his phone and wallet were sufficient temporary identification until his dental records could make it official. And despite the decomposition, they could still see the bullet wound where Bruce had shot him between the eyes.

Everybody at the station congratulated them on a job well done. But as they filled out the paperwork and wrapped everything up, something Marissa had said kept rattling through her head like an earworm.

I knew what he was capable of.

Was it just a turn of phrase, or did Marissa really have reason to believe Bruce was capable of blackmail and worse?

Once the bulk of the paperwork was done, she dug into the case file from the day Miguel Navarro had been shot, and pulled up the parking garage footage. She played it several times, but couldn't glean anything more from it. The camera was just too far away.

But no, dammit, she wasn't going to let it go at that.

She grabbed Arnett and the video and marched into the tech lab. Marzillo and her team were still processing Bruce's car, so she grabbed another tech, whose badge identified her as Priscilla Harvey, and asked her if she could zoom in at all on the car. She did her best, but they still couldn't see the driver.

What they were able to see was the passenger's hand on the dash, bracing against the momentum of the turn, wearing the same unique figure-eight turquoise ring Marissa wore.

CHAPTER EIGHTY-THREE

Marissa admitted everything as soon as they asked. She couldn't stand another sleepless night, she needed to be rid of the voice in her head forcing her to hear the truths she couldn't deal with.

Yes, Bruce had killed Miguel. Once the second mortgage paid off the gambling debts, he told her Miguel had to die. Sara would inherit, and Marissa would ask her for the money.

She refused, of course, but he tried to manipulate her emotions. Went on and on about how Miguel had abandoned her and made her go through Sara's teen years as a single mother. How she should have gotten the house in the divorce, but no, she'd had to settle for a smaller, older dump.

Marissa told him if he kept on, she'd leave him.

She'd wanted to for some time, anyway, and Debbie had been encouraging her to leave since she married him. But it wasn't that clear cut. Debbie had a reliable husband who loved her and took care of her. Easy for her to *say* Marissa should just get a job and support herself, but it wasn't that easy to *do*. Marissa didn't have a college degree, so the only thing she was qualified for was flipping burgers or greeting people at Walmart, and that was the sort of mind-numbing bullshit that would make her want to kill herself. So she self-justified, and when he stopped trying to convince her to kill Miguel, she stayed with him.

But the money disappeared far faster than she thought it would, and suddenly the day when the bank would take her house was no longer just a distant, theoretical speck on the horizon. Bruce brought the scheme back up. She refused again, but even to her own ear her refusal didn't have the full ring of conviction it once did.

He didn't tell her ahead of time. Just picked her up one night and said they were going out for dinner. He had someone else's car—she should have known then.

You did know, a voice whispered in Marissa's head. *You just didn't want to admit it.*

She asked why he had a different car, and he said he'd swapped with a friend from work who needed something more reliable in the snow to visit his mother in Maine. They'd get their car back on Sunday night. She'd trusted him.

No you didn't. You just needed to believe.

He drove her into a parking structure downtown, but left the car running after he pulled into a slot. He said they were early for their reservation, so they might as well listen to a little music while they passed the time. She'd felt anxious, like she knew something wasn't right.

Of course you knew.

Then Miguel stepped out of the elevator. Bruce fired up the car and floored it, tires squealing through the garage. He pulled out a gun and unloaded an entire clip. Several shots missed, but it only took one, and Miguel collapsed to the floor, dying.

That's the part that made her retch: The sight of him, sprawled on the gray-cement floor, brown eyes wide, a swath of red blood pouring from his head.

Bruce laughed as he flew out of the lot. "There's a drive-by once a week downtown. The police'll never spend time on it. But the important thing is, now you're an accessory. If they come for me, they come for you."

She should have gone to the police right then. But she didn't trust that they'd believe her.

No. You didn't go because it was easier.

She sobbed as she remembered—because the voice was right.

She looked up at Detective Fournier as she finished, searching for understanding. "I took the coward's way out. I told myself it was done and I couldn't undo it, so I might as well benefit from it. I'll sign whatever you want, it doesn't matter if I spend the rest of my life in jail. I let him do this, and I should have known he was going to kill my baby. I'll never be able to forgive myself."

Detective Fournier's face had softened, and she started to say something—but then she stopped and her face hardened again. The other detective, Arnett, told her they'd have a statement written up for her to sign.

Then they left her, alone.

CHAPTER EIGHTY-FOUR

As Jo and Arnett worked their way through the new batch of necessary paperwork, Jo kept staring at her monitor, typing nothing, her mind racing.

Arnett noticed. He rolled his chair over to her desk and leaned in to whisper. "Jo. I can finish this off myself. Go take care of yourself."

"I want you to be able to enjoy your Easter dinner."

He gave her a come-on-now glare. "Dinner's at six. If I'm a little late, it won't be the end of the world."

She started to object again, but he cut her off. "I get that people grieve in different ways. But the common thread is actually grieving, not burying yourself in a cloud of denial. You're gonna have to go home sometime." He pushed himself back over to his desk, making it difficult for her to respond without being overheard.

She fought down the fear that rose up into her throat. Now that the case was over, she had no excuse. He was right, she was delaying the inevitable. And she wasn't helping him by just staring at the monitor, regardless.

She slipped on her blazer, grabbed her phone and her keys, and left.

But her mind kept racing around the same circular track—she couldn't wrap her head around what Marissa had done.

She prided herself on trying to understand people, on never judging without walking in their shoes. That was one of the keys to her success as a detective, her ability to recognize that people almost always thought they were good and had done the right thing—people were the heroes of their own stories, never the villains, even if their deeds were judged as villainous by others.

And she wasn't a mother. She kept reminding herself of that. Vigorously. The week that she was aware of a child growing within her did not qualify her for that.

But the feelings she'd had about her own baby, however difficult they'd been to label and classify—when she thought about that child, a fiercely protective being rose up inside her, ready to destroy anything that threatened it. She couldn't reconcile those emotions with the idea of using her child as a conduit for a dirty inheritance, let alone blackmailing her, even without the intention of following through. And she'd never, ever put her child in a situation with someone she knew was a dangerous killer just to make her own life a little easier.

She shook her head. She'd seen worse things during her time on the force, mothers involving their daughters—far younger daughters—in schemes much more nefarious than this. These emotions must be a side effect of the hormones her doctor warned her would be out of balance for several weeks after the miscarriage.

Her phone rang, and Matt's number displayed on her dash.

Her first instinct was to ignore the call. But this wasn't just a man she was dating, this was also the doctor working on Marissa's case. She pulled to the side of the road and answered the call. "Matt. It's good to hear from you."

"Happy Easter."

"Happy Easter. Are you with family?"

He laughed his rich, sexy laugh. "I am. My sister's hosting, and I'm on my way now. You?"

"My family celebrated early. We just about an hour ago wrapped up Marissa's case." She gave him an abbreviated recap. "So you nailed it, really. Psychological trauma, and even when her memory began to return, her mind protected itself from the actual murder."

His voice turned somber. "I'm sad to hear it turned out that way. What do you think will happen to her?"

Jo stared out the windshield. "You know, I usually have a sense, but in this case I just don't. The DA may decide she's been through enough and let her take a plea. If she goes in front of a jury, it'll be one of those cases that will be won or lost during *voir dire*. For some people, the video will be damning. Others will see her as a victim."

"What do you see?"

"I was trying to figure that out when you called."

A silence lingered between them for a long moment.

"Well. On a different topic, I called to see if you'd like to have dinner with me this week."

Jo ran the possibility through her head. She wanted to want to, but just couldn't bring herself to face anyone at the moment. "I'd love to, but I'm going to have to pass this week."

He paused another second. "Is this an *it's-not-me-it's-you* conversation?"

She laughed a genuine laugh. "Not in the way you mean. I do want to see you again. But I have some things I need to sort out. I didn't mention it in my recap, but I was injured when we apprehended Bruce and Marissa."

His voice took on a doctor's edge. "Injured how?"

She hurried to reassure him. "Don't worry, I'm fine. I was shot in the arm, but it's superficial."

"Who did the surgery?"

She hesitated, thinking of the other details included in that night's write-up. "Doctor Tercero at Oakhurst General. And I suspect you consult there, so I need you to promise me this is a line we don't cross. No poking into my medical records without permission, and I promise not to run background checks on your ex-girlfriends."

His sexy laugh returned. "Deal." He paused again. "So what I'm hearing is, I should let you take the lead."

Jo's brows shot up—this was new. Men usually ignored the hints she put down, or rebelled against them. But he was respecting her needs without letting his ego interfere. "On the nose."

"I can do that. But I can't say it'll be easy."

They said their goodbyes, and she hung up.

She thought for a moment, then pulled up her text conversation with Eric. She'd intended to call him, but the circumstances had changed once again. She couldn't face it, but it also wasn't fair to keep him waiting any longer. She typed in her long-overdue reply to his last message.

> I'm sorry, Eric. I'm not good at these things, and I haven't handled this well. I thought I made it clear to you that I'm not at a point in my life where I want anything serious. I was good with how things were, but you weren't, and the closer you tried to pull me to you, the harder I pushed back. You broke things off, so when you texted me again, I wasn't sure what to say or do. Not my finest moment, and I apologize. But I think we just want different things, and I don't think it's a good idea for us to try again.

She waited for a reply. Five minutes, then ten. He didn't respond. Which was fair enough.

She turned the car back on, and pulled out onto the road. But at the next light, she made a U-turn.

*

Ten minutes later, she knocked on her mother's door.

"Josie, I—" Elisabeth stopped, then stepped back from the door. "Come in."

Jo crossed into the living room, then dropped into one of the sofas and clutched a gray-and-white pillow to her abdomen. "No Greg?"

"Since we had our Easter on Wednesday, he decided to play golf and then visit his sister in Beverly."

"You didn't go with him?"

"You know how I feel about golf."

Her mother felt about golf the same way Jo felt about wedding planning—the very thought of it made her eyes glaze over and all of the bones in her body turn to rubber. Jo nodded, then pretended not to notice her mother watching her, probably fighting the urge to tell her to stop slouching and sit up like a lady.

"Can I get you anything, honey? Something to drink? I just made a fresh pot of coffee."

"I'd love a glass of wine," Jo said.

Elisabeth nodded, and left the room. Jo's eyes followed the crown moldings around the ceiling until her mother returned carrying two wine glasses the size of mini globes, each half-filled with red wine. She handed one to Jo, then sat on the other end of the couch.

"You don't usually drink before dinner," Jo said, then swallowed a mouthful of the wine. It tasted like olives and black pepper, and conjured up memories of romantic pasta dinners in Italian restaurants. She took another long swallow, finished the glass, then set it down on the coffee table.

Her mother raised her eyebrows, sipped, then put her glass down as well. "We all have our secrets, dear."

Jo examined her mother's face. On any other day, she might have taken the comment to be a jab. But something about Elisabeth's tone and expression signaled something very different today. Her mother was telling her she understood. That it was okay, and there was nothing to explain.

Something about that unexpected release from the web of family obligation and guilt opened a floodgate within her. Tears that hadn't existed a moment before overflowed her unblinking eyes and streamed down her face.

She met her mother's gaze. "I don't understand. How is it possible to feel so utterly destroyed over something I didn't have yet? Something I wasn't even sure I wanted?"

Elisabeth leaned forward and pulled Jo to her. As her mother's arms closed around her, Jo broke, too strong for too long, frightened and without direction. Sobs wrenched out of her with the ferocity of a wounded animal.

Her mother rocked her gently back and forth. "I know, baby. I know. But you're going to get through this."

Jo gripped her mother tighter and allowed herself to be enveloped in the childhood faith that her mother could make everything okay again.

A LETTER FROM
M.M. CHOUINARD

Thank you so much for reading *Her Daughter's Cry*. I hope you enjoyed reading it as much as I enjoyed writing it, and if you did, then you'll love my other Jo Fournier thrillers, *The Dancing Girls, Taken to the Grave* and *The Other Mothers*. If you have the time to leave me a short, honest review on Amazon, Goodreads, or wherever you purchased the book, I'd very much appreciate it. I love hearing what you think, and your reviews help me reach new readers—which allows me to bring you more books! If you know of friends or family that would enjoy the book, I'd love your help there, too.

If you'd like to keep up-to-date with Jo Fournier or any of my other releases, please click the link below to sign up for my newsletter. Your e-mail will never be shared, and I'll only contact you when I have news about a new release.

www.bookouture.com/mm-chouinard

My grandmother was diagnosed with Alzheimer's disease when I was a teenager. Through the progression of her disease, I learned how fragile memory is, and how much we take it for granted. What I saw also left me with so many questions: How does memory work? Why does it malfunction? How much of who we are would remain if our memories were gone? How much of our personality, and our morality? These questions were part of my desire to become a research psychologist, and plague me to this day. *Her Daughter's Cry* allowed me to explore some of those issues.

Memory (and the brain in general!) is an incredibly complex and fascinating subject. If you're interested in an approachable read about some of the peculiar ways it can go wrong, I highly recommend the work of Oliver Sacks, particularly *The Man Who Mistook His Wife for a Hat*. You can also connect with me via my website, Facebook, Goodreads, and Twitter. I'd love to hear from you.

Thank you again, so very much, for your support of my books. It means the world to me!

M.

🖥 www.mmchouinard.com

📘 mmchouinardauthor

ⓖ author/show/5998529.M_M_Chouinard

🐦 @m_m_chouinard

ACKNOWLEDGMENTS

First and foremost, thank *you*. Writers are nothing without readers—and I appreciate every person who takes the time to read one of my books. I'm also deeply thankful to those who take the time and effort to review them and blog about them. Your help is invaluable!

I'm endlessly grateful to the team at Bookouture for helping me make this book what it is. Leodora Darlington nursed it from start to finish; Alexandra Holmes, Jane Eastgate, Nicky Gyopari, and Ramesh Kumar all helped edit and produce it; Kim Nash and Noelle Holten tirelessly promoted it; Jules Macadam and Alex Crow helped market it; Ellen Gleeson helped with the audiobook; and Leodora Darlington, Oliver Rhodes, Ruth Tross, Jessie Botterill, and Natalie Butlin helmed the ship that transported the product to its readers. So much time, energy, and heart!

Harley Killien—what can I say? I've warned you repeatedly to no avail!

Thank you very much to the NWDA Hampshire County Detective Unit for their help. Any errors/inaccuracies that exist are my fault entirely.

Thanks also to early readers whose feedback was crucial: Brian, Erika Anderson-Bolden, Ronna Jojola Gonsalves, and Dianna Fernandez-Nichols. And, D.K. Dailey and my fellow Bookouture authors have been an immeasurable help in more ways than I have space to list.

My husband has made it possible for me to pursue my dreams; there is nothing I can do or say to ever repay that. I couldn't ask for a better partner and best friend on my path through life.

And as always, thanks to my furbabies, whose cuddles keep me warm while I write, and whose demands for food and walks remind me to rejoin the real world!

Made in the USA
Coppell, TX
30 September 2020

38958375R00194